THE EXECUTIONER BOX

Also by Matt Hilton

The Cautionary Tale Series

WICKED JENNY *

The Grey and Villere Thrillers

BLOOD TRACKS *
PAINTED SKINS *
RAW WOUNDS *
WORST FEAR *
FALSE MOVE *
ROUGH JUSTICE *
COLLISION COURSE *
BLOOD KIN *
FATAL CONFLICT *
COLD FIRE *

The Joe Hunter Thrillers

RULES OF HONOUR
RED STRIPES
THE LAWLESS KIND
THE DEVIL'S ANVIL
NO SAFE PLACE
MARKED FOR DEATH
THE FOURTH OPTION

The Korvix the Axe Warrior Series

CLASHING BLADES
KORVIX AND THE TREASURE OF PYRE
AGAINST THE CRIMSON GODS

Standalone Novels

THE GIRL ON SHATTERED ROCK
WILDFIRE
THE GIRL IN THE SMOKE *
DEATH PACT *

* *available from Severn House*

THE EXECUTIONER BOX

Matt Hilton

SEVERN
HOUSE

First world edition published in Great Britain and the USA in 2025
by Severn House, an imprint of Canongate Books Ltd,
14 High Street, Edinburgh EH1 1TE.

severnhouse.com

Cover and jacket design by Piers Tilbury

British Library Cataloguing-in-Publication Data
A CIP catalogue record for this title is available from the British Library.

ISBN-13: 978-1-4483-1582-6 (cased)
ISBN-13: 978-1-4483-1869-8 (paper)
ISBN-13: 978-1-4483-1583-3 (e-book)

All Severn House titles are printed on acid-free paper.

Typeset by Palimpsest Book Production Ltd., Falkirk,
Stirlingshire, Scotland.
Printed and bound in Great Britain by TJ Books,
Padstow, Cornwall.

The manufacturer's authorised representative in the EU for product safety is Authorised Rep Compliance Ltd, 71 Lower Baggot Street, Dublin D02 P593 Ireland (arccompliance.com)

Praise for Matt Hilton

'Folk horror meets psycho thriller in this grim tale of murder, madness and slithering things in dark, hidden places'
Paul Finch, *Sunday Times* bestselling author of *All the Devils Are Here*, on *Wicked Jenny*

'A tightly wound tale . . . on the way to a finale of gut-clutching violence'
Booklist on *Death Pact*

'Completely apocalyptic . . . With characters who are truly mad, bad, and dangerous'
Kirkus Reviews on *Death Pact*

'Hilton grabs readers from the outset'
Publishers Weekly on *The Girl in the Smoke*

About the author

Matt Hilton worked for twenty-three years in private security and the police force in Cumbria. He is a 4th Dan black belt and coach in Ju-Jitsu. He is the author of thirteen novels in the Joe Hunter series, ten Grey & Villere thrillers, and *Wicked Jenny*, the first in the Cautionary Tale series.

www.matthiltonbooks.com

Dedicated to my parents, Jacky and Val.

ONE

'Stop complaining, Ben,' said Helen King. 'We're here now, so you may as well make the most of it.'

Ben Taylor muttered under his breath while steering his Range Rover across grass churned to mud in places by the hundreds of vehicles already lined up opposite the decommissioned Kirkholme airfield to the west of Carlisle in northern Cumbria. 'I've better things to do with my Sunday mornings than scratch through other people's rubbish.'

'Well, I sure as hell am not tearing you away from church,' his wife pointed out. 'What else did you have in mind?'

'It's my only day off work this week. I wanted to chill out, maybe catch up on a bit of TV I've missed. The last thing I wanted was a bloody busman's holiday, trawling through more junk.'

'One man's rubbish is another man's treasure,' Helen quoted back at him.

'What exactly am I going to do with old VHS tapes and dead men's shoes? Anything decent will have already been snapped up by the other dealers.'

'So we should have come sooner, like I wanted to. Anyway, you're looking for stuff others might not recognise as worthwhile. You never know, you might even find something valuable.'

'We'll see.' Ben parked the Range Rover alongside a battered white van, choosing to reverse into a slot in front of a half-collapsed drystone wall where he wouldn't get blocked in, plotting a quick escape route.

'I knew you'd come around.' Helen showed him a self-satisfied grin.

Ben mumbled under his breath, but it was for effect. He turned off the engine, then reached round into the back seat to grab his coat. As Helen climbed out of the vehicle, she peered eagerly across the field to where rows of trestle tables were surrounded by droves of bargain hunters picking their way up and down the aisles. Beyond the impromptu boot market area were the stalls, wagons and vans of the professional market traders. Helen had no interest in the stalls selling cheap warehouse clearance goods, fake perfume, vegetables or home-baked produce.

'Come on, Ben, we'll start over there and make our way up and down.' She pointed out their route, then set off without waiting. Ben rolled his eyes skyward, thinking better of adding another complaint. It was like Helen said: they were there now, so he might as well go with the flow. Dragging his heels would only mean he'd have to spend longer trailing behind his enthusiastic treasure-hunting wife.

It was the last Sunday in May, and the spring bank holiday weekend, but the temperature was still cool in the north. Pulling on his coat, he said, 'Let's get this done then.'

Helen barely looked back, certain in the knowledge that Ben was following. He went after her, a smile edging on to his lips. His complaints were more for show than anything, because, if the truth were told, he was experiencing the buzz of anticipation he regularly felt when he was on the hunt for obscure and rare items of interest. He moved around churned-up sods of grass and mud with alacrity, until he met the weathered asphalt that marked a route out to the abandoned runways. The airfield had been an active hub during World War II, as evidenced by the number of hangars squatting on the near horizon, and old red-brick buildings fallen to ruin beyond where he'd parked the Range Rover. Back then it was a maintenance station under control of Coastal Command and was used primarily for storing new aircraft. Twice the Luftwaffe had bombed the aerodrome, but twice they'd failed to destroy it. Now, more than half a century later, it was all but out of use, and the acres of tarmac and concrete had grown cracked and broken by weeds taking root. Most of the old airfield was deserted, apart from in one corner where a distribution company had erected a compound for their trucks, and another small area where a sewerage treatment plant had been housed to serve the nearby seaside town of Kirkholme. Only during spring and August bank holiday weekends did the airfield see similar numbers as it had in its heyday, when the current landowners opened it up for the county's largest gathering of car-boot marketeers.

A rough estimation of the vehicles in the adjacent fields told

Ben there were upwards of a couple of thousand people prowling the rows of tables, all seeking out bargains, trying to barter down the canny stallholders. The practice had become an English tradition in the last couple of decades, and had made his job all the more difficult. 'Bargain hunting' TV programmes didn't help; there were so many now that there was a proliferation of armchair antiques experts, and Ben supposed they were all at the market today. But, as Helen had pointed out, in the main they were all seeking a Clarice Cliff ceramic, a Royal Doulton tea set, a previously undiscovered L.S. Lowry painting, or – if they were particularly fortunate – a Ming period vase. They probably weren't seeking out the kind of obscure items that appealed to him or to his clients.

The smell of fried onions wafted across the field. It was an aroma that Ben associated with car boot sales. That and exhaust fumes from all the cars lined up and waiting to get into the parking area. He supposed it was better than smelling the effluent treatment plant. As he approached the first row of tables, he heard a stallholder giving it his best Del Boy patter as he tried to convince a florid-faced woman that she wouldn't find wares cheaper than his anywhere else on the site. Ben shook his head in disbelief as the woman handed over cash. She need only progress a few stalls in and she could have purchased the same tat at half the price. He didn't begrudge the stallholder the profit: it was a tough climate, and if he could grab a few extra quid then good for him. The woman seemed happy enough as she pushed by Ben clutching a carrier bag full of God-knows-what as she headed deeper into the market.

Helen was out of sight.

No surprise there.

Ben went his own way, strolling through the sea of bargain hunters, only taking marginal interest in the wares laid out on the trestle tables. As usual people were trying to offload their rubbish for a few pennies. Occasionally, where an object had caught his interest, he stopped and had to nudge past the elbows of other browsers, but his perusal was only momentary before he'd evaluated and then discarded the items as uninteresting.

He passed faces he vaguely recognised. Not surprisingly other dealers were out and about. Some of them smiled at him; some frowned; others winked in good humour and made brief hellos, all the while remaining guarded about the bagged items they clutched. It was a full half-hour before he came across Helen, who was chatting over a collection of brass ornaments with a thin-faced man who carried a nasty scar on his left cheek. The man appeared to have suffered skin cancer, and the surgeons hadn't done a neat job of excising the melanoma. His hair was thin, combed over a mottled pate, and it looked as if he hadn't stood too close to his razor when shaving that morning. Bristles stood in patches on his chin, beneath the folds of his nostrils and in the deep groove of his philtrum.

'All right?' Ben asked when the man looked up at him.

'I'm awreet,' the man replied. He had the twang of a local farmer. His interest didn't hold on Ben, but returned to Helen. Ben didn't think it was his wife's good looks the man was captured by, but the fact she was turning over a brass object in her hands. 'Can let you have it for a tenner, lass,' he urged.

Ben never interrupted his wife when she was dealing, and he held his peace. But he was happy to hear her say, 'It's worth about two pounds for scrap. That's all I'll give you.'

'Two pun? You're having a joke, reet?'

'Two pounds or you can have it back,' Helen said.

'Mek it a fiver,' the man wheedled. 'Things have been a bit slow th'day.'

'Not surprising at the prices you charge, Willie.'

Evidently Helen knew the man. She'd done deals with him in the past, Ben guessed, and he trusted her to handle the old skinflint correctly. He touched her on her elbow. 'I'm going to have a walk down here, Helen. I'll see you on the way back.'

Helen only glanced at him, gave him a nod, but she was caught up in the haggling game and that was all the attention Ben was going to receive. 'I'll make it three pounds.'

'Come on,' Willie the farmer said. 'Mek it fowwer and we've got a deal.'

Helen went to place the object on the table. Ben could see that it was a squat item, somewhat like a candlestick. It was archaic now, a stand for a hot poker. They already had half a dozen of them back at the shop, but for a few quid Ben wouldn't complain. 'Three's my last offer, Willie.'

'Aach, give it here then. I'll tek your three pun.'

Ben continued on, smiling to himself at his wife's skill. She'd clean the brass and then mark up the price to around the twelve quid mark: a decent enough profit. Alternatively, she'd add the poker stand to her own growing collection of brass art. She'd be happy with the deal whatever the final outcome.

Dogs barked close by.

Ben wondered what their owners were thinking, bringing their pets with them, but dogs were often a feature at boot markets. They caused bottlenecks in the foot passage when punters had to move aside for dogs straining at their leashes to get at the others of their kind. Largely the dogs were well behaved, but now and again a fight broke out, and it was accompanied by the angry complaints of their respective masters. He couldn't see the dogs, but knew where they were judging by the hard press of people a little further ahead. Ben paused at a stall to allow the backlog of people to clear.

He saw a number of worthless items arranged on a wallpaper pasting table: old toys, sweet jars filled with nails and screws, some of the ubiquitous VHS tapes that *nobody* wanted, an old radio/cassette player, some mismatched clothing, a few tatty paperback novels now yellowed and curled at the edges. Under the table there were a couple of cardboard boxes filled with bric-a-brac, and more videotapes and books.

'You can take the lot off my hands for twenty pounds.'

Ben didn't look up at the sound of the reed-thin voice, but was conscious of a small bird-like woman sitting on a deckchair beside the open doors of a canary yellow Transit van. He shook his head at her offer.

'It's not worth a thing to me. Sorry.'

'Ten pounds. It'll cost me as much in diesel to take it to the tip.'

The old woman's haggling style wasn't exactly hard sell.

'It'll cost me the same,' Ben said. Yet he didn't move on. In one of the boxes something had caught his eye, and he tried hard not to allow his excitement to show. He must have failed.

'Leona-Marie? Leona-Marie! Pull out that box and let the mush see what's inside.'

Ben finally met the old woman's gaze, and was taken aback

to find her peering at him with eyes that were thick with cataracts. Her attention wasn't on his face, but marginally over his right shoulder. How the bloody hell had she noted his interest when she was obviously blind? Did she possess the fabled Second Sight of the Romany, because it was obvious at first glance, if not hearing, that the old woman was a Traveller? Her mode of dress wasn't a giveaway, because she wore a bog-standard anorak over a blue sweater, a grey skirt and flat black shoes. She wore a lot of gold jewellery, though not in any clichéd sense, but she bore similar features to other old travelling women he'd dealt with over the years. Plus the use of the term 'mush' to denote a 'man' in traveller cant spoke volumes to him.

'Which box?' A young woman moved around the side of the van.

Ben clawed his gaze from the old woman's rheumy eyes to alight on those of her female companion. Hers were crystal clear, the shade of spring light on water. She was average in height, slim but with an athletic musculature that Ben guessed came from a life of hard labour. She wore bleached jeans, artfully ripped on the thighs, and a tight white T-shirt partially covered by a short, bolero-style jacket. Her hair verged on white it was so blonde, and was neatly plaited and hung as low as the small of her back. Her jewellery extended to earrings, formed of strings of small silver coins. She wore no make-up. In Ben's opinion she didn't need it. Hers was a natural beauty. Her only undoing was the curl of her lip when she saw the box he was interested in.

'Do my grandmother fair, mister,' she said, her tone carrying a none too subtle warning.

'She said I could have the lot for a tenner,' Ben said, and the woman's sneer twisted tighter. 'Don't worry. I'm not going to rip her off. If there's something I like, I'll give her a decent price.'

The woman bent at the waist, and Ben caught a flash of milky skin as he tried not to peek down her top. She pulled the box towards her and then lifted it with a grunt of exertion. The muscles in her forearms stood out with the strain, fine blonde hairs ruffling as though tickled by an electrical charge. She placed the box on the paste table, on top of some folded clothing.

'Don't be bothering the country mush,' the old woman said. 'Go on, Leona-Marie. Stand out the way here while he has a good deek.' She flapped her hand alongside her. Obedient, the young woman moved to stand where she was told. Both women then watched Ben as he opened the flaps on the cardboard box. Ben glanced at them and wasn't sure which scrutiny he felt was more disconcerting, the unfocused gaze of the old woman, or the crystal-clear one of her granddaughter.

Ben looked inside the box and again felt his heart leap.

Wedged between two paperback books was the item he'd first spotted. To many, they'd think the amulet worthless, costume jewellery at best. But Ben recognised the piece as being genuine topaz in a gold and platinum setting. The chain was white gold. Worth a small fortune. He fingered the amulet without lifting it out of the box.

'Anything there that you like?' the old woman asked.

Ben met her gaze. Before where it had been unfocused, it was now stuck on his with what almost amounted to laser intensity. Maybe she wasn't as blind as he'd first assumed.

'I, uh, think I might take this.' He pulled the amulet out, but only enough to flash it momentarily before pushing it down inside the box once more.

'Take it with my thanks,' the old woman said, 'but at the right price.'

'What have you got in mind?'

'You said you'd be fair,' Leona-Marie reminded him.

The old woman reached across, grasping her granddaughter by the hand. 'Hush, now. Let the mush make his offer.'

'Granny,' the young woman said in hushed tones, 'please let me take it to Shay like I asked—'

'You said I could have the lot for a tenner,' Ben jumped in quickly, fearing he was about to lose a bargain to whomever Shay might be. 'How about I match that but just for this box?'

Leona-Marie opened her mouth to speak, but Ben saw her eyelids pinch as the old woman squeezed her hand – old as she was, she'd also known a life of manual labour and was probably stronger than the lie of her frail appearance.

'Ten pounds for a beautiful piece of jewellery like that?' The old woman's head shook in mock remorse.

'It's nice,' Ben agreed, 'but you do know it's fake? It's just a paste jewel, and gold plating.'

'You don't think I'd have put something valuable in among that old stuff if it was real?' The old woman chuckled at his apparent ignorance.

'What do you say then? Does a tenner sound about right?'

'Tenner and a couple of pounds for luck?'

Whenever Ben had made deals with Travellers before, they'd all added the caveat that an extra donation was always made to the seller. It was deemed rude not to, and incredibly unlucky for the buyer.

'Tell you what . . .' Ben brought out his wallet and peeled off a ten- and a five-pound note. 'Here's fifteen quid and we'll agree on the deal.'

'Go take the money off the lovely man,' the old woman told her granddaughter.

Leona-Marie came forward. Her gaze never left Ben's as she held out her hand. He placed the notes in her palm, but before he could let it go, she snapped her fingers around his. 'It's yours now,' she said in a whisper, and the warning tone had returned. 'And remember I told you to play my grandmother fair.'

'I was fair. I even gave her more than she was asking.'

'And you country hantle call us Travellers thieves,' Leona-Marie said scornfully.

Ben picked up the box, holding it tightly to his chest. He watched as Leona-Marie backed away and handed the fifteen pounds to her grandmother. The old woman stuck the folded money in a coat pocket as if it was worthless paper. It seemed neither woman had anything further to add, so Ben simply nodded his thanks and walked away. His satisfaction at finding a valued item was somewhat dampened by guilt, but it was an emotion he only suffered until he met with Helen once again and told her how he stood to make several hundred pounds' profit on the amulet.

'So you're happy you came after all?' Helen was laden down with plastic bags containing her own purchases.

'Turned out not a bad morning.' Ben grinned. 'Best I've had in a while.'

'We could make it even better. Pub lunch and a bottle of wine, seeing as you're going to be rich?'

'Steady on, the amulet isn't worth that much.'

'You might be able to swindle an old woman, but not me.'

Swindle? Ben hadn't swindled the woman, he'd given her more than her asking price, so where was the problem? Still, as he drove them towards a favourite pub, he couldn't help feeling the knot of guilt that grew again in his stomach.

TWO

Under the current tough economic climate, extra days off during a bank holiday didn't apply to self-employed businessmen like Ben Taylor. He had to open his shop when the prospective customers were out and about. In fact, he found that holiday Mondays were good for business; there were more people in town than usual, and – because they had time on their hands – the punters were more inclined to browse and therefore buy. He arrived at work a little before 10 a.m. and found Rachel Quinn – his part-time salesperson – already inside, and getting on with the important task of brewing a pot of coffee.

'You read my mind,' Ben said. 'I've a tongue like the bottom of a birdcage this morning.'

'Heavy night?'

'You might say I imbibed a few more sherbets than usual.'

'Celebrating?'

'Just enjoying the company of a good woman,' Ben said. Then with a wink he added, 'Just don't tell the wife about her, eh?'

Rachel chuckled as she poured out two mugs of strong coffee. Ben took his coffee black, and she handed it over before spooning in a mound of sugar to her own, then splashing in milk. He nibbled on a ginger snap biscuit.

'So what's on today, boss? You want me to hold the fort or to finish labelling and cataloguing the stuff downstairs?' Rachel cupped her mug beneath her chin, peering up at Ben through the misted lenses of her glasses. She was in her mid-twenties, carried a few extra kilos around the hips, and wasn't exactly the most fashionable of girls. She was also one hell of a saleswoman, was funny and easy-going, and an asset to the shop.

'Look after the till for me?'

'Yeah, sure,' she said, sounding a little less enthusiastic.

'There's a few things I need to do, but I'll relieve you so you can grab some lunch in a couple of hours.'

Rachel was conscious of her extra weight, but unperturbed by it. 'I can live off my reserves till the end of day, don't worry.'

Shaking his head at her self-deprecation, Ben supped his coffee as he moved towards the front door. The shop was cluttered and he had to search for somewhere to put down his hot mug. He chose a space on a shelf displaying carved wooden African figurines and Japanese ivory netsuke.

'There's a few things to bring in. I'll go get them before we open for the day.'

He'd parked his Range Rover around the corner from his shop, beyond Carlisle's pedestrianised high street. In the back of his car were a few procurements that Helen had made at yesterday's boot market, plus the box he'd purchased from the elderly woman. After they'd toasted their successful day over a pub meal and a couple of pints, Ben had driven them home. They had then cracked open a bottle of wine while they'd both looked over the amulet. They'd toasted to a good sell-on. He decided they'd sell the amulet by private auction, while the rest of the clutter could go to the shop. They'd ended the night on a couple of glasses of whisky, and a kiss and cuddle had turned into some of the most energetic love-making Ben could recall in years. No wonder he was feeling so stiff, sore and dehydrated this morning.

He picked up the cardboard box, then looped fingers through the handles on the couple of carrier bags containing Helen's stuff, juggling them all while closing and locking the back door of the Range Rover. He returned to the shop and pushed inside.

'Ooh, what have you got there?' Rachel asked. 'Some new goodies?'

'A load of old tat,' Ben said, 'but our customers needn't know that, eh?'

'You are shameless, Ben Taylor.' Rachel grinned.

'It's what makes me a successful entrepreneur and such a wonderful boss to work for.'

'Speaking of wonderful bosses, isn't Helen coming in today?'

'She's gone round to see her mum, but she should be in later. That's if her mum doesn't keep her chatting. When they get together and start gossiping, they can go on forever.'

'You know what it is: they're talking about how terrible a husband you are for Helen while you're out of earshot.'

Ben laughed. Rachel was absolutely correct. There was no love lost between Ben and his mother-in-law, Gloria King. When her daughter had agreed to marry him, Gloria had not concealed her displeasure. It wasn't that she disliked Ben as a person, just that she thought he wasn't good enough for her daughter. Helen should have married a doctor, a pilot, or a professional footballer; anyone but a junk-shop owner. Ben had tried to convince her that he was actually a purveyor of exotic and esoteric objets d'art, but she was having none of it. 'Mere trinkets and baubles,' she'd argued. 'If it were objets de vertu then at least *that* would be something.' Well, as far as objects of virtue went, the inscribed topaz necklace pretty much fitted the definition, and he hoped that Helen would mention it to Gloria: that'd shut her up for a while.

His shop couldn't be described as spacious. Rental and commercial rates on any larger unit on the high street was beyond him. There were two private apartments above the shop to which he had no access, but he'd been given use of the basement at no extra cost. The basement was easily three times as large as the shop space, extending beneath the two units to either side of Taylor and King Curiosities. Neither of the other stores – a women's hairdresser and a mobile phone shop – shared the basement, because long ago, Ben had padlocked the doors leading from those premises, claiming the space for his exclusive use. The only access to the basements were via a steep staircase at the rear of his shop, and a coal chute once employed when the building was a single large Victorian dwelling. The chute had long since been locked and a steel security grid fitted over it.

The basement was dim and musty, the overriding aroma being damp cardboard and cleaning fluids. It was laid out with aisles of metal racks, on which were stacked boxes that Rachel had already sorted and catalogued. Most of the objects were destined for online auction; some of it was clutter that needed to be disposed of. He flipped a light switch and striplights *pink-pink-pink*'d into life. He placed the box and bags on a large table towards the rear of the basement. He used the table as a workbench where he sorted through boxes and crates purchased from the various house clearance companies he dealt with. Even with the glow of the overhead striplights, shadows were prevalent. He switched on a lamp and angled it towards the table, and began fishing objects from Helen's bags. She'd gathered a few ornaments and old agricultural tools, plus the brass poker stand purchased from Willie the farmer. Nothing of much interest or sell-on value, but they'd do to fill a space on the shelves upstairs. In her second bag he found a set of horse brasses: cleaned up they'd do OK – there was still a market for them, and he even had a prospective client in mind, a pub manager who held strictly to Olde-Worlde décor. He cast his eye over the small pile of items, evaluating them and decided that after paying for lunch, the bottle of wine and half-bottle of Scotch they'd downed, he'd pretty much break even. But that was discounting the topaz amulet and necklace. Taylor and King Curiosities would be quids in.

The thought brought with it a pang of guilt. He had recognised the amulet's value at several hundred pounds – on a bad day – and maybe even more than a grand to the right buyer. Yet he'd happily conned the old woman out of it, making the deal seem all the sweeter by the addition of a few extra pounds. Normally he wasn't prone to guilt, his business depended on making deals in his favour, yet the fact he'd liberated the woman of her necklace for a fraction of its value left him feeling itchy.

'Do my grandmother fair, mister,' Leona-Marie, the granddaughter, had warned.

Well, Ben had *done* her all right, but totally unfairly. The thing that worried him most was that Leona-Marie knew it too. He recalled the look she'd given him, and the reminder that he should have been fair. What was it she'd said? *You call us Travellers thieves*, or words to that effect. What perturbed him most about her final words on the matter was that she'd almost appeared to smile, as if she'd expected nothing less from him, but it had rapidly slipped, and he thought there'd been nothing left but resolution in her gaze. As he'd hitched up the box to move away, he had caught the two women glancing at each other, followed by an almost imperceptible nod from the old woman.

Oh, to hell with them. They probably thought they were offloading a worthless piece of junk on him. So what if they lost out? Their loss was his gain, and that was the way of business. They should be pleased that they'd got a few quid in their pockets, and that he'd taken a box of their junk off their hands. Less for them to dump, so he'd saved them the inconvenience.

'May as well see what tat you've dumped on me,' he said aloud, pulling the box towards him.

As he expected, there was little of value in the box. There were some old paperback novels, dog-eared and water-stained and designated directly for the rubbish bin. A couple of cheap ceramic ornaments and a chipped mug. He binned the mug but set the ornaments aside. There were dead batteries; some wires from an outmoded piece of electrical equipment; the head off a garden hoe; a few more books. One of them was a hardback – missing its dust cover – which he turned over a few times in his hands. He opened it and found it to be an early twentieth-century textbook on *The Gentleman's Self-Defence Art of Jujutsu*, and thought that to a martial arts practitioner interested in the history of combat arts, it might be worth something. He set it aside for later scrutiny. In the bottom of the box was what he at first thought was a folded, but empty, carrier bag. He almost disposed of the box and bag together, but as he lifted them off the table, he realised there was something of weight inside the bag. Placing the box down again, he leaned in to retrieve the bag.

It was a well-worn 'bag for life' from a supermarket chain, now with half the colours worn away. Ben didn't think that there'd be anything of value inside it, but the treasure-seeking buzz went through him. and he unfurled the handles and opened the bag. He peeked into it rather than inserting his fingers – he'd learned his lesson before, and there was plenty of wisdom in the old adage that you should look before you leap. One time he'd delved into a box only to prick his fingers on a used syringe. A few weeks of nervous anxiety had gone by before he was given the all-clear from the hepatitis and HIV tests he'd subsequently undergone.

A brick-shaped object lay at the bottom of the bag, wrapped in a thin sheet of bubble wrap. Taking the bag by its bottom corners, Ben tipped the carrier bag out and the bubble-wrapped object slid heavily to the tabletop. The bulb in the angle lamp beside him emitted a soft pop and went dark.

'Bloody hell!'

Ben must have shouted louder than intended, because he heard the clump of feet at the top of the stairs and Rachel called down. 'You all right down there, boss?'

'Fine. It's just these lights blowing again. Remind me to get an electrician in to check the wiring, will you?'

'I've been saying it for long enough.'

'OK. Good job I listen then.'

Rachel retreated. He could imagine her shaking her head in amusement.

Moving the box out of the way, allowing more of the overhead light to spill across the workbench, Ben reached for the wrapped package. Tightly bound Sellotape secured the bubble wrap. He turned the package over in his hands and saw a handwritten note had been fastened to it. The lettering was almost child-like, scratchy block capitals poorly formed. The ink was faded, making things difficult to read. He angled the package to get more light, and exhaled slowly as he deciphered the words. DO NOT OPEN.

'Yeah, right,' he said. He picked up a pair of scissors from the workbench and snipped through the tape, directly through the centre of the warning note. To his fingers the packaging felt a bit greasy. As he teased open the folds, he wondered what he'd find: not much, he assumed, because judging by the writing it had been put together by a child.

He realised that he was stalling from opening the final fold.

It wasn't through any feeling of anticipation, but something else . . . something more like dread.

He shook his head angrily. He wasn't the superstitious type, and wasn't about to be deterred by a frigging handwritten note.

And yet . . .

Leona-Marie's warning had not been subtle.

But what was he worrying about? She'd been referring to his dealings over the topaz necklace, not the object in the wrapping. He doubted the woman had even known that it was buried at the bottom of the box.

So what was he waiting for?

He snorted, and reached for the last fold of opaque bubble wrap.

He clucked his tongue in mild disgust. So much for discovering a mislaid treasure, but that's what he deserved for being so bloody greedy.

All that the wrapping contained was a roughly hewn wood and copper box, about twenty centimetres long, twelve wide and ten deep. It had a sliding lid recessed in grooves and a tiny copper clasp. Ben had made one just like it in woodwork class when he was about twelve years old. A bloody pencil case of all things!

In disgust he almost cast the box in the bin, but three things struck him at once. There was writing the likes of which he couldn't understand etched into the lid; a silver nail had been driven through the lid and clasp to keep it locked, and something heavy shifted inside it when he made to toss the box away.

'Hmm, what have we here then?' he said in a pantomime voice.

He picked up the box, first checking out the silver nail-head. It was actual silver, blackened with time, not your bog-standard nail picked up in a DIY superstore. He studied the writing. He could pick out letters among the chicken scratches, but couldn't make head nor tail of the wording. It looked like a cross between Sanskrit and Greek, or a blend of both.

He turned the box in his hands and there was more of the same weird writing on the bottom, as well as along both long sides, though they had been worn faint by the touch of many hands. The wood looked aged, stained dark in places, and the copper was dotted green with verdigris. He reassessed his description of the box: this was no schoolboy's carpentry project, but something much older. Gently he shook the box and heard whatever was inside shift and thud. Best he didn't shake it too hard in case the item inside was fragile. He held the box steady, peering again at the lettering on the lid. Among the jottings he could make out one term, more recently inscribed than the others: Mulé.

'Mule,' he intoned. 'What, like a donkey?'

The box shifted in his hands.

He yelped, dropping it on the table.

The movement was sudden, subtle, but it had definitely *moved.*

Impossible, he thought. Likely whatever was inside was uneven in shape and had toppled over, thus causing the box to tip. He gently wobbled the box from side to side, and did indeed feel several items moving within. He glanced over his shoulder, checking that Rachel hadn't caught him being startled. His assistant took great pleasure in creeping him out, sometimes sneaking up on him while he was down in the cellar, touching him on the back of the neck, or jumping out and shouting, 'Boo!' She'd love to have seen the look of surprise on his face right now.

But Rachel wasn't in sight. Actually, he could hear her upstairs, speaking with a customer.

Ben placed the box down and reached for a pair of pliers.

Do not open.

The warning came to mind, but he shook it away with a laugh at his own expense.

'Jesus, Ben! Are you man or fucking mouse?'

He picked up the box in his left hand and guided the pliers to the head of the nail. He was just about to jiggle the nail out when, from that angle, he made out recognisable words. In fact, if he weren't mistaken, he could read his own name. BEN. What were the chances? He studied it a moment longer and saw that he'd been mistaken. The name was actually incomplete. When seen at a slightly different angle there was a 'G' after it. BENG. Immediately before, but with a slight space between the lettering was an 'O'.

'O Beng?'

Having no idea what the phrase referred to, he shrugged it off and leaned in with the pliers once more. The silver was soft enough that a simple nip of the pliers removed the head of the nail. Ben picked up a small screwdriver, inserted it beneath the lip of the lid and prised upwards enough so that the copper hasp popped off the stub of silver and he was able to slide it open along the grooves.

'What the hell?'

Ben averted his face as moisture spurted from the box. It was dark grey, speckled with motes as black as coal, and it puffed upward a good half a metre. There was a stench he couldn't define, the closest he could get to it being the sweetness of decay. He almost threw the box away, but made do with setting it down while he wafted away the cloud hanging in the air. In the lambent overhead glow, it was as if the mist swirled and avoided the touch of his fingers. Ben swore under his breath. What the bloody hell kind of trick was this? Then the cloud dispersed and he was left wondering if he'd imagined it; if not imagined, then exaggerated the size of the cloud due to his revulsion. Yet the tang of rot still hung in the air. Holding his breath, he leaned forward and peered into the now open box.

He couldn't see within it.

It was as if the box was much deeper than its outer dimensions suggested. Frowning, Ben pushed the box along the workbench so it sat directly under a striplight. Now he could tell that the weird effect was some kind of optical illusion. The inner surface of the box was a uniform black, dull matte, making it seem like he was peering into a deep hole in the ground. An illogical fear went through him: he had no desire to insert his fingers in the box, and this time it wasn't for fear of pricking a finger on a used needle. Instead, he tilted the box towards him and laid it on one side. Using the screwdriver, he took care to tease out whatever lay within.

First out of the box came a lock of hair. It was aged, brittle, and tied securely with a thin strip of white ribbon – now yellowed with time. Out next was an unadorned gold ring, nicked and misaligned, as if deliberately bent out of shape. It was large enough to fit a man's pinkie, or a woman's wedding finger. Ben had no idea what the third item was. It was as black as the box's interior, the size of a bird egg, but withered to ridges like on a plum stone. It was desiccated too, and minute flakes broke from its surface and floated to the workbench. Ben wondered if the puff of moisture had been as a result of the item slowly disintegrating within the box, and as he released the lid, the accompanying pressure change had jetted out the fumes of decomposition, carrying with it some of the flaking substance. A trickle of unease went through him: what if the motes in the mist were mould spores and he'd breathed some of them in? He'd heard that some forms of black mould could be bad for your health.

Unconsciously he wiped at his lips with the back of his left wrist.

It was obvious to him now that there was nothing of real value in the box – the ring was good for nothing but scrap – but curiosity got the better of him. Holding his breath, he leaned down to study the strange withered form. Closer, he still couldn't make out what it was. He used the screwdriver to roll the thing over. It was unvarying in its weirdness, and its identity continued to elude him. Probably an ancient piece of fruit or something equally mundane, he poked a bit harder with the screwdriver.

The thing hissed and rolled away.

Startled, Ben recoiled. He took a couple of ungainly steps backwards and banged up against the nearest storage rack, rattling it the length of the basement. He must have shouted in dismay as he could hear the clump of feet as Rachel came to investigate.

'Hey! You all right down there?' his assistant called from the head of the stairs.

Was he all right?

Damned if he wasn't startled, but physically he was fine. That was if he discounted the pounding of his heart and the tremor in his hands. He gripped the screwdriver as if it was a knife he required to defend himself.

'I'm . . . I'm OK, Rachel. I, uh, only tripped.' He had no idea why he felt the need to lie to her. But who would admit that they'd been terrified by a bloody dried-up prune or whatever? When he jabbed it, he must have ruptured something, and the resulting hiss of air had caused the thing to roll away. That had to be it.

But if that was the case, then the air within it must have been under high pressure because there was no sign of the thing on the workbench.

When it had initially rolled, the movement had only taken it a few centimetres, no more. So where the hell had it got to?

The skin crept up Ben's back. The short hairs at his nape stood on end. His vision almost tunnelled. Every fucking cliché in the book, he thought. And with them he felt foolish. He bit his lip, and would have scolded himself aloud if not for fear a customer might overhear.

And yet he didn't approach the workbench again.

He backed away, still holding the screwdriver like a knife.

When he was midway through the basement, he turned quickly and practically fled up the stairs.

THREE

The crap showing on telly was even worse than usual. Five hundred channels and nothing on. At least nothing that Jason Halloran wanted to watch. Round about now, if indeed he was out of bed, he could normally count on a laughing fit from the show hosts Phil and Holly, but they'd gone their separate acrimonious ways now, plus the schedule was all off with it being a bank holiday Monday. Friggin' bank holidays didn't mean much to someone who wasn't in employment. Every day was a day off work for Jason. Why'd they have to mess with the schedule, anyway? The routine television programming was his clock; it kind of told him where he was in his worthless day-to-day existence.

He checked the digital clock on his mantel. It said 9.40 a.m. He hadn't adjusted the clock since last winter, and it was now running a full hour fast . . . or was that an hour slow? Slow, he decided. But why bother changing it if he only had to put it back or forward again in a few months' time? 'Daylight savings time' was bollocks to someone who had nowhere to go and no time to be there by. A quick calculation told him it was officially 10.40 a.m., still an early rise for him. Usually he scanned through the adult pay-per-view channels, bouncing between the ten-minute freebies that came on the hour, or watching some skank miming oral sex with a cell phone while jiggling her butt at the camera, well into the early hours. Most nights he didn't retire until three or four a.m., but he couldn't actually be sure about that: usually he was rotten by then on cheap cider, and the clock was just a blur. Last night, though, he'd gone to his bed earlier, loaded up on beer. If anything, holiday Sundays were good for a piss-up, and some of his pals even managed to put their hands in their pockets to pay for a round or two.

He'd got back to his flat around midnight. Because there was no access via the front street, he'd had to climb the stairs at the rear of the junk shop. His upstairs neighbours were back and making a racket as usual. He had no idea how many Polish immigrants called the upper flat home, but he was sure he'd counted at least six different blokes coming and going since they'd moved in. Jason didn't speak to them. Not that he had anything against them – they were welcome to the shitty jobs at the fish-packing factory he was unwilling to perform – but that he feared them. They were a closely guarded group, dour bastards who didn't as much as say 'hi' if he met them on the stairs. He thought if he tried to be pleasant, they would stick him with a blade and leave him to bleed out in his doorway. He half expected that the noise they were making would keep him awake, but no. He'd fallen asleep in his easy chair in front of the telly, waking up this morning to find a hole the size of a credit card in his shirt where his cigarette had fallen from his slack lips. Good job his shirt was damp with spilled beer, or he might have gone up like a torch.

Thinking of his near miss didn't put him off smoking, it sparked his nicotine craving and he reached for his pack and lighter. He only had two ciggies left and had been trying to make them last. He thumbed one to his lips and lit up. He exhaled slowly, allowing the smoke to wreathe up past his features as he peered around the room, searching for his mobile phone.

'What the bloody hell is keeping you, Belinda?' he wondered aloud.

His girlfriend should have been here by now. She'd promised that she'd be at his flat for ten. If she'd said she was going to be later, he could have had another hour in bed.

He tapped numbers on his phone and then juggled it to his ear.

'Hey! Lind, where the hell are you at?'

Belinda Sortwell said, 'I'm trying to score. Where d'you think I'm at?'

'I need more fags, how long you gonna be?'

'Nothing's stopping you going to the shops yourself.'

'Aye, right, and how d'you suppose I do that with no money?'

'So nick some, it's not like you haven't done it before.'

'I would but I'm banned from all the shops around here. Fuckin' security guards are on me like flies on shit the second I step through the door.'

'Must be great to be so popular.'

'You're not funny,' Jason growled.

'Neither are you, you're a miserable twat. Now stop complaining. I'll be there soon, OK?'

Jason took out his cigarette and found it almost gone. A qualm went through him when he realised he was down to his last one. 'Make sure you do.'

He hung up.

He went back to channel hopping; anything to kill time and to keep his mind off cigarettes and booze. From below him, through the thin carpet and warped floorboards, he could hear the murmur of voices in the junk shop. Ordinarily he couldn't make them out, but they were raised. He wondered if something was going wrong, if some unhappy customer was giving Ben Taylor what for, but that wasn't it. There was no anger in the raised conversation. To him it sounded like excitement. Lucky bastards!

He stamped his foot on the floor.

'Shut up down there, you inconsiderate shits!'

He was frightened of his Polish neighbours but wasn't worried about the likes of Taylor or his specky-four-eyed assistant. Mind you, he wouldn't mess with Taylor's missus, not unless it was between the sheets. That Helen King was a tough bitch, but she was a good-looking one, he'd give her that.

Below him the shopkeepers fell silent, but it lasted only a few seconds before they began talking loudly again.

Jason thumbed up the volume on the telly.

FOUR

'So where is it?'

'I'll show you. Come on.' Ben locked the front door, turning over the 'Back in Ten Minutes' sign, then led the way to the basement stairs. Behind him he knew that Rachel was smiling at his apparent foolishness, quite probably shaking her head in mock reproof. He ignored the urge to turn and catch her in the act, and went down the stairs, taking them slowly and carefully as she followed.

'It's over on the workbench. At least it was. It moved.' Now that they were in the basement, Ben halted to look at Rachel. He would risk ridicule for the sake of peace of mind. He wanted Rachel to check out the strange box and the items he'd taken from it, if only to reassure him that it was just a random collection of junk that should be binned.

'How could it have moved?'

'I told you already. I went to touch it with a screwdriver and it hissed at me and rolled away.'

Rachel blatantly shook her head at his craziness. 'You're saying it was *alive*?'

'No. Of course I'm not.' Ben wasn't convinced by his own words, and neither was Rachel.

'You think someone was playing a trick and put an animal in the box? A mouse or something?'

'No. That wasn't it. By the look of things, the box had been sealed for a while. No way that a mammal could have survived any length of time without air, food or water.'

'An insect, then? They can last for ages.'

'It wasn't an insect and it wasn't a bloody mouse. I'm telling you, Rachel, it was . . . well, it was *weird*.'

They moved through the basement as they considered the identity of the strange thing from the box. Neither of them was particularly keen on being the first to arrive at the workbench. They stood closer and more intimately than Ben had with any other woman than Helen in years, with Rachel hanging on to his left bicep with both hands.

'You've got me creeped out,' she whispered. 'Aren't we going to look like a pair of idiots when we find an old golf ball or something?'

'It wasn't a golf ball,' Ben said.

'Where is it?'

Pointing out where he'd left the box, the lock of hair and the ring, Ben said, 'It should have been right there.'

'Did you actually poke it with the screwdriver?'

'Only gently. Not enough to make it roll the way it did. I thought perhaps I'd punctured something and the air came out.'

'You said it was round and withered. That's maybe it. An old balloon or something.'

'A balloon would have just popped. This thing *moved*.'

'Are you sure you aren't just having me on? This isn't some ploy to get me down in the basement alone with you so you can have your wicked way?' Rachel bit her bottom lip, batted her eyelids. It was all an exaggeration so he knew she was kidding. Not that Ben believed she was. He suspected that Rachel had a bit of a crush on him, and her teasing was only half-meant. He'd caught her watching him when they were alone in the shop, and the look was one of more than adoration for her boss. Rachel was chatty and, yes, when he thought about it, a bit touchy-feely, but whenever Helen was around she ensured she was busy with some small task or other at the other end of the shop. Sometimes when speaking with Helen, Rachel would even blush for no obvious reason. Ha! Maybe he'd read things wrong and Rachel's crush was for his wife.

'Don't worry, I'm always the consummate gentleman.'

'I trust you,' Rachel said. 'Thousands wouldn't. Not sure I trust your crazy imagination, though. Are you sure you aren't just having me on?'

'Rachel. I'm not making this up. If you don't believe me, you go first.'

'Some gentleman,' she said.

'Just expressing my support for gender equality.'

Rachel pushed him forward.

With some trepidation, Ben went to the workbench. Now that

the bulb in the lamp had blown, he suddenly felt that the overhead lights were wholly inefficient, as if the shadows had taken on an unnatural density. He checked out the worktop, could see the box, the lock of hair and the ring, but of the withered object there was no sign.

'Can you see it?' Rachel asked from the safe distance she'd adopted behind him.

Ben shook his head. He leaned in further so that he could see where the bench met the wall, expecting to find that the thing had rolled to the back and perhaps dropped into the small gap there. He found a collection of odds and bobs, but not what he was looking for. He glanced back at Rachel. The striplights were reflected on her glasses and on her teeth. Her mouth was hanging slack, in awe of the situation. Despite herself, she was buying into the fact that something horrible might indeed be nearby. She had no love of spiders, and was perhaps fearful that some ghastly arachnid would crawl out of hiding and skitter up her leg. Ben realised she was as frightened as he was, but it wasn't a satisfactory conclusion. *Jesus, Ben! Man up!*

Feeling a little embarrassed now, Ben poked among the stuff on the bench. He moved the lock of hair and the ring out of the way. Then he flicked at the bubble-wrap packaging he'd cut off. Nothing. He then picked up the box and was surprised when something moved within it: the same tilting sensation as he'd felt before. He tipped the box up and the strange withered thing fell on the desk. 'It went back inside the box,' he said in a whisper.

'What? It was in the box? It must have rolled there when you prodded it.'

That must have been it. When he'd poked it with the screwdriver, the thing had simply rolled and ended up back in the open box. But Ben was sure that he'd set the box to one side, and that the thing had rolled in the opposite direction. But the proof was right there before him. He'd tipped up the box and out it had fallen. He could only put down his mistaken memory of the event to having been startled. After all, when he thought the thing had moved of its own volition, he'd jumped back. Had he really seen it roll towards the back of the bench, or only *assumed*? The object wasn't exactly cylindrical, so it wouldn't have rolled away smoothly. It was tapered at one end, so it was more likely to have rolled in a shallow arc, which could have sent it back inside the open box.

'That must have been it,' Ben concurred, but his tone said he wasn't entirely convinced.

Rachel moved closer to his side. She clung to him, one hand on his shoulder, the other gripping the clothing at his waist.

'Can you tell what it is?' she said barely above a whisper.

Ben peered down at the withered husk.

'Well, one thing I'm certain of: it isn't a deflated balloon.'

'Poke it with the screwdriver again.'

Ben puffed out his cheeks, not keen on the idea.

'Go on,' Rachel urged. 'Apparently it isn't anything of value, so it's not as if you're going to do any harm.'

'What if it is a living thing?'

'Ben . . .'

'All right. But stand back, OK? Just in case.'

While she shuffled to one side, Ben positioned the screwdriver so that he was gripping it at the end of the handle. He had no wish to get too close to the thing, if indeed it was some kind of exotic insect. God knew what it might do if threatened. He made an exploratory probe and the item remained inert. He poked a little harder, and though it moved, it was only through the pressure being placed upon it. Relaxing into his role of valiant hero, Ben pressed harder and buried the tip into the thing. He half-expected it to squirm, to hiss, to lash out with a venomous stinger, but it didn't. After only modest resistance the outer skin gave way and the tip of the screwdriver dug into the flesh beneath. A waft of decay shrouded Ben and he had to resist giving in to his gag reflex.

Rachel wasn't as stoic.

She made a retching noise, and moved quickly away. 'Oh, my God! That's disgusting!'

'At least we know it isn't a living creature,' Ben said.

'Trouble is,' Rachel said, her face twisted in revulsion, 'I'm not sure we can say that it never was alive.'

Now that it was obvious that his imagination had been working overtime, Ben was braver than before. He fully impaled the withered thing on the screwdriver, so it was like some sort of repulsive toffee apple. He turned quickly to Rachel. 'Want a lick?'

Rachel shrieked. 'Ugh! Keep that thing away from me.'

'Go on. Bet it tastes delicious.'

'Throw it in the bin.'

Chuckling at her discomfort, Ben did as commanded.

FIVE

The basement of Taylor and King Curiosities was Rachel Quinn's favourite workspace. To see her through university, she had taken on two part-time jobs that she could fit between her studies, and she'd held onto those jobs after her schooling finished. Some afternoons she waited tables at a greasy spoon café, which she despised with a passion, but it was a wage. Other days she fitted in around Ben and Helen at the shop, working the occasional morning, afternoon, or as vacation cover as and when required. She knew that Ben and Helen valued her as an employee, and she was comfortable working alongside either of them. They often commented on her work ethic and how good a saleswoman she was, and she took their praise modestly or responded with a self-deprecating joke. It was all a front. What they didn't suspect was that she was introverted, that she lacked self-confidence, and avoided meeting customers for fear of ridicule or embarrassment, and at any given chance would disappear downstairs to help with the sorting of the newly procured stock. In the basement there was less chance of having to deal with strangers, and instead of the confident act she put on serving at both the café and upstairs, she could be herself, withdrawn and happy with her sole company.

Neither Ben nor Helen was in the habit of turning down her offer to work downstairs. As they did all the buying and carrying of the stock, the last thing they wanted to do was rummage through it while at the store. Rachel had spent most of last week downstairs, sorting and cataloguing the goods from some recent house clearances, and had hoped to do the same again for a few more days. Earlier, when Ben had turned down her offer to sort through his latest acquisitions, she had to put on a happy face and work in the shop. Luckily for her, there had only been a few, largely uncommunicative visitors before a shaken Ben had appeared from below with a weird story to share. She'd been happy to accompany him downstairs, and planned on staying there to take over the basement duties.

However, that was then. Now she wasn't as keen.

Even if things had proven to be mundane, she was infected by Ben's overreaction to the incident with the withered thing from the box, and now her safe haven had taken on a different aspect altogether. Not that she bought his tale of the hissing, animated thing, putting the entire event down to his overactive imagination, she couldn't help but be creeped out. Somehow it was as if the lights had dimmed, the shadows had grown denser, and the disgusting smell of decay had invaded every corner of the basement.

Ben had taken no convincing to go back upstairs. Rachel had reminded him that his coffee was cooling on the shelf and that she'd take over while he drank it, or made a fresh one. Once he was upstairs and his mind engaged on other tasks, he'd forget about coming back down and he'd leave her to clean up. Before going upstairs, Ben had dumped the withered thing in the trash and had then piled in the discarded bubble wrap, before placing an empty cardboard box over the top of it and tamping it down. But she could still smell the rot and thought about emptying the bin and sealing the black bag. For now, she avoided approaching the rubbish bin, preferring to work without going anywhere near it. Yet, she couldn't help taking an occasional glance at the bin, and each time she did, she half expected to see the withered thing come creeping, worm-like, over the rim. It was absurd, pure nonsense, but that was how much she'd been affected by Ben's outlandish tale.

To shake off the freaky thoughts she made herself busy, moving and opening boxes, sorting through the goods inside and moving them to their rightful places on the racks. Usually, when engaged in the task, she would take her time about it, studying each article for wear and tear, taking satisfaction in discovering an object worthy of display in the showroom upstairs, but today she worked vigorously and without interest in the items she shelved. She always enjoyed the task of sifting through other people's belongings, rarely considering that the previous owners were largely dead and buried now, but this time she experienced no pleasure. The task of sorting merely became a means to keep her mind off the withered thing.

Her hard work paid off.

She had made her way through half of the boxes in need of sorting before stopping for a rest. Somewhere along the way, her mind had drifted off Ben's strange tale and on to the job at hand, and a quick glance at her watch told her that she'd killed more than two hours while she was at it. She stepped back from the shelving, fisting her hands on her hips, and nodded in satisfaction at her industriousness. From overhead came the ringtone of the telephone. There couldn't have been any customers in the shop because Ben picked up the call. She heard muffled conversation, but couldn't make out the words. She was only partly distracted.

Then she heard a scrape from behind her.

Instantly the weirdness of earlier assailed her, and she spun around, mouth open in a silent shriek, fully expecting to see a blind, squirming monstrosity heaving itself from out of the trash.

There was of course nothing crawling from the bin.

'Bloody hell! Get a grip, will you?' she admonished herself.

The scraping noise hadn't even come from the direction of the bin, but from the workbench.

She peered at the small pile of stuff that Ben had removed from the cardboard box. A short stack of books and an assortment of other things had been piled to one side, and next to them the wooden box, its lid, the ring and the lock of hair. Nothing unusual. Nothing that could have made the noise. Rachel wasn't alarmed. Many times she'd heard odd scrapes and knocks in the basement. Badly stacked objects occasionally shifted under their own weight, or were nudged over by a mouse or rat that had found its way inside. Sometimes she would swear to have heard disembodied footsteps ringing through the cellar, but had discovered that it was noise carried in from outside when the tenants of the flats above the shop came and went by the rear fire escape.

She shrugged off the sound as extraneous. It was probably that pisshead, Jason Halloran, who lived on the first floor, sloping off on a shoplifting spree, his usual afternoon activity if the local shopkeepers were to be believed. She didn't doubt it; the few times he'd been in the shop he'd acted furtively, and she was sure he'd been trying his hardest to nick something. If Ben or Helen were staffing the shop, they chased him out, and he now only came in when Rachel was on duty. She didn't have the bottle to tell him to leave, and the creep knew it.

'Hey, Rachel, how are you getting on down there?'

Rachel jumped at the question, more spooked than she'd like to admit.

It took a moment to get some moisture into her mouth.

'I was just about to come up for some lunch,' she told Ben.

'Yeah, come on up. But do you mind holding on for another half-hour? You aren't going to believe what Helen did on her way back.'

Rachel glanced again at the workbench. Nothing moved. There were no more strange scraping sounds. Yet she responded a tad quicker than normal when asked to watch over the shop floor.

When she reached the top of the stairs, she closed the door to the basement securely behind her. Ben didn't notice as she sighed in relief.

In fact, Ben's attention was elsewhere entirely. He grabbed his coat, pulled it on and started for the front door. Then he turned around. 'Where are my car keys?'

Rachel shrugged.

Ben dug in his coat pocket and pulled out his keys. 'Ah, right. Look . . . I won't be long.'

'What is it? Nothing bad, I hope?'

'Only for Helen's car.'

'Oh, no? She hasn't crashed?'

'No. She stopped at the filling station. I've told her a dozen times. It's a diesel car, not a bloody petrol one.' Ben grimaced, angry but concerned at the same time. 'Luckily she realised she was pumping in the wrong fuel, and stopped quickly enough and had the sense not to try starting the engine. I need to go and pick her up, and arrange to have the car towed back to a garage so it can be drained and cleaned. Hopefully it won't take long. Look, if you get too hungry, just lock up for a while, OK. Things aren't panning out as busy as I thought.'

Ben was babbling. Rachel went to him and guided him out through the door. 'Go and help Helen. I'll be fine here; I'll look after the shop.'

Ben smiled sheepishly. 'Been one hell of an unusual day, hasn't it?'

'It has been an odd one, I'll give you that. Now, go on. I'll expect you when I see you.'

Rachel shoved him out of the door and Ben headed directly for his Range Rover. As soon as he was out of sight, Rachel shot the bolt and turned around the 'Back in Ten Minutes' sign and retreated into the depths of the shop. Ben's leaving was an unexpected boon. If he happened to return sooner than expected, then she'd claim to have only closed for a few minutes for something to eat – as Ben had instructed her – but in the meantime it meant she could avoid customer-facing duties for a while longer. Not that she was about to shirk on the job. She fully intended carrying on working, only she'd maybe spend a little while upstairs. As much as she hated admitting it, Ben's story and the scraping noise had rattled her.

She made herself busy, pricing ornaments on a shelf. When that was done, she moved about the showroom, repositioning goods on the shelves to make more attractive displays. A customer came to the door and rattled the handle. Guiltily, Rachel considered opening up, but her irrational fear of speaking to strangers while she was alone like this won out. She kept her back to the door and pretended not to hear. After a long half-minute, she was sure that the customer had given up, but she didn't dare look. Eye contact would be enough to guarantee that she'd have to open the door. Better that she remain ignorant, bury her head in the sand and move further into the store.

As she walked towards the back, she heard a muffled thump from below her feet.

Had something fallen over? She was sure that she'd stacked everything safely on the racks. Yet something had caused the noise and this time it was more substantial than the possible scratching of a mouse.

Indecision clutched her throat: Acknowledge a possible customer and allow them in the store, or go down and check for damage in the basement while she was alone? She almost looked back at the front door.

She pushed open the door to the basement and peered down into darkness. Ambient light from behind cast her shadow on the steps, but nothing else was distinguishable. She reached for the pull cord and below the striplights blinked to life. She craned out, hoping to see if anything was lying on the floor at the bottom of the steps. Nothing. She started down, holding her breath and not knowing why.

At the bottom of the steps, she peered between the racks. At the far end she could just make out the workbench and the unusual box.

'What? I didn't leave it like that . . .'

When she'd all but fled the basement, she was sure that the box had been lying lengthways, as it had been while Ben fished the withered thing out and put it in the bin. Now the box stood on end. The interior of the box was towards her, and if there was such a shade darker than night, then the inside was that colour.

The effect must be a trick of her eyes, or her overwrought imagination. How could the interior of the box be darker than everything else around it? The glow of the striplight nearest was at an angle that it should have highlighted the inside of the box, not made it a deeper shade of black. Intrigued, Rachel stepped forward. There were three overhead lights between her and the workbench. Each cast a cone of light on the floor. Between each were pockets of shadow, but even these weren't dim enough to hide anything. She couldn't see anything that might have fallen and caused the noise. Perhaps her ears had played tricks on her and Jason Halloran made the thump in the flat above. No, that wasn't it. Not only had she heard the thump but she'd also felt it through the floorboards. Nothing had fallen, not unless gravity had gone skewed, because whatever had made the sound had bumped *up* against the basement ceiling.

There was the scratch earlier, and now a thump, and logically only a trapped bird could have caused both. She wondered if a bird had made its way inside, which neither she nor Ben had noticed, and had taken up roost in the rafters. She began scanning the joists overhead, looking for the avian's hiding place. But there was no evidence of a bird. No loose feathers. No crap dappling the beams or on the floor.

In her peripheral vision something moved.

Rachel spun towards it, but whatever had shifted in the darkness had already moved on. It had barely been a flicker of movement, a vague disruption of the shadows. Rachel's heart beat a drum solo in her chest. She scanned back and forward, seeking the source of the movement. This time a shadow flickered to her left and she turned with it. Yet again the movement was elusive, and she couldn't focus on it. She grew conscious of her breathing, the noise like a rasp on metal.

Something fluttered overhead.

She took a step back, her hands coming up to clutch at the front of her shirt. A high-pitched wail escaped her lips, even before she understood what she was looking at. A bloody moth! The bug battered relentlessly against the striplight above her head. When it was close to the light, its shadow was exaggerated and was cast on the ceiling and walls. Rachel exhaled, almost deflating in relief.

If there was a rolled-up magazine to hand, she'd have squashed the moth flat, but she decided against it. It was her own stupid fault that the moth's shadow had disturbed her so much; nothing to do with the little creature and its mindless quest to reach the light. She shook her head and moved away. Now that she'd discovered the source of the movement, it helped bolster her against her illogical fear of the box on the workbench. She moved quickly towards it, telling herself she *must have* set it on end while moving stuff about earlier. She grabbed the box, intent on laying it down. A tangible weight shifted inside the box. In reflex she dropped the box and it tipped towards her. The withered thing rolled out onto the workbench.

'What the hell?'

Rachel glanced at the trash. She had watched Ben skewer the thing on the screwdriver and then scrape it off against the rim of the bin. He'd then dumped the cardboard box and wrapping on top of it. She'd watched him and was certain he hadn't covertly sneaked the thing back inside the box. Why would he? So how in hell had it got from the bin to its resting place? Ben had been certain that it was a living thing, and now Rachel had to credit the thing with life, too. No. That was insane. The simplest answer was that there were more than one of the withered objects in the box, and this was a different one. She leaned down, peering through the bottom of her bifocal lenses and bringing the thing into clarity. She could see where the screwdriver had been driven through the wrinkled skin into the fleshy pulp beneath. A drop of thick viscous goo leaked from the wound. A breath escaped her like air from a punctured tyre, misting before her as if the atmosphere had grown frigid.

There was no 'as if' about it. The temperature had dropped. It was icy cold and, with a sense of incredulity, Rachel watched frost form on her glasses. She rubbed at the lenses and the ice smeared, fogging her vision. Freezing wind blasted her, blowing her hair about in its ferocity. Questions clambered over each other in her mind: what, how, who, where? She back-pedalled, and her head swung to check the old coal chute. Other than the stairs from the showroom, it was the only access through which a blast of cold air could have come, but the chute doors were closed tight. Outside, someone might have opened the doors, exposing the metal grate and allowing a breeze in, but the doors would have rattled at the bottom, such was the intensity of the wind that hit her. The doors stood inert.

She was kidding herself in the hope that the wind was coming from outside. She knew it wasn't. The wind originated right there, directly before the workbench. Directly from the open box, and the deepest, darkest gulf contained within it.

Rachel let out a wordless cry and ran for the stairs.

She barely made it three paces before the furthest striplight exploded into sparks, raining glass. Rachel skidded as she tried to stop. One heel went from under her and she tumbled to the floor. Cursing, kicking and scrabbling for balance, she made it over on to her backside. The second striplight exploded, and this time the tinkling glass and sparks dusted her from head to feet. Rachel threw up her hands in reflex, but the action was too late to stop the debris hitting her face. The glass was thin and fragile, most of the shards bouncing off her flesh harmlessly, but some were sharp enough to pierce her cheeks and forehead. She tasted the white dust from within the striplights and distantly recalled that it was toxic. She gagged and spat, rubbed at her cheeks to dislodge the stinging shrapnel.

Rachel bounded up, and then the third striplight blew and the basement was plunged into darkness. The only source of light to guide her was from the open door at the top of the stairs. Rachel rushed towards it.

The door slammed shut.

Ink. Night. The soul of the devil. Nothing came close to how dark it suddenly felt to Rachel. 'Felt' being the correct term, because it was as if the darkness had taken on malignant life; one that pulsed and throbbed around her, and enfolded her with an impenetrable shroud.

Rachel screamed.

She scrambled for the stairs, recalling from memory in which direction they were. She was off angle and crashed into the metal racks on the right. The collision caused boxes to shift, and some fell in a thunderous clatter behind her. Rebounding from thc rack, Rachel took another few staggering steps and then her toes caught on the bottom stair and she fell against them, banging an elbow, barking a shin, almost biting through her bottom lip when her chin smacked painfully against the boards. She cried out, not so much in pain but in her need to get out of there. She began hauling at the stairs with her hands, kicking at each step with her feet.

Two hands grasped her by the shoulders and pressed her down.

Rachel screamed in terror.

The hands clutched at her, trying to hold her firm, to halt her escape. She threw her arms back, felt a lessening in the pressure and squirmed around. She drew up her feet, forced her palms tight against the weight of darkness upon her.

Someone was in the basement with her!

Someone was *attacking* her!

They must have gained access through the showroom, and entered the stairwell while she was inspecting the box. Slammed the door behind them so that they could have their way with her untroubled.

That had to be it.

Rachel was shy when facing strangers, but never had she been afraid to stand up for herself in a fight. She kicked her feet and thrust with both hands. She felt no impacts, and yet the weight still bore against her, crushing her against the stairs. Rachel screamed, now in fury as much as terror, and struck out blindly. Again, she didn't feel the satisfying smack of her hands against any face or body. But someone loomed over her. Faint light leaked around the doorjamb above her, filtering down the stairs, and she could make out a pitch-black form that was blacker than the black around them both. And yes, she could make out eyes, too. Dim, pale orbs that appeared stark against the background. They didn't blink. They made a target for her fingernails and Rachel raked at them with both hands. Still she felt no resistance to her tearing nails. She squealed in a long yowl of desperation, and began crawling upwards, backwards on her heels and backside up the steps.

The form looming over her jammed up close, and she felt the breath get forced from her lungs. Her glasses had been knocked askew in the struggle. One lens was over an eye, but the other had been pushed up onto her forehead. Her vision was impaired, unable to focus either eye, but Rachel still *saw*.

A face pressed close to her own, almost intimately, and she could feel the ice of its breath on her chin and lips. Rachel screamed again, and those hands that had earlier grasped her now pressed hard against her biceps, pinning her to the stairs. The face was indefinable, black on black, but Rachel knew that the mouth opened widely and she steeled herself for teeth chewing into her flesh. But the ripping sensation didn't come. Instead, the mouth continued to widen, to elongate, and it took on an unimaginable size to be that of a human mouth. From the open maw came a blast of air, and Rachel, even caught in that moment of abstract terror, understood that the open mouth was the source of the freezing winds that had already assailed her. It was the same bottomless gulf contained within the ancient, curse-marked box. And Rachel felt herself tip and then fall towards it, and if she could not save herself then she would fall for an eternity, sinking deeper and deeper into those hellish depths.

SIX

Over the inane chatter of the talking heads on TV, Jason heard the screaming. Living on the high street, near the pubs and nightclubs, it wasn't unusual for him to hear screaming. Often it was good natured, drunken ribaldry, but sometimes a brawl kicked off and voices were raised in anger or consternation. But it was early afternoon on a bank holiday Monday and the screeches were out of time and place. Distractedly he wondered if some sort of accident had happened and someone had been hurt, but his interest wasn't piqued enough to drag him out of his chair. He was more concerned by what was keeping Belinda and his cigarettes. For fuck's sake! He'd smoked his last tab and was now ready to crawl up the frigging walls!

Another scream rang out and he sat up straight.

What if that was Belinda he could hear? What if some twat was trying it on with her, or worse, trying to steal his fags?

Galvanised by the latter thought, he stumbled up from his chair and went to the front window. Peeling aside nicotine- and tar-stained curtains, he craned for a look down onto the front street. Outside a few people had paused, concern on their faces for the screams that continued unabated. He could see no sign of who was screaming, but still couldn't be sure that it wasn't his girlfriend. He rushed across the room to the rear window, where he could see out onto the fire escape and down into the cramped yard through which he accessed his flat. He could hear the screams there too. If anything, they were louder. *Bloody hell*, he thought, *has someone followed Belinda into the alley?*

He pulled open his door and stepped out onto the rickety staircase. Another holler rang out, from down below him. He leaned over the edge of the stairs, looking for Belinda. Above him, two voices muttered in conversation. Jason looked up and saw two of his Polish neighbours standing in their doorway. They both met his eyes, casting accusing frowns at him.

'Hey, this has bugger-all to do with me! The shouting's coming from down there. The junk shop.' For clarity Jason stabbed his finger down, then made a play of shrugging a few times and tilting his head from side to side. The two Poles appeared unimpressed. One of them went back inside, while the other continued to glare at Jason.

Jason said, 'You think we should check it out?'

The Pole sneered at him, said, 'Wanker.' Then he went indoors and slammed the door behind him.

Now that the guy was out of sight and hearing, Jason flicked him the two-fingered salute.

Feeling braver, he leaned out, searching for the source of the screams. He was certain that it was one of the women, hot-stuff King or that pudding-faced girl, Rachel, that worked for her, that was raising hell down in the basement, rather than Ben. He decided that it was most likely Rachel; to him, the squeals sounded too girlish to be those of the mature woman. For a moment he wondered if Ben was the cause of the girl's terror; maybe he had tried having his way with her and she was fighting him tooth and nail. His momentary bravery waned: he didn't want to get involved in other people's troubles, he had enough of his own, but more so he was worried that he might invite a beating from the antiques seller if he stuck his nose where it wasn't wanted.

The screams became whimpers.

Jason tentatively picked his way down the corroded metal stairs.

There was no back entrance to the junk shop, and even Jason had wondered in the past how Taylor and King got away with not having a fire exit – to satisfy his curiosity, he'd even checked for one at the side of the building that was perhaps shared with the mobile phone shop. He had found none – but had subsequently learned that the basement could be accessed via several different shops at one time; maybe anyone in the basement could access one of those exit routes in an emergency. He approached the cover on the archaic coal chute. A test pull told him that the wooden cover was rotting and loose and could easily be wrenched off in an emergency; however, the wood sheet covered a more permanent fixture in the shape of a barred grille. He crouched so that he could pull up one corner of the board, and spied between the bars. It was black as pitch inside, not even the hint of a light showing.

'Hello? You all right in there?'

The girl gave another series of squeals, these short and eardrum-piercing.

Jason sat back on his haunches, looking around, bewildered by what he'd heard.

He wasn't the heroic type, but there was nobody else around, so it was firmly on him to do something to help the obviously terrified girl.

'Is somebody hurting you?' he demanded.

The sound of weeping answered his question.

'Hey, whoever's in there and hurting that girl, you'd best get the hell away from her. I've called the coppers and they're on the way here. You know what's good for you, you'll piss off, quick like!'

The girl – he was convinced that it was Rachel, the shop assistant – scrambled through the darkness of the basement towards his voice. She crashed into something that fell and clattered on the floor.

'Please, please, whoever you are,' she cried out, 'you have to help me.'

'The coppers are coming,' he said, even though he was yet to call them, but he didn't want her attacker to know that.

'I'm stuck in the basement and the door's locked and all the lights have gone out. Please, get some help.'

'Uh, where's Ben?'

'He isn't here.' She hiccupped out a wet sob. 'He had to go and help his wife, Helen, after her car broke down.'

'Who's in there with you then?'

'No one.'

'But I heard . . .'

'You heard me panicking. I'm, uh, really afraid of the dark. When the lights went out, I was taken by surprise, and when I found the exit door jammed, well I—'

'So there's nobody there who's hurting you?'

'No. It's only me.'

'What if I pull off this cover and—'

'Yes! Do it. Please let some light in so that I can see!'

'Aye. All right. S'long as Ben doesn't have me done for criminal damage.'

'He won't.'

'He treats me like a criminal any other time he sees me.'

'Is that you, Jason? The lad from the flat upstairs?'

'Who else is it gonna be?'

'Right? Thank you for coming down to help me.'

'Yeah. Good job you weren't relying on those gits from up above me.'

'I'm thankful you heard me and decided to help.'

'Aye. Right. Better stand aside in case anything falls in on you.'

He grasped the edge of the board, taking a firmer grip than before. Fleetingly he wondered if he should demand some kind of reward for helping her, but he decided to wait, maybe bring it up once she was safe and back in the light of day. He yanked up with the entirety of strength left in his emaciated body. The board ripped easily away, tearing off at three corners, where the screws holding it were tougher than the board. He cast the cover aside.

Rachel blinked up at him from the darkness below. She'd somehow lost her spectacles, and her eyes brimmed with unshed tears. She gave Jason a strained smile of acknowledgement, but then peered longer into the darkness beyond her shoulder.

'You sure you're down there alone?' asked Jason, apprehensive still.

'There's nobody else here,' she assured him.

He could recall her screams though, and they had not been issued simply from a girl surprised by a sudden power cut. The skin on her neck was blotchy in places, flushed in others, and her round cheeks were also flushed as though from exertion. Her hair gave no clues if she'd been in a fight; it was too short, and tight with curls, to look dishevelled. Her clothes were a bit ruffled, but not torn or yanked aside as he'd expect following an assault. In her urgency to escape the basement, though, she had clambered up the old coal chute, risking barking her knees or shins on the rough concrete. More convinced than ever, Jason believed there had definitely been an attacker down there with her, but where had he got to since?

Rachel grasped the grille with both hands. She tried to raise it, but it wouldn't budge. 'Get me out of here,' she whined.

Jason tried to lift the grille, but it was wedged in a metal frame. A padlock fixed it firmly to the outer frame. Checking it, he saw there was no key; the hole itself was corroded and probably wouldn't work even if a key was used in it.

'I . . . I don't know how to help,' Jason said. He cast about looking for something heavy that he might use to break the padlock.

'Get outta the way.'

Behind him the two Polish lads had come down the fire escape. While concentrating on the girl's plight, Jason had been unaware of their descent.

He looked up at them over his shoulder, a bit perplexed.

'Outta the way.' The curt order was repeated but, before Jason could respond, the one who had earlier sworn at him grasped his shoulder and pushed him aside. Jason collapsed onto his backside.

'Hey!' he squawked, but the young men ignored him.

The second man carried a short crowbar. He jammed its end between the padlocked hasp and frame, and then used his heel to bear weight on the opposite end. The bar spat loose.

'Pass me that,' he said, and his friend grabbed part of a broken brick, and this time the lever was braced over it. This time, when the man stamped down, the hasp broke free from the frame, making the lock redundant. His friend grabbed the grille and hauled it open. Rachel clambered out on her hands and knees. The man with the crowbar bent over the opening, threatening the darkness below with the bar, even as Rachel scrambled up and into the protective arms of his friend.

'Are you OK?' the man asked in perfect English.

'Yes. I'm OK.'

'Nobody was trying to hurt you?'

'No. I just got locked in and freaked out in the dark,' she explained.

'You're safe now. There's no need to be afraid.'

'Thank you, thank you,' she moaned in gratitude, addressing the man with the bar too. 'I don't know what I'd have done if you hadn't come to help.'

Rachel pawed at wet cheeks with hands turned black from clawing her way up the chute. Her elbows and the knees of her jeans were also pitted.

She again thanked her rescuers, then bent forward to place her hands on her thighs, and she coughed out a string of bile-tinged saliva from her strained throat. The first Polish male placed a hand on her back and gently patted her, telling her again that she was safe.

To one side, Jason sat on his backside in the dust, forgotten and ignored. Initially he was disappointed, but it was a feeling that didn't last; after all, he was often forgotten, dismissed, or physically pushed away, so this was nothing new.

'Stuff you,' he grumbled under his breath, and wondered what was keeping Belinda with his ciggies.

SEVEN

Observed by Rachel and Helen, Ben tested the door to the basement.

It swung open easily.

When he pulled it shut again, and used a little force to hold it in the frame, it easily opened a second time with the slightest of shoves. He'd ensured that the door was fitted loosely in the frame, and that the only thing holding it shut was a ball catch. Trusting that the heftier padlocks he'd fitted to the coal chute grille and the access doors from the neighbouring shops sufficed when it came to external security, he didn't see a need to make the internal door secure: he preferred that he could shoulder it or nudge it open with a knee whilst carrying stuff downstairs.

'I can't understand how you couldn't open it,' he said.

Rachel didn't argue, reluctant to disagree with her boss perhaps.

'Try it from the basement side,' Helen instructed on her behalf.

'I will, but I bet it opens just the same.'

Ben went through the door and down a few steps, before turning and pushing the door shut.

For a moment he felt the same creeping menace that must have freaked out Rachel, but it was only the density of the darkness at the top of the stairs after all the lights had gone out. Within a few seconds, his vision began to adapt and he could see the faint glow edging the door in its frame. Immediately the creeping shadows retreated, and he pawed for the handle on the inside of the door. It was set lower than usual, so that it was easily reached by someone still ascending the stairs. He gently drew the door open towards him, and peered out at his wife, who'd moved closer to the door. Beyond Helen, Rachel chewed her bottom lip.

'I don't get it,' said Helen, with a glance back at their assistant.

'Maybe something inside got wedged under the door,' Rachel offered weakly.

'Nothing here that I can see,' said Ben after a cursory check on the stairs. 'It was probably just down to panic. Maybe you missed the handle and tried pushing your way out instead of opening the door towards you?'

'Yeah,' Rachel said. 'Maybe that was it.'

None of them was convinced.

'Did you get the lights working again?' Helen asked.

'Rachel said that the bulbs blew.'

'You're saying all the striplights blew at the same time?'

'Well, maybe not. Maybe there was a power surge and the fuse tripped. Let me check.'

He'd resisted calling in an electrician, despite going through a constant stream of bulbs in his desk lamp: he'd entertained the idea that it was the lamp at fault, not the system, because replacing the lamp with another picked up in a house clearance would prove less expensive than hiring a tradesman. Now he couldn't put off the truth any longer, not if the entire electrical circuit had crashed in the basement. Long ago, before he'd taken possession of the property, the basement's electrical supply had been routed via the master fuse board in what was now their second-hand shop. It suited Ben, because he didn't want to allow his neighbours access to the basement, in case they got designs on using some of the space themselves. Taylor and King Curiosities had been on site now for almost a decade, and there'd never been an incident where either neighbour had required access, and he hoped to keep things that way. The fuse board was hidden inside a cupboard behind the sales counter. He crouched and tugged open the door and began running his fingertips over the switches: sure enough, one of them had tripped. He flicked the switch and instantly the basement was alive with striplights popping to life. Ben grinned over at the women. 'There you go, problem solved, eh?'

Neither Helen nor Rachel entered the stairwell. Rachel blinked in confusion at the now steady glow from the striplights. 'I could have sworn one of the bulbs blew but . . .' she said, her voice petering out.

Ben checked the fuses a second time, just a cursory tap of his fingertips over each switch. It occurred to him that the fuse controlling the striplights had been tripped, and yet the one for the sockets had not, as should have been the case if the desk lamp was causing the outages. He mentally shrugged off the contradiction: he wasn't an expert in this stuff; his domain was in other people's discarded treasures.

He joined the women at the head of the stairs.

They hadn't gone down a single step.

Had Rachel since told Helen what had happened to her?

She had pulled Ben aside when the owners had arrived back at the shop, telling him about an uncanny incident with the shrivelled thing from the box seemingly moving . . . and how she'd been freaked out when the lights went out and her screaming had brought help from their neighbours. Ben was under no illusions; she had given him only part of her story, and it was frightening enough, but he believed there was more to it. He had so many questions, but Rachel had pleaded with him to keep the incident with the shrivelled thing between them, as Helen was stoic in her scepticism about anything supernatural or otherworldly, and Rachel didn't want to lose favour in her boss's eyes. In the past, Ben had shown he was more open to discussing the weird and the wonderful, so apparently she wasn't too worried about skewing his opinion of her.

Standing close to both women, he wasn't so certain that Helen's scepticism was as firm as it used to be, because she hadn't made any attempt at taking a step down into the cellar. Rachel, he noticed, stood with her arms wrapped protectively around herself, and visibly shivered. There was a network of vivid scrape marks on the back of her neck. They looked as if she'd been clawed with a bird's talons, and yet in the next instant she reached back and plucked subconsciously at the wounds: probably they were self-inflicted.

'Let's see what kind of damage we've to deal with, eh?' Ben prompted.

Neither woman moved.

'After you,' said Helen.

'Haven't I had to play the hero once already today?' he asked.

'Some hero. All you did was have the car towed to a garage.'

Ben pushed between them and onto the stairs. He wasn't keen on going down the stairs, but wouldn't admit it in front of the women. 'Stand aside, ladies,' he said in an exaggerated voice, 'this is man's work.'

'Sexist Neanderthal,' Helen called him.

'Caveman-ist,' he retorted.

His attempt at levity fell on deaf ears. He went down the stairs, taking undue care. The floor below was largely clear, but in her panic Rachel had knocked over some items, and kicked her way through some stacked boxes, spilling some contents. As he gained the basement level, he used the sides of his feet and shins to clear safe passage through. He checked for anything strange, but nothing caught his eye. He knew that Rachel had played down what had happened, and also that she'd been seriously spooked because of that damn thing in the box he'd released. He approached the far end of the workbench. The box stood on end, and again he couldn't help feeling that the darkness within went far beyond a natural density. He picked up the screwdriver he'd earlier used to poke and then skewer the black, shrivelled thing, and used it to knock the box over on its back. It clattered on the worktop. He saw the hank of hair, the deformed gold ring, but of the *thing* there was no sign. There shouldn't be: he'd dumped it in the bin then piled the old bubble wrap and stuff on top. Hearing the scuff of feet, he turned towards the stairs. Helen was on her way down, and Rachel followed with visible trepidation, one hand on Helen's shoulder for support. Helen's nose was wrinkled in distaste.

'It smells like death down here,' she said.

Ben had got used to the smell but, now she mentioned it, he could again detect the faintest tang of decomposition, the same smell released in the air when he'd originally poked the withered thing.

'Look at the mess,' Rachel croaked.

'It's nothing,' Helen reassured her.

'I promise I'll get everything tidied up before I go home.'

'Don't be daft, Rachel. You've already stayed beyond your time. Don't worry about a thing, Ben will have the place ship-shape in no time.'

Ben blinked in surprise at his wife. Why send Rachel home when she was happy to work? You don't buy a bloody dog and then bark yourself. But when he thought about it, it would take him all of a minute or two to put the place back to normal, and besides, he was more concerned with the possible damage done to the grille over the coal chute than he was to a few inexpensive gewgaws that might have broken in the toppled boxes. Leaving the women talking next to the bench, he crossed the room to the archaic chute. Looking up he saw daylight, but it was crosshatched with iron bars: the grille had been lowered once Rachel had been helped out by her rescuers. Ben made a mental note to fully secure the hatch before leaving for home.

Rachel began weeping.

Helen tried comforting the girl, enfolding her in a hug.

Ben approached them, and saw something at their feet. He bent down and retrieved Rachel's spectacles. One arm was slightly bent at the hinge, but the lenses were fine. He held them out.

'I think you might need these, Rachel,' he said, and Helen released her so that she could take them.

Wet-eyed, Rachel settled her glasses on her face. She sniffed back mucus, then used the back of a sleeve to wipe her face. 'I'm sorry for causing so much fuss,' she said in a tiny voice.

'Don't be daft,' Helen told her again. 'You've had quite a scare. If it had been me locked here in the dark, I'd have run right through that door and left my shape in it like a cartoon character.'

Helen also aimed for levity, but the mental image she painted barely raised the corner of Rachel's lip. Helen reached for her and teased an unruly curl off the girl's glasses and tucked it behind her ear. Rachel ignored the gesture; she looked up at the ceiling fixtures and frowned.

Ben followed her gaze.

All was in order as far as he could tell, but Rachel frowned harder, her forehead rucking and she muttered something under her breath.

'You OK?' Ben ventured.

She shook her head. 'I have to go. Sorry.'

She spun away and almost ran for the stairs.

Helen, concerned, went to follow, but Ben clutched her wrist, holding her back. 'Just let her go. She's embarrassed and needs some space. Wait till tomorrow and she'll be back and totally fine again.'

'I hope so. She's a good one and I'd hate to lose her over something as stupid as a bloody avoidable power cut.'

'Me too,' he admitted, though he knew that something beyond Rachel's fear of the dark had been behind terrorising their assistant. His gaze crept to the carved box surrounded by the few trinkets it had held. Evidence of the strange, shrivelled item he couldn't see, and was grateful for the tiny mercy.

EIGHT

She was twenty-five years old, worked two jobs, and still lived under her parents' roof. Other women of Rachel's approximate age were still engaged in full-time education, were in training or had begun their careers, or had already started their families. Some were even climbing the property ladder, usually helped along by cash boosts from grandparents living – via trust funds – or deceased – through inheritances. Rachel's dirt-poor grandparents had left nothing in their wills for her, so her parents tried making up the deficit with kindness. In doing so, her parents tried to give her the space she required, and in return for their ongoing support and generosity, she helped out where she could with the housekeeping money. They usually refused the handouts from her or, if they did take it, usually dribbled it back to her over the coming weeks by way of paying for her home delivery meals, or settling her mobile phone and TV streaming subscription bills. Their house wasn't huge, but her parents generally stuck to the ground floor until bedtime, and she kept out of their way by staying in her bedroom unless it was breakfast or dinner time. Arriving home mid-afternoon and immediately disappearing to her room was not unusual, but her haste to get inside and lock out the outside world must've caught her mum's attention. Amanda Quinn followed her upstairs and gently knocked on her bedroom door.

'Can I come in, Rache?' she asked.

'I'm OK, Mum.'

'It didn't look OK, not the way you ran upstairs just now.'

'I just needed the toilet.'

'Urgently?'

'I was bursting to pee.'

'Yet you haven't been yet?' The shared bathroom toilet was on the upper floor, but Amanda had watched her daughter flee up the stairs and enter her bedroom, and she hadn't left in the thirty-or-so seconds since.

'The feeling left me,' said Rachel.

'Can I come in?'

'Why, Mum?'

'Because we both know you're lying and that something is wrong. I only want to help you, love.'

'Mum, I'm not lying to you. Something freaky *did* happen to me at work today, but I'm OK, and you needn't worry about me, honest.'

Amanda tried the door handle. 'Will you please unlock the door, Rache.'

There was a moment of hesitation before Rachel answered. 'I'd rather be left alone.'

'Just for a minute sweetie, so you can convince me I'm only being an overprotective mother, then I promise I'll leave you alone.'

Rachel uncoupled the sliding bolt from its retainer. She thought about how her dad, Geoffrey Quinn, had installed the slide bolt at Rachel's insistence when she was a child entering puberty. Back then, she'd demanded strict privacy, and would have been mortified for her parents to have seen her any less than fully dressed, so enforced a locked-door policy whenever she was in her room. The practice had subsided as she'd entered her latter teenage years, and had been non-existent since. If she wasn't mistaken, this was the first time that she had bolted her door in the past five years: her mum's instinct was right, something decidedly wrong was troubling her daughter.

Looking small and vulnerable, Rachel peered up at her mother through the couple inches gap she'd allowed between the door and jamb. She had taken off her spectacles, to make dabbing her swollen eyelids with a tissue easier. Her cheeks were streaked with dried tears; some of them had made runnels in dust as black as soot – which invariably it was, from the coal chute.

'What happened?' Amanda said, and without asking permission, she stepped forward, causing Rachel to instinctively open the door and allow her in. Her mother placed a comforting arm around her shoulder and assisted her back to sit down on her bed.

Rachel sat, her mum beside her, and that was when Amanda noted the rash of scratches on her neck.

'Who did this to you?' she demanded, her voice strident.

'Did what?' Rachel touched the back of her neck. She winced, and her fingertips came away dotted with blood.

Amanda pulled down the collar of her daughter's top, checking for more evidence of an assault. The scratches were deeper on her back, some of them having broken the skin and bleeding droplets of blood.

'I, uh, did it to myself,' said Rachel.

'You tore your own skin off?'

'Don't exaggerate, Mum.'

'I'm not exaggerating! Look at you! Is there more . . . are you hurt anywhere else?'

'Mum.'

'Who did this? Was it Ben? The bastard! Did he—'

'Don't be stupid, Mum. It wasn't Ben. Ben's kind to me, he'd never hurt me.'

'Then who was it?'

'I told you. I scratched myself . . . subconsciously.'

'How? How could you do this much damage without noticing?'

'There was a blackout when I was in the shop's basement. I was freaked out and couldn't find my way out. I think maybe I was clawing my neck with frustration.'

'Frustration? Are you kidding me? Those scratches reach halfway down your back. How could you have—'

'Mum,' Rachel snapped, and immediately regretted her tone of voice. 'They're a few superficial scratches, will you just let it be?'

'If I thought for a second that—'

'*Nobody* hurt me,' Rachel wheezed. But then she slumped forward, her face in her palms and she sobbed.

Amanda patted her daughter's shoulders, then faltered when Rachel squirmed uncomfortably from her touch, as if her wounds were painful. Awkwardly, she tried leaning in so that their heads touched, but Rachel again drew away.

'Mum,' she said in a tiny voice, 'I just need a few minutes to feel sorry for myself. So . . . can I just be left alone and I'll be down shortly, and we can prepare dinner together, OK?'

Amanda paused for several seconds.

'OK, but if you need me, call me.' Amanda stood and backed

away again to the open door. She lingered a moment longer in the doorway then, when Rachel peeked up at her, she nodded, crossed her arms and turned away.

Her mother's footsteps receded down the stairs. Her father asked what was going on.

Rachel rushed to close the door.

Experiencing a burning sensation in her spine, she pressed her back against it, for fear her mum might return and try pushing her way inside. For only the second time in years, she slid the bolt into its retainer. She moved away, and began pulling out of her sweater. Underneath she wore only a bra. She angled her body so that she could see the entirety of her back reflected in a full-length mirror. Normally, she was conscious about the extra weight she carried, and used the contradictorily named vanity mirror for moments of self-loathing. This time she was oblivious to her size, concentrating fully on the wounds in her skin instead. The scrapes and scratches around the back of her neck were superficial, but those her mother had spotted struck deeper into her flesh between her shoulder blades. She ignored them all, more concerned by the deeper wound in her lower back, from where the pain radiated. It sat directly over her spinal column, a raw hole in her skin about the size of a two-pound coin. Her skin had been opened, and the red flesh, and the pinkish-white layer of fat beneath were exposed. She couldn't recall knocking against anything sharp enough to cause the injury, and besides, she knew it had nothing to do with catching herself on a sharp corner. More like something had tried burrowing inside her, and though she tried to deny it, in her heart she knew the truth: the black shrivelled thing had tried to bore into her as if it was an overgrown blood-sucking tick. Thankfully, when she'd fought against it on the basement stairs, and she'd managed to twist around onto her back, she must have rubbed the little monster loose, and escaped its hallucinatory influence when Jason and those Polish lads broke open the coal chute hatch.

Hallucinatory!

She aimed tremulous fingers at it, and before they reached the gaping wound it closed, the edges pinching together like the lips of an old toothless man sucking on a piece of sour fruit.

Panic seized her again, and she almost cried out.

What if the shrivelled thing was some kind of burrowing creature, and it had deposited tiny parasites into her bloodstream, and even now they were swimming through her veins, latching onto her organs, tunnelling through her brain?

She touched the remnants of the wound, and it faded under her fingertips. Frowning, she rubbed it, circling where the pain had been before and where now she only felt a soft tingling sensation. If she had been somehow infected, would the pain and the awful sensation of violation fade so quickly? The open wound must have been psychosomatic, caused to appear on her body by her own overwrought imagination, like some type of ungodly stigmata. Yet now it had faded to a pinkish mark. So, what did that mean?

The entire horrifying sequence must have been hallucinatory?

The thought persisted even as the wound dissolved and her skin returned, unblemished. Even most of the scratches on her back began to fade, though they didn't disappear altogether, so maybe she had unknowingly scraped herself on the stairs.

Yes, a hallucination had to be the answer. The wound to her lower spine – and even the terrifying belief that some *entity* had physically assaulted her in the shop basement – must surely have been some kind of waking nightmare that had persisted until now, perhaps induced by inhaling those black spores that Ben claimed had spurted from the thing when he'd accidentally punctured it with the screwdriver. Had she been given an extra dose of dream-inducing fungi spores when Ben had playfully held out the skewered thing to her and offered her a lick?

Yes, again, it had to be the answer.

Something had been troubling her about the entire incident since she'd stood with Helen at the head of the basement stairs, watching as the striplights each *pink-pink-pinked* to life once Ben threw the fuse switch. During the frightening experience downstairs, she'd swear that the lights blew sequentially as she'd tried fleeing, and that she'd not only heard the tinkling glass but felt tiny shards land in her hair or bounce off her shoulders. How hadn't she noticed at the time that she was under the influence of a hallucinatory substance that forced her to believe a lie; hell, striplights don't explode, and besides, if somehow they had, the bulbs themselves were under clear plastic covers that would have caught any falling glass.

She dashed her hands through her hair. Some dust filtered to the floor, but no glass shards. She retrieved her discarded sweater, and a quick inspection showed that it was dirty with soot and cobwebs, but there were no bloodstains, and no slivers of glass stuck in the material.

The horrible incident and her injuries had mostly been a hallucination, then, but knowing so didn't make things any less terrifying or troubling.

NINE

Belinda Sortwell had finally delivered on her promise to fetch Jason some cigarettes, but that had been hours ago and already he'd made his way through the pack and was down to the last couple, and now she wanted him to share.

'I've only got two left,' he groaned.

'I only want one.'

'Yeah, but if I give you it, that's me down to my last.'

'Give me a smoke, Jace.'

'If I do, you'll have to go and get me some more from the offy.'

'I'm not going to the off-licence, I've been barred.'

'The shop at the petrol station, then.'

'D'you know how much they charge for fags there?'

'I know, but maybe you'll be able to get us some cider while you're there.'

Belinda shook her head. It was currently in Jason's lap; the rest of her skeletal frame was stretched out across his dingy settee. He sat with one arm draped over her back while his other hand clutched an almost empty can of cola. It was a cheap knock-off brand, with the bittersweet taste of saccharine, although Jason had chosen it for its supposed sugar content: he needed something sweet to fight his other cravings.

'I've no money for cider,' Belinda said.

'So nick some.'

'All well and good, but how does that get your ciggies?'

'I'll come with you. You can cause a distraction, and I'll grab some from behind the counter.'

'You know they keep the ciggies in those bloody lockable cabinets these days?'

'Yeah, but from what I've seen, there's nobody who actually keeps the little doors locked. If you can get the cashier out from behind the counter, I'll be in and out, quick like.'

'We're talking about going on the rob, Jace, not having nooky.'

She sniggered, but Jason didn't find it funny. Intercourse these days was lacklustre at best, but Belinda should think herself thankful he gave her even a few minutes in the sack: her alcohol and drug addictions hadn't been kind on her looks.

Having brought up the subject, albeit as a joke, Belinda turned her head slightly and nuzzled his privates.

'Give over,' Jason said, and pushed her face aside. He squirmed out from under her, and allowed her to drop back fully on the settee.

'Suit yourself,' Belinda told him, and closed her eyes. 'I'm too tired for nooky, anyway. You should go to the petrol station on your own, I'm too knackered to move.'

Before he'd made up his mind whether to go alone or not, Belinda snored softly, making the decision for him. He couldn't understand how she could sleep with the telly so loud. He grabbed the remote and thumbed down the volume. Belinda snored louder.

'Yeah, you stay there,' he grumbled, but was secretly thankful for the escape before he had to hand over one of his remaining ciggies. He lit up the one she should have got, and left the apartment to stand on the metal steps at the back. It was quiet overhead for a change, his Polish neighbours having gone out for the evening, making the most of the holiday weekend before duty at the fish-packing factory called. They were probably out celebrating their heroics, having stolen his thunder earlier. Pushing him aside like dirt, they'd taken over busting the hasp and lifting the grille so that Rachel could scramble out. The pie-faced girl had been shocked, frightened of her own shadow or something, and had clung to the Polish lads as if they'd slain a bloody dragon during her rescue. She'd forgotten all about Jason's inclusion, and he doubted that anyone else had dropped his name to the owners. Effectively, they'd ripped away any hope of a monetary reward he'd planned on begging from Ben Taylor.

Sucking his cigarette all the way down to the stub, he flicked the filter over the edge of the stairs and into the backyard below. He watched the yellowed filter tumble through space, all the way until it hit the dirt and rolled, to join dozens of other used stubs that had formed a drift against a wall. Ben Taylor had asked that Jason not discard his fag ends in the yard, but it wasn't Taylor's sole property, and his access and parking rights said that Jason could also use the yard, so fuck him. He thought about lighting up again, to give himself a bit of a boost on his walk to the petrol station; it would help pep him up and bolster a little false courage for the planned theft. But if he lit up and failed to snag any cigarettes, then he'd have none left. Panic rose in his chest and pinched his throat. He left the sole cigarette in the battered packet in his shirt pocket.

There was no guaranteeing that he'd get an opportunity to slip behind the counter and raid the cigarette lockers at the petrol station, not without Belinda helping him and causing some kind of distraction. Why'd he ever think it was a good idea to go alone, other than because desperation was guiding him? He didn't have to make the trek to the station, of course, because there were other shops and other ways to nick what he needed. He smiled in the knowledge and immediately went down the stairs. They creaked and groaned underfoot, but it didn't matter: the Polish lot weren't home, and Taylor and King had shut up shop early and buggered off too. He went to where the sheet of plywood had been re-laid over the grille to the coal chute.

A quick jab of his shoe told him that the wood had only been laid over the opening, and not re-secured. As he recalled from when he'd ripped it up the first time, the screws had come away easily, the corners of the board rotted and flimsy: perhaps Taylor had it in his mind to secure it again, but with more appropriate materials. He crouched, grasped the board and lifted it aside. Propping it to the left of the chute, he turned his attention to the padlock hasp: the hasp had been broken off by the Polish lads and was yet to be replaced. His heart hitched in his chest, his pulse excited by his change of luck. All that Taylor had secured the grille with was some twisted copper wire. Again, Jason believed that the owner had probably done enough to secure the hatch for the night, with the intention of making things more permanent in the coming days, and for now trusted that nobody would know the padlock was missing.

He hadn't counted on Jason knowing. For the first time, Jason was pleased that his thunder had been stolen; Taylor probably didn't even know that he'd been involved in Rachel's rescue and had learned of an easy access route into the shop.

Checking over his shoulder every few seconds, he crouched

and began tugging at the twisted wires: undoing them was more difficult than he first expected, and his fingertips grew sore before he could unwind the thick wire from the grille. But he was persistent, and soon had the wire hanging in a loose coil at his side. Conscious that his fingerprints might be lifted from the wire if he set it aside, he scrunched it up into several longer loops and shoved it in his pocket, of a mind to discard it well away from the yard once he'd finished there. Pulling his abraded fingers into his sleeves, he grasped the grille and hauled it open, setting it upright on its hinges against the wall. He peered down into the archaic coal chute.

Evening had crept up on him. It wasn't dark yet, but the shadows had grown long and dense and he could barely differentiate between the chute and the ground that swallowed it. Taking care, and with another cautious glance around, he set his heels at the edge of the chute, then sat on his backside. His addictions meant that he wasn't a heavyweight, though he wasn't yet verging on skeletal the way his girlfriend was, so there was no fear of becoming trapped in the chute. Rachel had climbed out, so he was confident he could wriggle down through the same space. Scrabbling about for purchase on the slope with his heels, he allowed gravity to assist him, and he slid downward on what felt like a galvanised tin sheet. He fell for less than his body length, and then his feet found empty air. He slapped at the walls either side of him to slow his descent, and felt ancient bricks against his palms. His fingertips were punished a second time, and then he had a hold of the edges of the tin sheet and his back arched over the edge, his feet dancing a few inches from the basement floor. Grunting at the effort, he let his weight down and settled his feet on a softly undulating floor.

The basement was in complete darkness. He staggered a moment, feeling as if he stood astride the deck of a boat wallowing on the tide. Then his right hand found the wall to his side and he steadied himself. He closed his eyes, then slowly opened them, taking in the density of the darkness and coming more in tune with it. The rocking sensation faded, and he allowed his knees to flex and took an exploratory step forward.

It felt as if he stood at the centre of a great void.

Stretching out both hands, he groped for the touch of something familiar. His fingers groped like blind worms, and then he found the hard edge of a workbench, and using one hand to steady himself, he dug in his pocket for his cigarette lighter with the other. Flicking on the lighter, he aimed its flame to one side then the other, and was able to orient with the workbench and the bottom of a set of steps up to the shop. He quickly followed the receding shadows as he marched towards the steps, assuming that he'd find a light switch at their base.

He didn't.

The only switch he discovered was situated at the top of the stairs.

His lighter had grown so hot it threatened to scorch his hand.

He let the flame go out.

Then, after a few seconds, he touched the metal roller, and hissed when it burned his thumb.

A few more seconds passed in depthless darkness, and then he rapidly rolled the wheel against the flint and it sparked the fuel alight.

The darkness danced away from the flame like flitting bats.

He climbed the stairs cat-footed.

He was fairly confident that the shop was empty, but what if he was wrong?

At the door he paused and set his ear to it to listen.

He detected a low mechanical hum, but that was all. There was no hint of life beyond the door. He tested the handle and found that the door easily swung towards him. He peered into the shop but was afraid to enter it properly. It was one thing gaining access to the basement, but he believed that the shop itself might be protected by an alarm system, perhaps with PIR motion detectors situated in the ceiling that he'd trip the instant he crept out onto the shop floor. He doubted that Taylor or King were the types to leave good money sitting in a till drawer when the shop was shut, and there was nothing on the shelves he could see nearby that could easily be lifted, let alone sold to any of his contacts: he hoped instead to find something valuable out of sight and mind down in the basement. Retreating, he closed the door and sought a lock, but there wasn't one. He'd rather secure the door than leave it easily opened: he hoped to stall anyone entering the shop from quickly coming downstairs should he need a few seconds' grace to make an escape. There was nothing he could see at first, but then he noted a small wooden peg – perhaps it had been used to wedge open the door at one point, to make accessing the basement easier – and he forced it under the door to make opening it difficult and noisy. With that done, he groped at the pull cord and waited while the striplights flickered to life.

Before he was banned from entering, he'd snooped around the curios shop plenty of times, seeing what he could thieve, but he had never been in the basement before. It was much larger than expected, and a simple approximation told him that he'd heard correctly, that it extended beneath the two units either side of the curios shop as well. Taylor had taken control of the entire basement, the way he kept on trying to with the backyard, and it pissed Jason off. If he didn't find anything nickable, he'd smash up the place before leaving, maybe even take a dump on the floor and leave something for the greedy sod to dig through seeking golden nuggets.

He snorted, and with the exhalation fled his temper.

He wasn't being serious about crapping on the floor, that'd be overstepping a line, but, yeah, maybe he'd knock over some of those racks and shelves on his way out.

He made his way past the first racks. There were items stacked on the shelves, but from what he could tell they were ornaments like his old granny used to display in her china cabinet, and not something any of his contacts would be interested in buying. He spotted some brass objects and wondered if there was any scrap value in them. Yeah, he decided there probably was, but where could he weigh them in during a bank holiday Monday evening? *Nowhere* was where.

Ignoring what was on the shelves, he looked for a safe or a strong box, something that might hold Taylor and King's most precious curios, but couldn't see either. There was some kind of funny-looking box standing on end of the workbench.

He approached it, and let out a hiss of triumph on spotting something next to it worth boosting. A small gold ring, not large enough to fit his fingers, but maybe on Belinda's, had been hung on a small upright stand with several limbs. He grabbed the ring and studied it: even he could tell it was old, and of a good gold content, probably near enough eighteen carats, although it was slightly misshapen. He looked for symbols inside it, but couldn't see any, not even a stamp to authenticate it as gold . . . possibly older even than he'd assumed, and possibly foreign made. He admired the gold a moment longer, then safely tucked it away in his shirt pocket alongside his other treasure, his sole cigarette.

He checked around and saw what looked like a hank of hair, the colour dulled by age, tied with a faded ribbon. The lock of hair and the ring had come from a corpse, he deduced. He'd had a basic education, actually he hadn't paid much attention in classes, but from watching so much TV over the years he'd heard of certain things, like the Latin term memento mori, and understood it to be the term for keepsakes taken from the dead. He was only partially on the right track: the phrase was actually a reminder that mortality was fleeting and all must die, but in his perception it meant something to remember the dead by. It didn't matter; he wasn't superstitious and would happily dig the gold fillings from a corpse if he got the opportunity. He wondered what else belonging to the dead had come into Taylor and King's possession. He had no idea that he was practically surrounded by items gained from house clearances; pretty much all were dead people's trinkets.

He touched the unusual box, and snapped away his fingertips.

'It's like bloody ice!' he croaked under his breath.

He reached again, more tentatively, and when he touched the wood it was indeed cold, but not as sub-zero as he'd first thought.

He gave it a nudge.

It rocked slightly, but remained upright.

He pulled his hands into his sleeves and used the barrier of the material to protect his abused fingers. He picked it up and held the box close, peering inside, and was confused by the way it seemed to shift in his grasp. It was as if something heavy rolled from one end of the box to the other, and then, without him tilting it, rolled back the way it had just come. He turned the box over but nothing tumbled out. He shook it with the same negative result. Perhaps the crudely crafted thing wasn't balanced at its centre point. He noted the scratchings in the wood, and that they were infantile attempts at words. His reading ability wasn't anything to brag about, but it was a skill developed slightly more than from his schooling through the reading of subtitles and advertising banners while watching the TV into the early hours.

'What the fuck's OBENG mean?' he wondered aloud.

There were other words, mulé being one, and something that looked like Ruffie, and Jason had no clue what those words meant either.

The words, he supposed, were unimportant. The box itself was old, and not very pretty to look at. He thought it might have been crafted as part of a larger collection of storage containers at one time, but was now just a mismatched piece of junk. He saw that there was a lid, and found that it slid shut on twin grooves in the box. He held it shut with a thumb and forefinger, and gave the box a shake: again he sensed that weird over-balancing sensation of it, but otherwise there was nothing further of interest regarding the old box. He tossed it aside and it clattered on the workbench.

Jason caught his breath. What the hell was he thinking? For certain there was nobody upstairs to hear him, but he should take more care while effectively burglarising the place. In fact, his earlier idea of taking out his frustration on Taylor by wrecking the place no longer sounded like a good idea: he should leave the place as if untouched, and take only what he could conceal about his person, and perhaps he'd get another chance at robbing something valuable during a future burglary. He reached for the box, about to take off the lid and set it upright again as he'd found it. Remarkably the box moved from his grasping fingers. It stood upright of its own volition, and the lid flipped like an ejected slice of bread from a toaster out of the grooves.

'What the . . .' Jason took a deep step back, one hand going to his throat. The other he balled into a fist held over his shoulder, as if he would hammer the box into kindling if it dared move again.

The box remained still, standing on one end as it had when he'd first spotted it.

He shook his head.

No, he hadn't seen the thing move like some sort of poltergeist's plaything! The box must be some kind of toy, a trick; something spring-loaded that, after being knocked over, returns to an upright position by itself.

Yeah, that had to be it, because any other explanation was just too crazy to contemplate.

He poked shaking fingers at the box, but they fell short by several centimetres. Again he could feel the coldness of the box, but this time it emanated outward, freezing his skin even over a distance.

Scraaaatch!

The sound came from inside the box.

Jason stood open-mouthed.

Had he heard the spring-loaded mechanism resetting or something?

Scraaatch!

The sound repeated, and he leaned forward, squinting into the depths of the container, trying to make out—

A black bolt shot towards his face.

Jason screamed and stumbled back. He swept his arms at whatever had launched at him, but he had lost sight of it, it moved so quickly. Thankfully it had not struck his face, but neither had he felt it strike his arms, or land on the floor behind him.

He did feel something worming under his collar and slither down his back.

He stumbled around the basement, trying to wrench his shirt off his body, slapping at a nipping sensation as if tiny claws pinched him, trying to rid his flesh of whatever had invaded his clothing.

He tripped and fell on his backside, crying out.

He scrambled away from the workbench, clawing at his back, trying to dislodge the thing that latched onto his spine. The sharp pinpricks grew agonising; the thing was chewing a hole in his flesh!

It was a living nightmare, and Jason screeched in terror. He'd never experienced anything so hellish in his life.

Until the lights flickered and true horror struck.

TEN

Rather than park in the backyard, Ben pulled his Range Rover up on the paving outside the shop. This part of the street had been pedestrianised, but it was early evening on a holiday Monday, so his injudicious parking wasn't exactly impeding any foot traffic. He stuck a handwritten note on the dash – claiming to be unloading – to stave off the traffic wardens.

'Wait here,' he instructed his wife, 'let me check things out first.'

She nodded, but Helen wasn't the type to take instruction by the letter, especially when coming from her husband. As he opened his door and got out, she mirrored him to stand on the pavement closest to the shop. She bent to peer through the window, but couldn't see any movement inside.

Shaking his head at her, Ben hurried around the car, juggling the shop keys as he headed for the door.

'Maybe we should wait for the police,' Helen suggested.

'We could be waiting forever,' Ben grunted, sounding as if he had a low opinion of the local force. 'I'm pretty sure it's just a false alarm and something has tripped, maybe with us resetting those fuses earlier.'

Helen moved closer and cupped her hands around her eyes as she put her face to the window. 'I don't see anything.'

Ten minutes ago, they had received a call from their security monitoring service, alerting them to a silent alarm being activated within their shop. Sooner than waiting for the police to check things out, Ben had elected to go and ensure the shop was secure – in his mind, he hoped it was some type of false alarm, but feared it was something to do with that damn *thing* he'd released from its cage earlier. He hadn't shared his concerns with Helen, because neither he nor Rachel had come clean to his wife about the shrivelled monstrosity seemingly moving of its own volition. He certainly had not mentioned it to his security service, and wouldn't to any responding coppers either: they'd think he was insane.

'You remembered to secure the hatch to the basement, didn't you?' Helen wondered aloud.

'Yeah, I fixed it with some wire for now.'

'Wire?'

'Yeah, the thick kind.'

'Oh . . . right. Must've worked. I don't see anybody,' said Helen, peering into the dimness. A sole security light had come on as darkness fell, but it barely cast enough illumination to the back of the sales floor. 'But what if they are downstairs?'

'I'll check,' he promised, 'but after we make sure the safe hasn't been tampered with.'

He unlocked the door and went inside.

He progressed no more than two paces before halting and listening keenly.

He was unsure if the silent alarm had already been reset by the monitoring company, but had to go through the process of keying in a code on the alarm's panel. The panel was to his right, concealed behind a plastic flap on the wall. He turned down the flap, saw an array of steady green lights and a single red one, winking like a demon's eye from the depths of the pit. Each bulb represented a different location in the shop. The blinking red light covered the passive infrared motion detector situated directly above the door down to the basement. Unlike the other PIR's set in each corner of the ceiling, this one was recessed, and specifically directed down on the doorway. Anyone entering via the basement and making their way to the upper floor would have no idea they'd tripped the alarm, not without a concerted search for the detector – Ben and Helen had invested in the security device rather than spend more money to cover the entirety of the basement.

Seeing that the door had been opened and something had emerged from the basement gave him pause, but a quick check confirmed there was nobody lurking nearby, and there were no obvious signs that anything on the sales floor had been tampered with. He keyed in his code and the red light went green. Looking around, he saw that Helen had entered the shop. She flicked switches, and light flooded the sales floor.

'I asked you to wait,' he croaked.

'Yeah, but you also said we could be waiting forever. You

know how impatient I am.' She shrugged. 'Besides, everything looks in order.'

'I have to check downstairs,' he reminded her.

She nodded, but immediately headed towards the sales counter and the small safe on the wall behind it.

Ben joined her. The safe was resolutely closed, and there was no hint that it had been fiddled with. But he wouldn't be happy until he'd made certain. He dabbed at the buttons on the safe. Code accepted, the safe unlocked and he pulled open the door. Inside sat the gold, platinum and topaz amulet he'd practically swindled the old woman out of. He exhaled through his nostrils.

'All's well?' asked Helen.

'Yeah. It's still here.' He closed the door and heard the electronic locks engage. Standing, he again checked that nothing else had been messed with. Everything appeared to be in order.

'If anyone got in downstairs, I'm pretty certain they skedaddled the second we turned up,' said Helen.

'You're probably right,' said Ben, but didn't approach the door to the basement.

'Are you going to look then?' asked his wife.

'Yeah,' he said, but again didn't move.

'Bloody hell, what's got you so rattled?' said Helen, exasperated, and she stepped towards the door.

'Wait on,' said Ben, and he grabbed her elbow, hauling her to a stop. Once he was sure she wasn't going to pull out of his grasp and charge downstairs, he looked around and spotted where Rachel had left a sweeping brush and pan sitting in an alcove. He took the brush, wielding it as if it was some kind of spear and he was off to slay an ogre.

When he pushed the basement door open, struggling slightly against a wooden peg that had somehow become wedged under it, he immediately saw that the lights were on.

He knew for certain that when they left earlier, he had turned off the lights again, rather than allow them to burn all night. Somebody – or *something* – had turned them back on. He sucked in a steadying breath. No creepy little shrivelled plum had got to the pull cord and turned it on; turning them on had to have been achieved by a human agent.

'Somebody there?' he demanded in his toughest voice. 'You'd better get the hell out of here before the police arrive.'

No sounds of panicked flight responded to his threat. He went down a couple of steps, the brush held out as if he could hold back an attacker with its soft bristles.

'See anything?' Helen asked and Ben jumped.

She was immediately behind him on the stairs.

'Jeeeeesus,' he wheezed.

There was nobody in sight.

There were few places for a person to hide in the basement, and from their vantage they could see the blocked entrances to the other shops. Nothing had been disturbed.

Except that the wooden box he'd found in bubble wrap now stood on end, the lid off, and it took all of about a second to tell that the buckled gold ring was missing from the tiny stand and the hank of ribbon-tied hair was now lying on the floor. Somebody – or again *something* – had been at play.

His attention was drawn immediately to the coal chute and, as he strode towards it, could feel the draft of cool evening air blowing into the basement. Dim evening light could be seen at the top. Somebody had removed the wooden cover and gained access by lifting the grille. He swore, cursing himself for not making the grille more secure with another sturdy padlock. This burglary was on him, and they were fortunate that no more than a practically worthless ring had been stolen.

'Some thieving rat's been in,' he told Helen.

Neither said it, but they both had their suspicions about who was responsible.

'I'm going to get that thieving scumbag evicted from his flat if it's the last thing I do,' Ben snarled.

Immediately he began retracing his steps, and he ushered Helen before him, up the stairs. He flipped off the lights and closed the door behind them. He'd a good mind to send the cops directly to Jason-bloody-Halloran's door but, without proof, he couldn't accuse his drug-addled neighbour of burgling the basement. All he could do was ensure that the thieving scumbag couldn't find easy access again before he could permanently fix the grille over the chute again. As memory served, he had a bicycle lock on one of the shelves upstairs that could be put to good use.

It took a moment to find the chain and lock, and to ensure that the key still operated it. He held it up to Helen. 'Do you want to wait in the car while I go round and fix the grille?'

'Give me the keys and I'll lock up,' she said.

He handed over both the shop and car keys, and left her to reset the alarm and to lock up. He went around the side of the mobile phone shop, down the shared alley and into the backyard. Seething, he glanced up at the metal fire escape, but from his vantage had no view of Jason's flat. From higher up, he heard voices. It seemed that some of the young factory workers had returned home and were standing out on the fire escape, smoking. Ben wondered if it was the same two that had earlier come to Rachel's rescue, and considered asking them if they had seen anyone crawling out of the coal chute since then. From what he'd gleaned from previous interactions, one of them had a good grasp of the English language, which was fortunate because Ben's command of Polish was zero. He let the thought escape, turning instead to inspect the coal chute. As he'd expected, the wooden cover had been set aside and the grille raised back on its hinges. He checked that nobody was crouching in the chute's mouth, then lowered the grille and used the bike lock to secure it better than before. He laid the wooden cover over the grille and stood. His knees made crunching noises, and he dug his knuckles in his lower back, easing aching muscles.

He thought that the antiques and curios business was perhaps better suited to younger men, but then recalled that he and Helen's love-making had been more energetic last night than in many a moon, and he grinned in salacious memory.

A woman screamed above him.

Instantly, the warm, fuzzy thought disappeared.

ELEVEN

Dozing off and on, the sound and colours of the TV occasionally impeded on her vivid dreams, so that Belinda was unable to differentiate one from the other at times. After Jason left on his mission to steal cigarettes, she'd stayed stretched out on the settee, but had transitioned somehow from one end to the other, at one point having jack-knifed up from one troubling dream, only to lie down again but with her head flopping at the opposite end to where Jason had sat earlier. She had pulled up her knees and wrapped her forearms around them, nestling into the sunken cushion. The old settee was stained with food and drink, and other unmentionable fluids, and it stank horribly, but Belinda had grown used to the smell, and besides, she wasn't too fresh either.

She was an unhappy girl. Her mum had died young, taken by an overdose, so as a child she'd known only poverty and abuse, and though the poverty continued she could at least count on Jason to care for her the way her stepdad hadn't. Jason, for all he had a reputation as a thief and rogue, was a sweet guy who would run into fast-moving traffic to save a kitten. He was her boyfriend, and she was his girl, though – sadly – not exclusively. Sometimes she had to turn tricks with other men to make enough cash to feed her habits; sometimes she had to pay Jason's way too, so how could she possibly be happy about her life? It was only when nestled up on his couch like this, warm and safe, and momentarily free of cravings, that she could sense what the possibility of a normal life might be. Soon though, the itching would begin, the spiders would start crawling through her veins, and in no time she'd be climbing the walls until she could get another fix. She hoped that Jason had been successful, not only in fetching them ciggies, but also some strong cider that would help stave off her other needs for the next hour or two.

Gratefully, she heard footsteps climbing the fire escape, slow and steady, and Jason came indoors. He pushed the door open and it banged on the interior wall. The sound was sharp and forced her to sit up, wondering why he was acting so forceful. Hopefully he hadn't failed to nick what they needed and had returned home frustrated: she didn't feel in a fit state to prostitute her body, and besides, who was going to pay good cash to her when it was obvious she hadn't bathed or changed her underwear in days? Sure, she could perhaps take a shower in Jason's bathroom, but she'd no spare clothing here and had no desire to return home to collect any: not when stepdaddy dearest might demand a freebie before she headed out on the game.

Jason paused in the doorway to the sitting room, his breathing ragged.

She forced herself to sit, one elbow braced against the armrest.

His breathing grew noisier.

'Y'all right?' she asked. 'Did you fetch me *something*?'

He raised both hands.

'What is it?'

Belinda was still caught in a moment of flux between the sound and colour assault of the TV and reality, and she looked without recognising what Jason held.

'Held' was the wrong term. Rather, 'wrapped' was a better description of how his hands were encircled by a length of heavy-duty copper wire. It was wound around his left hand, and a thick strand of it projected to a loop around Jason's right thumb. As her eyes focused on it, and her brain made some sense out of what confronted her, Jason took a long step into the room, and snapped the wire taut between both hands. Open-mouthed, Belinda watched him approach, and it took another moment for it to dawn that his intentions were not good.

'Wh–what's wrong, Jace? Didn't you manage to get any—'

He lunged, and rammed the tightened strand of wire under her chin. Stiff-armed, he shoved her backwards, forcing her back against the settee. The wire was as solid as a metal rod. Her throat was slim, and she possessed little tone or strength in it, and the force at which he rammed the wire home felt almost enough to decapitate her. Thankfully the old settee gave in under the pressure, so that she was buried into the upholstery, and not instantly throttled. Shocked, with barely any strength to fight back, she could only writhe in place, her balled fists beating ineffectively against his arms and chest. Jason reared in, forcing a bent knee into her stomach, holding her firmer. Standing on one foot he was less steady. Overbalanced, he fell against Belinda and, trying to right himself, he twisted to one side. For the briefest moment the wire sprang loose from across her throat, and she folded to the other side, throwing an arm between her neck and the wire. Jason growled deep in his throat, and again forced the wire towards her.

This time he crushed her arm against her head, and as she turned away, screwing her eyelids tight, she emitted a screech of terror. He grabbed at her arm, yanking it out of the way, and again bore in with the wire garotte, and threw both his knees over her thighs, pinning her. Belinda hadn't the strength to fight, and the wire dug deep into her flesh as he forced each hand in by increments. She felt it cutting deep into the cartilage of her larynx, and in her mind, thought he might saw her head off if he drove in any further. Instantly, all thought abandoned her as the oxygen supply to her brain was shut off, and Belinda fell into a blessed dark place.

Flash of light.

Sound.

Motion.

Red, the only colour in her vision.

More sound.

Violent motion. She was buffeted.

People swearing and shouting.

Belinda drew in a ragged breath, and it hurt so badly to breathe. She exhaled and it felt worse.

She cried out, pitiful and weak.

More shouts, more screams, and suddenly she was aware that Jason was no longer sitting astride her legs, and she herself was no longer on the settee, but was being dragged.

Instinct caused her to slap and beat at the arm around her, and it took a few moments more, and the urgency of the commands in her ears, to understand that somebody else had hold of her, and was trying to get her to safety. She sucked in more air, and was grateful that this time, she didn't experience agony. She made a keening noise, and again, the person – a man – holding her, spoke urgent but supportive words, and she submitted to him as he carried her from the apartment and onto the metal fire escape.

She went down on her knees, bent over, and she was only barely cognisant of the palms on her back, slapping gently, aiding her to hawk out a throatful of blood-flecked phlegm and to draw in life-saving air. From within the apartment, the sounds of conflict continued, and there were at least a trio of distinct voices raised in challenge. The racket swelled, and even in her dazed state, she understood that the fight was about to follow her outside. Her saviour understood too, and caught her under the armpits, hauling her to her feet, and sending her towards the uppermost step. He followed her down, one hand catching at her waistband, assisting her to stay upright, even as it forced her to keep moving. Her bare feet sucked at the old metal steps, and then she felt the texture change, and grit and stones began biting into her soles, and she finally understood she was on firm ground, in the backyard behind the row of shops.

She looked up, and saw the strained face of Ben Taylor, the co-owner of the curios shop, and it struck her that she now owed him her life. She opened her mouth to speak, but only a raspy hiss escaped. He pulled her head against his chest, in what might otherwise be described as an intimate gesture, but in this sense was more akin to a father cuddling a helpless infant. A strange sense of warmth pervaded her, but only fleetingly. She craned out of his embrace to look up; seeing Jason astride the landing outside his apartment ripped the warmth from her, and her blood ran cold. That face, contorted with rage and pain, those glaring eyes, and the horrible curses he roared, were not like her Jason's. He was obviously in the throes of some kind of psychotic breakdown, maybe reacting badly to a substance he'd taken that had sent him insane. Two figures struggled to contain him, and the other factory workers were bounding down from the uppermost flat to join their friends. They didn't treat Jason kindly, beating him with their fists and feet, but it was what it took to subdue him, and if they hadn't done that, she was fully certain that he'd have dragged them all with him down the metal stairs in pursuit of her, to finish what he'd started.

'Jason?' she cried, but what else could she say? He was in no fit state to answer for his behaviour, and hearing her voice only seemed to incense him. There were expressions on the faces of the men struggling to control him, as if they'd concluded that they'd bitten off more than they could chew.

And then it was as if a power cable had been yanked from its source, and all the wild energy driving him disappeared in an instant: Jason collapsed soundlessly. The men holding him stumbled, one fell to his knees on the landing. Another staggered down several stairs, holding his opposite elbow, then bent over the railing, gasping for air, showing how taxing the fight had been.

Belinda gasped, and began massaging her throat and jaw with one hand. The other still held onto the steadying presence of Ben Taylor. It was only once she'd checked that her throat wasn't cut open, and that her head was still atop her shoulders, that she stumbled towards the fire escape.

'No,' said Taylor, holding her back. 'Don't. He might try hurting you again.'

'Jason,' she squeaked, and was again lost for words.

Her word barely carried, and yet it had the strength to rouse her boyfriend.

Jason was still in the clutches of several of the factory workers, two of them kneeling astride him to ensure he couldn't rise, but his face was turned to the edge of the landing, and he could see over its edge to where Belinda stood below. He cried out, but this time his voice was forlorn, unrecognisable compared to the vehemence of only moments ago. He tried crawling one hand to the uppermost step, but his fingers fell short. He'd lost his hold on the thick wire garotte, but undoubtedly it was still wrapped about his other hand.

His bulging eyes were no less large, but they'd lost the volcanic flames of rage.

'Belinda,' he wept, 'what's happening? Why are they doin' this to meeee?'

She held up one hand to him.

'You don't have to explain anything to him,' Taylor said. 'We all saw what he was trying to do to you.'

'No,' she croaked. 'Jason wouldn't hurt me. Not . . . not normally.'

'There was nothing normal about his behaviour.'

'Maybe it's a bad reaction to something,' she countered, as if it might win him some pity. Jason tried to squirm out from under his captors, but they easily forced him down. One lad thumped him in the ribs, and Jason yelped like a kicked dog.

'Stop it! Don't hurt him!' Belinda cried.

'After what he did to you?'

'It isn't like him, I'm telling you. Just let him go.'

'Like hell we will,' said Taylor, and he checked to his right, and Belinda noted his wife and business partner standing at the mouth of the access alley. She had her mobile phone to her ear, and she nodded, confirming Taylor's unspoken question.

'I'm not pressing charges,' Belinda snapped adamantly.

'He just tried killing you.'

'No. You're wrong. He didn't, he—'

'It doesn't matter whether you press charges or not, the police are coming and are going to take him away. He can't be trusted not to go berserk again, and who knows who he might try hurting next time.'

'Belinda, *pleeeease*,' Jason called down. 'It wasn't me. I swear to you, I'd never deliberately hurt you. You've got to believe me. Something got into me.'

'You don't . . . bloody well . . . say,' Taylor grunted.

TWELVE

Ben rarely took any strong alcoholic drink before bed; an ingredient in the brew always made his dreams weird, sometimes downright nightmarish, and that evening he had the fodder to feed the weirdest of nightmares without extra stimulation. Yet he accepted the tumbler of vodka passed to him by Helen, and adjusted his position so that she could sit alongside him on their settee. A spooky movie was playing on the television, but neither of them was watching with any attention. Asked afterwards, neither of them would probably be able to recall the leading actors or the plot. He peered into the depths of the liquid in his glass; Ben had enough spooky thoughts creeping through his mind without the movie adding to them.

Jason Halloran had been arrested by the police and was handcuffed and placed in the back of a van for transportation to the local nick. He'd gone dejected and broken, with no sign of the violent monster of only minutes earlier. Belinda Sortwell, his intended victim, had been far more vocal and vehement towards the police, and had been threatened with arrest if she didn't calm down. Ben thought he maybe should have taken the girl aside and comforted her somehow, but decided he'd done his bit in saving her from her abuser's clutches, but she wouldn't thank him for any further interference. Belinda had shouted and cursed, then pleaded for Jason's release, then shouted and cursed again, then fallen into floods of tears. When Helen had tried to show her a kind word or two, the distraught woman had turned her curses on her, and Ben had heard enough. He'd encouraged Helen to join him back at their Range Rover, and a minute or two later had noticed Belinda trudging away, head down, feet shuffling in her dejection. She hadn't returned to the apartment; despite her near murder, something more imminent drew her away, and it appeared that even Jason's plight was no longer in her mind. Once he'd given his full details and arranged for a constable to visit and record his statement – the Polish lads apparently took priority before they had an opportunity to think things through and decide not to support an investigation – Ben had driven them home.

He and Helen had not talked much about what had occurred, both of them in a state of shock. While he'd taken to the settee and turned on the TV without much conscious thought, he'd been turning over the events in his mind, and quite often had come back to his parting statement to Jason.

'Something got into me,' Jason had whined, and it sounded almost flippant when he'd replied, 'You don't . . . bloody well . . . say.' He hadn't meant it to sound sarcastic. His skin had crawled at the possibility that Jason – thief, liar and druggie that he was – was actually telling the truth.

It had not yet been established that Jason had been the person to break into their basement, but Ben had concluded it. The fact that Jason had employed – as his intended murder weapon – the copper wire with which he'd earlier bound the grille shut spoke volumes. So what was the implication of being down there in the basement, and what had disturbed him so badly that he'd tried garotting his girlfriend? Earlier, Rachel had claimed some weird goings-on had occurred to her while trapped downstairs, and it didn't take a brain surgeon to figure out that both had been mentally disturbed by something they'd come into contact with.

Something that he'd inadvertently carried into the basement in that damned box alongside the amulet.

The horrible, withered thing.

Again, he must consider that when he'd pierced it with the screwdriver, and it had puffed rank-smelling air, that it might also have expelled some type of hallucinogenic fungus or spores. Where Rachel had been convinced she was under attack from some devilish force, Jason had gone a step further and claimed it had possessed him entirely.

Ironically, on the TV screen, some devil-infested girl levitated above her filth-streaked bed, spine contorted agonisingly, and Ben had to swallow hard to dislodge the notion of *possession* as if it was stuck in his throat.

Also on screen, the girl gurgled and spat and then ejected a stream of greenish bile. Ben slugged a mouthful of vodka, then reached for the remote control. Helen beat him to it, first muting and then finally switching off the TV altogether. 'I can't take much more of that,' she intoned, and Ben was in agreement.

He said, 'What exactly do you know happened with Rachel today?'

'Enough to know there was more to her story than she let on.'

'Yeah,' he said. 'I was going to keep this to myself, but she confided in me that she believed there was somebody down in the basement with her, and that she felt physically attacked. You don't think—'

'What, that Jason was down there all along and it was him who attacked her, the way he did Belinda?'

'No. That's not what I mean. Jason wasn't downstairs with her, in fact, and Rachel told me that too, he was the first to try getting her out through the coal chute before those other lads took charge.'

'She was frightened, in pitch darkness, it's unsurprising that her imagination played havoc with her.'

'That's the thing, Helen. I agree that it was probably all in her head, but I also think that something caused her to suffer such a wild waking nightmare.'

Helen looked at him for a breathless moment. Then she shook her head. 'What could do that?'

'I think I might have carried something harmful into the shop.'

'Like what?'

'Don't know for sure, but we might have to get the basement fumigated before it's safe to work down there again.'

'What are you talking about?'

'You know that amulet I bought?' he said. 'Well, it wasn't the only thing I found in that old cardboard box. There was other stuff, including an old wooden container with a few weird objects in it.'

'I saw the box on the counter once you got the lights back on,' she admitted. 'And there was a small gold ring and a lock of hair inside, wasn't there? According to Rachel, the ring was put on the stand and the hair and a ribbon were left lying on the worktop when she was working downstairs.'

'She told you that?'

'Yeah, when you were messing about with the door trying to find out how it could have jammed on her.'

He nodded. Initially he and Rachel had agreed to keep the weirder activity from Helen, but their assistant had had no reason to keep the more mundane facts a secret.

'There was something else in the box,' he said.

Helen waited.

'Something I can't quite explain.'

'Well, you could at least try, rather than keep me in the dark.'

He told her about the blackened, withered thing, and how he'd thought it a living creature at first, and had stabbed it with his screwdriver. 'I'm more inclined to believe it was some kind of exotic fungus or something and it released some spores when I jabbed it. Some mushrooms and toadstools can be incredibly toxic, can't they? You don't think this thing might have poisoned both Rachel and Jason's minds?'

Again Helen could do nothing more than stare.

'What kind of mushroom could make one believe they were being attacked, while making the other *into* an attacker?'

'I don't know. Maybe its effect has something to do with an individual's normal demeanour. Or maybe they reacted differently because of varying degrees of exposure.'

'Or maybe Rachel just panicked, and Jason took something else that made him high as a kite and psychotic?' Helen pursed her lips, waiting for him to argue.

He took another swallow of vodka, grimaced at its intensity, and then held up the empty glass. 'Want another?'

Helen handed over her glass and he went to refill their glasses.

On his return he sat beside her once more. He'd put only a tiny amount of alcohol in his own glass, but had not been miserly with hers.

'Ben Taylor, are you trying to get me drunk so you can have your wicked way with me again?'

'I'm not sure I have the energy after last night,' he confessed with a chagrined grin. He held up his tiny drink. 'I thought I'd best keep a clear head until after the police have been here and taken a statement.'

'Are you going to tell them about your hallucinogenic-fungus theory?'

'No way. Besides them probably deciding I'm a nutter, I don't want to give anyone a reason to think we're liable for sending them insane and trying to sue us.'

'Yeah. "Where there's blame there's a claim",' she quoted with a roll of her eyes. 'We certainly don't want one of those ambulance-chasing firms to get wind of this. But aren't we obliged to report it to the authorities if there's a chance the place is contaminated?'

'Like buggery. I'll ask around, see if any of my mates has somebody who'll come and do the fumigation on the quiet.'

'We've still got some face masks from when the lockdown restrictions were on,' she reminded him, 'and a bottle of bleach. I'd rather we just did a bit of a clean-up ourselves and not go overboard with this.'

'If that's the way you want to play things, then fair enough. But I'll do the cleaning up. I'm not letting you down there until I know that it's safe.'

'How sweet,' she said.

'It's not that, love, I just don't want you turning nuttier than you already are and trying to do me in.'

She playfully swatted his shoulder.

He chuckled, then knocked back the small measure of vodka in his glass. Through the window, he'd noted the arrival of a marked police car, parked awkwardly across their driveway, as if intending to block their Range Rover should they plan on escaping. The doorbell rang, and then, without waiting, the police constable drummed their fist on the door and a shiver raced up Ben's spine. Why, he wondered, should he suddenly feel as if he was responsible for everything and the true villain of the piece?

THIRTEEN

His boiler suit was too tight for Ben's husky frame, and he had to leave the uppermost button open or risk strangulation. When he walked, it was with his heels splayed. As well as the faded blue coverall, he'd donned a pair of wellington boots, rubber gloves, and gone way beyond a surgical-style mask by fishing out a firefighter's breathing apparatus and visor that he'd recalled purchasing as part of a job lot a couple of years earlier. As he stood at the threshold to the basement stairs, he paused, feeling as ridiculous as he must look. In one rubber-gloved hand he carried a spray bottle of disinfectant, and in the other a wad of cloth.

'Ready when you are,' announced Rachel, as she stood poised to shove open the door.

'When you push it open, try not to breathe in,' he said, his voice muffled and distorted by the mask.

Those were wise words, except he could hardly breathe in enough oxygen to feed his brain through the old respirator. The glass in the visor was scratched and pitted. Inside the mask, it smelled and tasted like burning horse hair, repulsive, and he thought this amount of caution was possibly beyond a joke. Rachel had put on a paper mask and tugged it up to the rims of her spectacles. Each time she breathed, the lenses misted over. Beyond them, Helen could barely contain a chuckle at their expense as she fetched a bucket of warm water, brimming over with soap bubbles to pass forward to her husband.

After shoving the cloths down the front of his boiler suit, Ben took the bucket and sucked in several inhibited breaths. Mind buzzing, he nodded at Rachel, and she aggressively thrust the door open. Rather than step back, she laid hands on him, and physically forced Ben onto the uppermost stair. It had surprised him, when Rachel had turned up for work as usual, with hardly any hint of the wreck she'd been when going home yesterday. It was as if she had forced the incident behind her, and was adamant that she'd display greater fortitude to her bosses. Perhaps she feared they would sack her for her wild behaviour, and was determined to show she was not the fruit loop they had witnessed after she had been locked up in the dark. Ben shrugged aside her concerns, because they weren't an issue, and instead found his own impeding on his resolve to disinfect the basement workstation.

Hands gently pressed him forward.

'Go on, nothing's going to bite you,' said Rachel.

Ben glanced back at her, but could hardly make out her features through the scuffed visor. He wondered why she had emphasised her words 'bite you'.

Finally, gravity and momentum helping, he chugged down the stairs in his wellington boots, the bucket sloshing at his side. At the bottom he halted and peered around, but again was largely foiled. He pulled in more strained breaths. He set down the bucket and spray bottle. Frustration won out, and he yanked and tugged loose the old breathing apparatus and set it aside. If the basement was contaminated, and he was affected by the hallucinogenic spores, then so be it: first sign of any madness and he'd hightail it out of the basement, before he was overwhelmed, and catch some fresh air. He stood, taking in shallow breaths, testing his thoughts for reason after each, and decided that doing so was a form of induced paranoia in its own right. Determined not to allow panic to take him, he turned and looked upward. He'd told Rachel not to breathe, and to close the door after he was safely on the stairs, but she hadn't listened. The two women crowded the doorway, looking down at him expectantly.

'I'll get going in a minute,' he pledged, 'I just need to pull myself together first.'

'Why did you take off your mask?' Helen demanded.

'I don't think I need it.'

'How could you possibly know that?'

'Do I look crazy to you?'

'You always look crazy.'

Ben caught the furrow in Rachel's brow and said, 'I'm not suggesting that you are nuts, just that something about *whatever-it-is* seems to have a weird effect on some folk.'

She shrugged off his comment, but her scowl didn't shift.

Rachel had returned to work, but her mind was not fully on her job. She certainly wasn't showing the same level of enthusiasm she normally did, but that was to be expected, he supposed. Hauling the bucket and spray bottle with him, he made his way along the workbench to where the wooden box sat. It still stood on end, the lid lying on the counter. As before, there was no sign of the buckled gold ring, and the lock of hair lay several feet away on the floor.

'Bloody thief,' he called Jason under his breath.

For all the gold value of the ring, and no way of proving that Jason had stolen it, he didn't intend making a fuss, but he was annoyed all the same. Each quid he lost on the other items was a pound lost on the profit he'd hoped to glean from the sale of the amulet.

He sprayed disinfectant in the general area of the box, then used the bottom of the spray bottle to knock it down on the bench. It fell with a rattle and sounded hollow. He gave the box another squirt, then aimed the spray inside, and only once it was doused did he pick it up in his gloved hands and squint inside. It just appeared to be a small wooden box, constructed by an amateur craftsman, by the looks of it, and completely empty. He tipped the box back and forth, but this time there was no sensation of anything rolling about inside. Happy that the withered thing had not somehow crawled back to its container, he inspected the lid next, after a liberal squirt of disinfectant. The words scratched into the wood still made no sense to him, but he committed some to his memory, intending to throw them through an Internet search engine later to see what he could learn.

Using the wadded cloth and soapy water, he wiped the workbench down, then retrieved the lock of hair and ribbon and placed them inside the box, before sliding the lid securely in place: if he'd a spare silver nail, he'd have knocked that in place too. He set them aside, and next went to the waste bin. He recalled dumping the withered thing in the bin and piling the old bubble wrap, cardboard and stuff on top. With no intention of delving inside, he pulled out the bin bag and secured it with a tight knot, placing it at the foot of the stairs for disposal once he went back upstairs.

'Are you OK?'

He looked up to find Helen standing in the open doorway.

'Yeah, totally fine,' he said. 'If that thing was full of toxic fumes or spores, it seems to have worn off by now.'

'You're sure you aren't feeling weird?'

'Actually, no. It felt odd the last time I was down here . . . not now.'

'It's gone.'

The latter voice was Rachel's. Her eyes sparkling with unshed tears beyond her lenses, she joined Helen at the top of the stairs.

'You're right, Ben. Even from here I can tell the atmosphere has changed. Whatever it was, that presence of evil has disappeared.'

Helen looked at her askew. 'Evil? You mean literally?'

'I know I might sound a little barmy,' Rachel admitted, 'but just ask Ben. There was something uncanny released from inside that box.'

Helen snorted in disbelief. 'I don't believe in that silly stuff.'

'Ask Ben. He can confirm it.'

His wife stared at him and Ben raised his eyebrows, his mouth downturned.

'Won't you need Holy Water in that sprayer instead of disinfectant?' Helen asked with a snarky twist of her lip.

Ben threw down the damp cloth. 'To be honest, I've come to the conclusion I don't even need to do this now. Whatever was here, as Rachel just said, has disappeared.'

'I'm, uh, happy to take over, if you'd like,' said Rachel, and she squeezed past Helen and began descending the stairs.

'Well, yes, if you think you're up to it?'

'I am. It's like Helen thinks, there's no such thing as evil stuff, not in a silly supernatural sense. Whatever bothered me yesterday, it probably had to do with being plunged into darkness and panicking. I'm fine now . . . as long as the lights stay on.'

'You'll still want these,' said Ben, showing her his rubber-gloved hands.

'Yes. And the disinfectant. I'll make do with my own mask, and you're welcome to keep hold of that boiler suit.'

Ben exchanged a look with Rachel as she approached. She was downplaying her fears for Helen's sake, but he saw the pain in her expression as she accepted the rubber gloves from him.

He said, loud enough for his wife to also hear, 'Let's do this between us and get it finished so much sooner, eh?' He looked up, caught the soft shake of his wife's head, and added, 'Are you OK watching the shop for now, love?'

'You want me to open up before you have the cleaning finished?'

'Why not?'

'I suppose you're right. We're already out of pocket, we may as well try and claw back some profit from sales.'

As Helen prepared to open the shop, Ben and Rachel exchanged looks.

'Are you certain you're up for this?' Ben asked.

'I hoped to have another word with you in private, and thought this was my best opportunity.'

He bent close, whispering, 'Something you don't want Helen overhearing?'

'We've managed to keep the weirdest things from her until now – do you want to keep things that way?'

'She's too sceptical for her own good.'

'Healthy scepticism is acceptable, it's cynicism I don't like.'

Ben grunted. He loved his wife and ordinarily would defend her to the nth degree, but had to agree that when it came to supernatural and paranormal happenings, Helen could be a complete – to the point of aggression – cynic.

Rachel nodded him away from the foot of the stairs. 'Can I show you something?'

'Of course you can.'

He followed.

For her return to work, Rachel had dressed in a fresh sweatshirt and black leggings. The leggings were tight fitting, almost a second skin. Ben could see the outline of her underwear through them when she angled her backside to him. He stuttered to a halt, wondering where the hell things were heading. She tucked her fingertips into her waistline and began rolling down her leggings, exposing several centimetres of pale flesh. Nervously he glanced back, ensuring that Helen couldn't see them, worried she might misconstrue things and think he was a willing participant in whatever Rachel had in mind.

'See it?' she asked.

'Rache,' Ben cautioned, one palm held out towards her.

Rachel angled her backside higher, and then Ben finally understood what it was he was actually supposed to look at.

There was a blemish at the lowest point of her spine where it met the swell of her backside. Under the artificial glare of the striplights, it looked livid, as purple as a ripe plum.

'Is that a bruise?' he asked, stupidly.

'It's more of a bite,' she replied.

'From what, a bloody mosquito on steroids?'

'From whatever you let loose from that box,' she corrected him.

He shook his head. 'No. No way, Rache—'

'Do you think I'm making things up? Look at the rest of my back.' She shrugged up her sweatshirt, exposing her back, and a network of faded scratches in her flesh. 'When I told you before that I believed I was being physically attacked, I didn't mention I also had physical *proof*.'

'Holy Christ! I saw some scrapes on your neck. Are you certain that—'

'Don't ask if I did this to myself. The weird thing is that yesterday I watched them fade from being vivid gouges, and convinced myself I must have hallucinated the attack, and that I must've scraped myself on the stairs. But I didn't, Ben. And before you ask, no! Does it look as if I could reach to scratch myself there?'

'I wasn't going to suggest you did it. I had wondered if, maybe, you were on your back on the stairs and maybe scratched yourself on the risers or something.'

'No, Ben, when I think about it, I wasn't ever fully on my back. I was forced down on my hands and knees, and it got its claws in me, and then I was terrified that it was going to try to . . .' Her words faded, unable to continue the suggestion that her attacker might sexually violate her. Then she shoved down her sweatshirt and yanked her waistband up, and faced him with a look of sheer desolation. 'It didn't rape me like *that*, but it bit me, and if I'm not mistaken, it tried to bore its way inside me by another route.'

Incredulous, Ben shook his head. 'Jeez, Rache, I'm not saying you're making this up, but—'

She jabbed a finger at the spot on her lower back where, he

had to admit, it had looked like some filthy lamprey had fastened on with its sets of concentric fangs. 'Did that bite look like a figment of my imagination to you?' she asked.

'No, but, well . . . we can sometimes misconstrue what has really happened.'

'I didn't do that to myself, and I didn't manifest it with the power of my mind like some kind of unholy stigmata . . . Something tried boring inside me, Ben, and we both know what it was.'

He was lost for words.

'That thing needs to be put back inside its box,' Rachel hissed at a whisper.

He nodded dumbly, then his head jerked up in realisation. 'It isn't here,' he croaked. 'You said so yourself, that whatever was here has gone. This thing with Jason, you don't think he was being literal when he claimed something had got into him?'

'Those were his actual words?' Rachel asked.

'Yeah. To the letter. After trying to throttle the life out of his girlfriend, he suddenly snapped out of the madness and said: "I swear to you, I'd never deliberately hurt you. You've got to believe me. Something got into me".'

Rachel exhaled loudly, puffing out her mask, and again painting the lenses of her glasses with moisture. Wiping them with her sleeve, she turned to where the box sat unattended on the counter. 'That,' she said, 'isn't an ordinary box, it's a container . . . a reliquary.'

'Aren't reliquaries used for keeping ancient relics?'

'Yeah, but I'm thinking of it in terms of a strongbox to keep something from escaping. Those words cut into the box, I bet they're warnings of some type, and when you broke that silver nail, it also broke whatever seal was holding that thing under control.'

'You do realise how ridiculous this sounds?' he cautioned, and again glanced to check that Helen wasn't eavesdropping, her lip set in a sarcastic sneer.

'If you've a better explanation for what has happened, I'm all ears.'

Ben moved and stood beside her. Together they stared at the box, neither of them making an attempt at touching it.

'Those words,' said Rachel, but didn't finish her thought.

'Mulé,' Ben quoted from memory. 'O Beng.'

'Does that read "amriya"?' Rachel asked.

Ben tilted his head from side to side. 'I can't tell. It's either amriya or armaya, but the writing's that crude it's hard to tell.'

Rachel indicated other words, again without touching the box. 'Mamioro? Ruffie?'

'Canni . . . kin?' Ben offered, reading another of the visible etchings.

'They're foreign words to me,' Rachel admitted. 'Or they're ancient.'

'You don't know your Rabbie Burns, then?' he asked, while rolling his Rs in a faux Scottish accent.

Rachel squinted at him.

'A cannikin's an old Scottish name for a wee drinking cup or vessel, usually one that has a lid and can be sealed. Unless I'm mistaken, Burns mentioned it in one of his poems. Or perhaps it was Shakespeare.' He shrugged. 'Maybe it's written on there because the box is some kind of vessel too . . .'

Rachel took out her phone and brought up the search engine. After a few taps she said, 'You're probably right, but it says here that Project Cannikin was an underground nuclear weapons test in Alaska.'

'Really? I was about to say we'll go with the vessel idea, but considering how dangerous it has proven, maybe we should handle it like it's a flaming nuclear warhead.' He was joking, partially, but didn't raise a smile from Rachel. She nodded agreement.

Upstairs, there was a crash of breaking glass.

It drew up Ben's head.

Helen emitted an agonised screech.

'What the hell *now*?' Ben yelped, and was immediately on the move. His rubber boots slapped the ground with each hurried step up the stairs.

Helen cried out a second time, this time lower, as if she was trying to suppress the pain.

Ben staggered out into the shop, with Rachel knocking up against his back, she was so close on his heels.

Helen turned towards her husband, holding her right wrist with her left hand. Shock contorted her features, and no wonder: blood dripped darkly between the clenched fingers of her right hand. When she slowly unfurled her fist, the blood spattered from a deep gash across the bases of her fingers.

The pain, the shock, the volume and sight of blood: Helen collapsed.

FOURTEEN

'You should throw that horrible thing away, first chance you get,' said Rachel, meaning the wooden box.

He understood without requiring further clarification, as it was on his mind while they sat in the overflowing waiting room at the Accident and Emergency department of their local hospital. They'd gone through triage, then sat for an age, but Helen had finally been taken through to have her wound treated. Ordinarily, Ben would've gone with her again, to keep her company and offer moral support, but she'd made it clear that she didn't need chaperoning by somebody who might faint at the sight of a needle . . . her way of deflecting the fact she had passed out on seeing her own blood.

'You're probably right,' Ben replied, 'it has brought nothing but bad luck since I found the bloody thing.'

'Maybe you should've taken more notice of that warning.'

He nodded glumly. He'd told her about the handwritten note attached to the bubble wrap: DO NOT OPEN. In hindsight, the warning had been there for good reason, but only if he really believed that the box and its contents had anything to do with the run of strange occurrences since opening it. He went back and forth on whether or not he truly believed that he'd released some kind of sentient *thing* when clipping the silver nail, or that everything since had simply been a series of coincidences. This latest event, with Helen slashing open her hand, couldn't possibly be connected to the shrivelled thing from the box, could it? While he and Rachel had whispered together downstairs, she'd gone through the routine of opening the shop for business. Although most of their stock was displayed on shelves and racks, some of the more expensive pieces were kept in lockable cabinets, and it was while unlocking one that the glass door had jumped out of its runners, and Helen, reacting instinctively, had tried catching it and halting its fall to the floor, only for the glass to shatter in her grasp and slice deeply into her hand.

'That bloody thing's ended up costing me a fortune,' he moaned.

Rachel exhaled at his words; to her, the trouble the box had brought them all went well beyond any loss of profit that Ben might suffer. However, a loss of profit to him meant a compounding of everything else that had gone wrong. In hindsight, he wished he'd never laid eyes on that bloody amulet. He had allowed greed to get the better of him, but by now, despite the profit he'd make on its sale, he was surely still going to be out of pocket. Already he'd lost the takings from the holiday Monday, and now he could count on losing another full day after aborting the clean-up to deal with Helen's injury.

'Better still,' said Rachel, 'you should burn it.'

'Not a bad idea,' he agreed. 'But first, I want to do some research, see what I can find out about those words that are scratched into it.'

'Earlier, while you accompanied Helen through triage, I used my phone to look online,' said Rachel.

'Find anything interesting?'

She see-sawed her head, then glanced around. 'Maybe this isn't the time or place to mention what I found.'

They were surrounded by dozens of patients waiting for the over-taxed emergency department to deal with their individual problems. All around them, people sat uncomfortably on seats pushed too close together, coughing, mumbling, groaning in discomfort; Ben was beginning to believe they should give up their seats to more deserving souls. He leaned closer to her. 'Any chance of a clue?'

Rachel kept her voice pitched low. 'You said you thought the old lady you bought the amulet from was a Traveller?'

'That's right.'

'Yeah, well, I looked and found that some of those words on the box are from the Romany language. Not all. But from what I learned, Scottish Travellers speak a different cant, and that's where the words Ruffie and cannikin come from.'

'You may as well tell me what they mean – nobody here is listening.'

He was correct. Everyone in the room had their own problems to contend with, and even if anyone was eavesdropping their conversation, so what?

Rachel took slow perusal of the nearest patients, and saw that – to a person – they couldn't care less what she had to say. She shrugged. 'O Beng is Romany, and Ruffie is Traveller cant, but they are interchangeable and mean the same thing. The Devil.'

'No way? As in . . . Satan?'

'Way,' she said with a grimace. 'Cannikin, again in cant, means "plague" or "sickness", while a mamioro is some kind of spirit that causes the illness.'

Ben stared at his folded hands.

'You're never going to believe what mulé means,' Rachel continued, lowering her voice to barely above a whisper.

'Go on,' he said, equally low.

'It represents the ghost of the dead, but not just any old ghost; it's a harbinger of doom.'

He shook his head, blinking.

Rachel turned and peered up at him through the smudged lenses of her glasses. 'I know it sounds ridiculous, but what if . . . no! It's too crazy.'

'What if I somehow released a captive ghost when I opened the box?'

He chuckled.

After a moment, Rachel chuckled too.

Except, neither of them found the situation humorous.

They sat a while in silence, each lost in their personal thoughts. The clock above the reception desk appeared to work on an extremely slow version of time. Finally the double doors that exited from the A&E department opened and out trudged Helen, holding her bandaged hand against her chest. She looked at the sea of pale faces that had lifted to greet her, trying to pick out the familiar ones, and both Ben and Rachel started to their feet. Ben was still dressed in the tight-fitting boiler suit and wellington boots, dotted with drops of Helen's dried blood. They had to traverse sideways to escape the rows of tightly situated chairs, and Helen moved to meet them.

'Twelve stitches,' she announced, anticipating their questions. 'And I was very lucky not to have sliced an artery, or worse still, a tendon.'

'How do you feel, love? Does it hurt?'

'What do you think?' said Helen with her usual snark.

'Actually, my hand's still numb from the anaesthetic, so it isn't sore at all.'

'It might be a different story tonight once it wears off.'

'That's something I'm not looking forward to.'

'There's still a little of that vodka left, isn't there? Some self-medicating might help.'

'No, I'll stick to paracetamol,' Helen said. 'Last thing I want is to get tipsy, fall over and break a bloody leg. I've had my fill of hospitals for one day. Come on, let's go.'

Helen and Rachel took the lead, leaving Ben to trip along behind them in his cumbersome wellington boots. If anyone might trip and break a leg it would be him, he thought dourly.

It was grey and overcast as they exited the hospital and aimed for the car park. Damp patches on the pavements showed that it had showered while they were inside, but had begun to dry up: a quick check of his phone showed that the process of having Helen's hand cared for had taken several hours. It was pointless even thinking about returning to their shop and opening for the couple of trading hours left in the day. 'We'll take you home, Rache,' Ben announced, 'unless there's somewhere else you'd like to be dropped off?'

'Aren't we going to finish cleaning the shop first?' she responded.

'No, it will wait 'til morning.'

Helen halted, and Ben almost walked into her. She said, 'Are you forgetting the blood? It was pouring from my hand and it dripped all over the place. Surely that needs cleaning up immediately?'

'Well, yeah, now that you mention it,' he conceded. 'Are you still OK to help, Rachel, or do you want to go home? I'm happy either way.'

'I feel as if I haven't earned my pay for days now,' said Rachel, by way of reply.

'Don't be daft. You're worth every penny and by the way, we both appreciate your help,' he told her.

Helen nodded her agreement.

'Let's get you home first,' Ben told his wife.

Helen agreed with a short nod. She turned her attention to Rachel. 'Make sure he does a good job. If it's anything like when he does the housework, I usually have to follow behind him and do it again, but right this time.'

The women grinned at Ben's expense.

He didn't mind being the butt of the joke, especially not if it kept Helen's mind off her injury, and Rachel's off devils and ghosts.

They approached his Range Rover, and Ben aimed his key fob at it, pressing the button and zapping open the doors. He went for the driver's door, while the women both angled for the passenger side.

'Oh, bother,' Helen swore.

'What's up?' Ben wondered.

Helen only scowled and nodded down. Rachel shook her head in disbelief.

Ben had to go around the car to see what had upset them.

Flat tyre.

He grunted at the inconvenience.

Then Helen aimed her bandaged hand at the back tyre: that was flat too.

'Are you bloody kidding me?' Ben hollered at the uncaring sky.

FIFTEEN

Ben sent Helen home in a taxi. Never in their motoring life had they experienced such bad luck as one car being put out of commission through Helen pumping the wrong fuel into it, and then for their other car to get not one but two bloody flat tyres at the same time. He couldn't see anything that had caused the tyres to deflate, and had to entertain the notion that the flats were the work of some nefarious prankster. Once he jacked up the Range Rover and manually changed the spare for the front tyre, he pumped air into the rear one and it fully inflated. Maybe the tyres had slow punctures, or he'd inadvertently parked up against a high kerb, nipping the tyres and causing air to escape from the sidewall. He would have the tyres checked for damage when he attended the garage to collect Helen's car; for the time being he would have to rely on his foot pump to get him from point A to point B. He'd again offered for Rachel to go home, sharing the taxi with Helen, but their assistant had refused. He could tell she had an ulterior motive for staying and it was not because he was sparkling company: she wished to continue the conversation begun in the hospital waiting room. After he lowered the jack, allowing the car to settle on all four tyres, he waited a minute, anticipating the rear one to slowly deflate once more, but it didn't. He went, grumbling about the exorbitant cost of the parking, and wondered why he hadn't called the parking company to inform them he had been inadvertently delayed through punctures: not that it would have won him a reduction in cost, he supposed, because they were greedy, uncaring sods. On his way back, it didn't surprise him to see that Rachel had already got in the front; she was bent over her phone, no doubt scrolling through Internet search results.

'Let's try this again, shall we?' he asked once inside, and he turned the key in the ignition. There was a tiny part of him that expected his run of bad luck to continue, and for the engine to fail to start. However, it rumbled to life, and he pulled away sharply enough for Rachel to rock back and forth in the passenger seat. She was unmoved by his aggressive driving, too wrapped up in whatever was on her phone screen.

Ordinarily a drive from the hospital into town would take about five minutes, but it was rush hour and the journey was slow, extremely slow, and over the car's radio they heard of a major accident on the ring road that was slowing traffic from leaving town. Perhaps forty minutes passed before they again pulled up outside the antiques and curios shop, and Ben set a handwritten note on the dash, deterring any traffic wardens with a claim that he was engaged in delivering stock. Approaching the door, he saw that the handle was smeared with Helen's blood: he'd tried staunching the flow by pressing his hands over hers, so it was little wonder that he'd daubed her blood all over the shop too. He must have smeared the handle when securing the shop behind them. He cringed a little, as if the same blood that hadn't bothered him earlier now sent a shiver of disgust through him. He used his keys to unlock the door, and pushed inside. There had not been time to set the burglar alarm on their way out, with a swooning Helen being practically carried between him and Rachel to the Range Rover. It wasn't dark, but the low clouds made the interior of the shop murky. He flicked on the lights, then moved inside, followed by Rachel. She was yet to inform him what had held her attention during the drive from the hospital.

The cabinet where Helen had badly cut herself still stood open. Inside were some of their more expensive trinkets. The cabinet was free of blood, but below it the carpet was dark and sopping, and great shards of bloody glass formed a pile. 'We should do something about that first,' said Ben, meaning the glass.

'I'll fetch the dustpan and brush,' Rachel said, and began shoving away her phone.

'Did you find anything else of interest?'

She took out her phone and peered at the screen again, as if she couldn't recall what she'd looked at before. 'There's loads, but I can't be certain how much of it is pertinent to that box, and how much is just made-up nonsense. From what I learned, the Travellers' cant is constantly changing and can mean different things from one extended family to another.'

'Why's that then?'

'I don't know. Maybe different families travelling around the country have different experiences, so adapt different words than another family might. The core language stays the same, it's just random stuff that's different.'

'What's the general consensus on the words on the box?'

'I don't remember them all, but the ones I already told you about seem universal and mean the devil, but I found out that both mulé and mulo means "the dead", as in the recently deceased, or "ghost of the dead" and, like I said, can represent a harbinger or warning. I told you cannikin meant plague, but it can also mean sickness, or how somebody feels if they are poorly, tying in nicely with the meaning of mamioro, a sickness-bringing spirit. Then there's amriya, a Romany term for "curse".'

Ben shrugged at her explanations. 'So basically, they all mean bad stuff?'

'When you boil it down to basics, yeah . . .'

'So maybe your idea of setting the bloody thing on fire is our best move,' he said.

She didn't reply, but her silence was enough.

He moved for the stairs down to the basement, and Rachel followed.

Earlier he'd hoped to learn more about the box, and the warnings etched on its surface, but in hindsight, he was better off shot of the damned thing. Learning what the poorly etched words signified didn't help put an end to the sequence of problems the box had trailed since he'd taken ownership of it; and besides, from what he knew of cursed objects – mostly knowledge gleaned from TV programmes and B-horror movies, and largely misinformed or hyperbolic – the best course of action was to reduce them to ashes.

They paused at the foot of the stairs.

The box remained standing upright.

The wind caught in Ben's lungs, holding him static.

Earlier, any sense of the weird or uncanny had drifted away, but now it was back tenfold.

'Do you feel that?' he croaked.

'It has returned,' Rachel said ominously.

Ben barely recognised her voice, and turned towards her to check it was actually Rachel who had spoken.

Her voice had sounded strange because most of her right fist was jammed between her teeth. She extracted it, glistening with saliva, to add, 'Do you think it has crawled back inside the box?'

Ben couldn't be certain, but felt she was right, and the horrible thing had crawled back inside like some demonic chicken gone home to roost.

'If it has, then that's good. It'll go in the fire with the rest of the shit.' Galvanised by his own words, he strode forward, wellington boots clomping on the floor, and snatched the box and lid off the counter. As an afterthought he grabbed the lock of hair and ribbon too, and stuffed it in the box before ramming home the lid in its slots – hadn't he done so already, once before? If he had a fresh nail, he would have willingly forced the bloody thing through the wood and hammered it home with the base of his fist if necessary. Earlier, he'd definitely thrown away the withered thing in the waste bin, but later removed the black plastic liner, so it should be in there – notwithstanding it had somehow found its way back inside the box – and, if memory served, he'd dumped the bag at the foot of the stairs in preparation for removing it. The bag was gone, but he doubted a supernatural explanation: distracted, he, or Rachel, must have later lifted the bag and discarded it with the other trash. The bin liner and the trash inside, he decided, was unimportant; if Rachel was correct and the thing had returned to the box, all that mattered was that they got rid of the box and its ungodly contents as rapidly as possible.

Carrying the box at arm's length, he headed for the stairs. 'Grab some cardboard and paper, anything that will burn,' he instructed, and Rachel nodded, diverting to where they kept some spare packing material, and grabbing up an armful.

He was most of the way up the stairs before she mounted them below him. She thundered upward, propelled by the intimidating atmosphere redolent in the basement. Ben paused, cringing inside, until she gained the step behind him, then continued up, offering his presence in support. In his hands, the small box felt as if it had gained several kilograms in weight. His forearms quivered with the strain of holding it away from his body, his shoulder muscles ached, but he persevered.

'We need a lighter or matches, or something to get a fire going,' Ben said.

Rachel didn't reply, but again he understood her silence.

'I'm certain there's an old petrol lighter in one of the cabinets, and if we're lucky it will still have fuel in it.'

Rachel set down her bundle of cardboard and paper, and darted to look. Interestingly, she headed directly for the cabinet with the broken door. Ensuring she didn't stand in the blood, or the shards of glass, leaning and reaching, she plucked out an old-fashioned Ronson table lighter. In this more enlightened age, smoking paraphernalia wasn't much prized, but this old lighter was historical, having ties to a famous local politician, and therefore having a collector's value attached.

Rachel held out the ornamental lighter. 'Helen had me put some fuel in it so I could demonstrate if a potential buyer wanted to see it working.'

'And you tried it?'

'Of course.'

Ben nodded, of course she had, otherwise why would she have gone for that particular item?

He headed outdoors, still holding the box like it was filthy, stinking and contaminated. Rachel followed, again clasping a pile of cardboard and packing paper to her chest, the table lighter clutched under her left armpit. They couldn't burn the box right there in the street, so Ben headed down the alley next to the mobile phone shop, into the shared backyard. Not only did the yard serve as an entrance to the flats above the shops, it also contained the rubbish receptacles for the dwellings, and a bunch of wheelie bins used by the shops. They were all made of plastic, and therefore useless to Ben and Rachel. However, sitting under the first landing on the metal staircase, there was an older bin, a relic from the days of coal fires and hot ashes. Ben had noted the old-style bin over the years, and had watched it progressively corrode and fill with rainwater and windblown rubbish. He set down the box on the metal stairs and ducked under the platform. Filled to the neck with stagnant green slime, the bin was full. Rather than try to drag it out while heavy, he warned Rachel to stand back, then shoved the bin over. It buckled, but retained most of its integrity, and splashed a tide of filth on the rough tarmac. Once mostly empty, Ben took hold of it as gingerly as he'd held the box, and upended the bin, to empty whatever nameless sludge lay at its bottom. A stench arose, and he gagged, wishing he'd had the presence of mind to bring the firefighter's respirator and visor out with him. Rachel, having set down the makings of their fire, also gagged, and threw an elbow across her face. A rat had drowned in the depths, and the putrid stench was intense.

Making faces of revulsion, Ben kicked the now empty bin out to the centre of the yard where it wouldn't pose a hazard to the surrounding buildings. Gasping at the horrendous stench, Rachel kept her distance, and Ben was forced to fetch the cardboard and paper. He didn't intend to try starting the fire with the contents inside the bin, so lay a small pile of wadded paper on the tarmac instead. He knelt down, hearing and feeling his knees complain, then held out a hand towards Rachel. Tentative, without inhaling, she approached and handed over the table lighter.

'Can you fetch me the box?' Ben asked.

She shook her head, fear flaring in her eyes.

'You'd best help me up then.'

Rachel assisted him to stand, and he groaned at the pain in his joints. He trudged over, wellingtons clumping, and reached for the box. The damn thing jumped and rattled on the metal stairs!

Ben grunted in alarm but, rather than retreat, he was spurred to action by it. He grabbed the box, felt something shift and roll inside, and he almost ran back to the makings of his fire. He immediately thrust the box into the old metal bin, and again crouched in front of the small bundle of paper. The old lighter was designed with ease of use in mind: a lever was pressed down with the thumb to spin the striking wheel against a flint, while also disengaging a pop-up compartment containing the fuel-soaked wick, which should, in theory, instantly ignite. Five lever-presses later and all he had achieved was a bruised thumb tip. He looked at Rachel.

She shrugged. 'I swear I put some fuel in it.'

'And it worked?'

'Yeah,' she said, 'about a year ago.'

'Was it displayed in its opened position?'

She nodded.

Most likely the fuel had evaporated a long time ago. He wondered if he could pull apart the components and maybe use the wheel and flint to strike a spark into his kindling bundle. It was a ridiculous notion, and his alternative was to send Rachel off to a nearby shop to see if she could purchase some matches. There was no way that he wanted to leave that box whole and unguarded while he went off in search of fire.

A smouldering cigarette stump bounced across the tarmac no more than a yard away. Sparks flew from it. Ben made to reach for the stump, hoping to blow it into life and use it to get a blaze going, but stopped, realising the cigarette had been thrown for another reason. Bloody Jason, taking the piss, after Ben had asked him to take better care of where he discarded his cigarette ends. But it couldn't be Jason, he must still be in custody at the police station. He turned towards the metal stairs, seeking the culprit, and had to crane higher when he found the landing to Jason's flat empty. One of the Eastern European lads leaned over the uppermost railing; 'Hey, Mister Taylor-and-King,' said the lad in a heavily accented voice, 'you need a lighter for your barbecue?'

'Do you have one I can use?' Ben countered.

'Yes. Hold on. I'll come down.'

'It's OK, just toss it down and I'll catch it.'

'I've to come down anyway,' said the lad dismissively.

The stairs creaked to each step as he descended.

Rachel grew bashful when the lad approached, grinning at her. 'How are you feeling now, miss?' he asked.

He was one of the two who had helped her out of the coal chute, and later helped to contain their drug-enraged neighbour, Jason. She didn't reply, but he was unperturbed. He looked quizzically at the small pile of papers in front of Ben. 'Where are the burgers and frankfurters?'

'Eh, we're not actually having a barbecue,' said Ben.

'I'm foreign, but I'm not stupid,' said the lad. 'I make a joke, but I see it went over your head.'

'Sorry,' Ben said. 'It's been a helluva couple of days and I'm not in a laughing mood.'

'So if not a barbecue, why do you make a fire?'

'Just getting rid of some rubbish,' Ben said.

The lad craned to peer into the bin.

'A pencil box? I had one of those as a boy. It's no good to you, I will take it.'

Ben shook his head. 'Ordinarily I'd say yes, but . . .' He paused, wondering how much he should confess, and finally said: 'It's contaminated.'

'What with?'

'Blood,' he said, and indicated the blotches of Helen's blood on his boiler suit and wellingtons. 'Helen had an accident earlier and bled all over it. Anything else, I would have just wiped it clean, but blood? No, I won't chance that it got into the seams or grain.'

'Does Helen have a disease?'

'No, but you do understand how bacteria spreads, right?'

The lad grunted, glanced at Rachel and caught a shy smile from her. 'Helluva couple of days, eh?' he mimicked.

'You can say that again,' said Rachel.

The lad handed over a plastic disposable lighter.

Ben lit the paper wad, and dropped it inside the bin, dreading hearing it sizzle in the dampness, but he turned and grabbed more waste packing paper, screwed it into bundles and dropped them in too. Soon he began adding cardboard, and the flames grew so high and hot that he had to stand back. He kept feeding the flames, and soon was certain that the box ignited amid the inferno, as a belching black cloud arose, and it stank almost as bad as the putrefying corpse of the rat had several minutes earlier. Both Rachel and the lad joined in, searching for fresh fuel, snatching up twigs and litter, and even the dismantled parts of an old coffee table behind the wheelie bins, and tossing it all onto the pyre.

Ben stood with the column of smoke rearing overhead, shivering despite the blistering heat radiating out from the metal bin. He wasn't totally convinced that their run of bad luck had been due to anything released from the box; to truly take it in, he'd have to accept that ghosts and devils and spiritual possession were real, and he wasn't there yet. He still believed that all could be scientifically explained, and that each seemingly supernatural event actually had an equally mundane natural explanation, and yet it gave him great satisfaction knowing that the cursed thing was currently being reduced to ashes, along with its foul contents. The flames, he trusted, would do their job. *Yeah, good riddance to it all*, he thought, as he fed more cardboard to the fire.

SIXTEEN

Hours later, when he peered over the edge of the fire escape, Cezary Nowak could still pinpoint the location of the bin in the darkness of the backyard. The fire had burned down, but cinders still smouldered at the bottom, and occasionally belched a few sparks when the ashes sifted and settled. After feeding it for about half an hour, Ben Taylor and his assistant had finally recalled they had work to complete inside the shop and had left him alone. He'd shoved in a few more sticks and then lost interest in the job and returned upstairs.

Cezary had mainly shown enthusiasm for the task of feeding their bonfire in order to get close to Rachel again. After helping her out of the coal chute yesterday, and again working with her to find flammable trash, he'd gained the impression that she was as interested in him as he was in her; actually probably more so. She was a bit shy, and though he'd appeared a bit brash and forward, he wasn't as confident as he liked to make out. He'd flirted with her, but had failed to ask her out on a date, but hey! It was a small blip in his road to dating her. He believed that he'd endeared himself to her, and when next he saw her, under different circumstances, she was sure to be open to his advance.

His friends had teased him mercilessly when he'd admitted to fancying the girl; they were more interested in those fakers posting sexy, doctored images on Instagram and TikTok than on a 'plain shop girl': their description, not his. They were indoors now, back from a tough shift at the fish-packing factory, laughing, joking, swearing, drinking, making too much noise for his liking. Sometimes he smoked only to take a few minutes' peace to himself. Sometimes his cousin Tymon joined him on the fire escape, usually to beg a cigarette from Cezary, as he was too tight with his wages to buy his own, but for now he had sole use. He drew in a lungful of more pleasurable smoke than had wafted from the bin-fire earlier, held it in his lungs a few seconds then allowed it to trickle out between his teeth. Hanging his hands over the railing, cigarette between two fingers, he stared down at the bin. Then he flicked his cigarette butt, aiming to sail it in a graceful arc to land in the ashes. The butt struck the bin and tumbled away in a shower of tiny sparks to land several metres away, in the company of several hundred more dead butts he'd flicked into the yard since moving into the apartment.

The butt had been of inconsequential weight or mass, and yet its simple collision with the can seemed to set off some type of cascade effect inside, with the last remaining burned sticks and cardboard ashes sifting and sliding and collapsing in on themselves, and a fresh cloud of smoke to puff heavenward, like the final gasp of a dying volcano. Cezary grunted. The smoke stank, most likely because it was tinged with whatever filth Taylor had failed to tip out when he first upended the water out of the bin. It smelt like . . . death.

He turned his face aside.

A moment later he snapped his attention back on the bin.

Something inside had moved. Something more substantial than charcoal and ashes.

He and Rachel had broken up several pieces of discarded furniture left to rot in the yard, and he'd pulled stuff from the wheelie bins to help feed the fire too, but he was certain that all had been consumed by the super-heated flames, before Rachel and Taylor had gone back inside. Since then, he'd only added those few twigs and they'd ignited the instant he threw them in. So what was substantial enough that it knocked against the bin when the ashes again tried settling?

He didn't really care.

No, actually, his interest was piqued, otherwise why question it at all?

He moved down the stairs, never taking his gaze off the bin.

He crossed the lower landing of his drug-addicted neighbour, and fleetingly thought how Jason's strength had surprised him and Tymon when the cousins tried wrestling him. Jason was a stickman, made of rags and bones, and very little meat. He should not have had the strength to resist, and yet Cezary knew that some narcotics lent desperate strength to their users even as they leached their other vitals, as did some forms of insanity. He shivered at the memory of Jason's contorted visage, and the hot spittle he'd spat all over Cezary's face while he ranted and raved. Cezary continued on, resisting wiping his face, the memory of the hot saliva disgusting. He hurried down the next flight of stairs and stepped out into the yard. From above, the yard – enclosed on three sides, and bounded on the last by high trees – had appeared darker than at ground level. There he had the benefit of the glow of streetlights filtering down the service alley and through the branches of the trees. He didn't need the meagre light, because the bin itself still radiated heat, adding its own form of luminosity as a guide. He moved forward, and leaned, taking care not to get too close: the heat could still be intense, and burn him if he was stupid enough to stick his face over the open rim.

The stench was bad.

He stepped back.

A second knock rewarded him.

'Co się kurwa dzieje?' He demanded to know what was going on, falling into his native language.

He returned to the bin, and standing sideways, he tipped to peer over the rim. The ashes had formed a pile in the base of the bin, easily seen because they still danced and writhed with embers. Seated upon the pile of twinkling ashes was Taylor's contaminated pencil box, slightly darkened, yet barely singed by the heat.

'Ty uparta istoto,' he called the box. Something his mother used to call him when he was a recalcitrant and rebellious child: You stubborn thing.

The ashes settled and the box moved, and it rang against the side of the bin.

'You don't want to stay there, eh?' he asked, reverting to English. 'What's wrong? Too warm for you?'

The box was old, and crude, with some type of writing on it he couldn't decipher. Taylor had claimed it was contaminated with his wife's spilled blood. Well, the heat should have solved the problem of contamination, and its rough-and-ready appearance only helped add to his nostalgia. He hadn't lied when he said he had been given a pencil box like it as a boy; it had been a handmade gift from his father, who had died shortly after. Cezary's original box had gone inside his tata's coffin with him when he was laid to rest.

Raising a foot, he set his heel to the rim of the metal bin and gave it a swift shove. The bin toppled over, spilling hot ashes across the yard, and momentarily he was blinded by a blizzard of sparks and lighter-than-air motes of ash. Blinking, then wiping ashes from his eyelashes, he checked and saw that the box had been spat from the bin as well. Avoiding a burn, he ensured he was out of reach of the hot metal, and again used his feet to first fish, then drag the box away from the hot ash. He slid the box along the tarmac until it was safely away from the bin, and then he crouched down to view it closer. He held his palm over it, checking for radiating heat and found none. Tentatively he reached closer, and again could sense no heat. Finally, he wet a fingertip and touched the box with the speed of a striking serpent. Skin contact was very brief but enough to assure him that the box didn't retain any blistering heat; in fact, if anything it felt cool to the touch. Ciekawe, he thought: interesting. He reached again and found that the wooden box had resisted the heat so well that the instant it was beyond the touch of the hot ashes, it had cooled to the ambient temperature.

He picked it up, flipping it between his palms, until he was certain there wasn't a hot spot that would sear his flesh. He carried the box with him and set it on the metal stairs. There was enough ambient light to study his prize under. He tested the lid and found that it slid easily in its runners, neither the lid nor sides warped by heat. It was crudely made, but impressive in its sturdiness, and once wiped with a clean rag would be a handy receptacle, and a nice reminder of his sorely missed tata. He thought slyly, perhaps, that it might make a good hiding place to put his cigarettes out of Tymon's view.

He took off the lid and set it on the step alongside the box, then tipped the container. Something moved inside, and he cringed slightly at the waft of decomposition that assailed his nostrils. With a tentative fingertip he inspected the thing within, finding it as desiccated and colourless as the box's interior, wondering how the box had resisted the scorching flames but whatever was inside had been charred to a black, withered lump.

SEVENTEEN

It had been hours since Jason Halloran was kicked back out on the street, after spending all night and the following morning in a holding cell. Although several of his neighbours had given statements to the police, Belinda had not made a complaint of assault against him. At first the coppers treated him as if they were going to throw the entire law book at him for attempted murder, but with nobody pushing the case, decided the best they could do was treat his attack on his girlfriend as nothing more than a common law breach of the peace. With the breach averted and therefore ended, they had nothing to charge him with: that didn't mean they released him immediately, as a duty of care was present so he was held until seen and cleared for release by the on-duty doctor. Proving he was drug and alcohol free, and of sound-ish mind, he was released on his own reconnaissance, allowed to return home. He didn't go home. Jason was too embarrassed and didn't want to face the music, should he meet Taylor or any of those Eastern European lads who lived in the upstairs apartment. He kicked around town, met with other guys with similar lifestyles to his, and ended up halving a two-litre bottle of strong cider with a down-and-out called Jeb. With a little Dutch courage on-board, he went in search of Belinda, but after hanging out outside her stepfather's place for ages without spotting her, he decided she'd probably already gone out on the game. It made sense; with Jason gone, she had to find somebody else to help bankroll her addictions.

He dawdled as he wound a path home, and when he reached the pedestrianised shopping area, he sat on one of the benches situated for the use of weary shoppers, and watched the lights go out in the shops and the last few stragglers head off home. There was no activity in the junk shop, and he saw the lights go on on the uppermost floor. It was inevitable that his neighbours would return home from the factory where they worked, and he gave them time to get settled in behind their closed door. Finally, hoping that Belinda might call around and give him an opportunity to apologise, he trudged towards the building he shared with the three shops and the bunch of Polish friends. As he passed Taylor and King's he peered inside, and felt a shiver ride the entirety of his spine. There was nothing about the sales floor itself to disturb him, but he had caught sight of the door down to the basement and it had ignited a spark of terror within him. He had little to no memory of his break-in after his first tentative search of the basement, and pilfering the gold ring – which must have slipped through a hole in the lining of his pocket, because it wasn't found when the cops searched him – and absolutely nothing would come to mind about trying to strangle Belinda with a length of copper wire, or of fighting Taylor and two of the Polish lads. The only thing of clarity about the entire horrible incident was when he'd abruptly snapped to on the fire escape, with a couple of burly lads struggling to hold him down, and crying out for help from Belinda, claiming he wouldn't hurt her, and that something had got inside him.

His words now seemed stupid.

Like, what the bloody hell was he talking about?

He had a crawling sense that there was something peculiar about that box he'd spotted on the workbench, and that the lock of hair and ring in it, were more than mere keepsakes. He couldn't help – at the expense of his sanity – feel that something else had crawled out of that bloody box and chewed its way inside him, taking control of his mind and using him like a demented sock puppet. He touched a sore spot at the base of his spine, just above the protrusion of his hips. He had felt a raw ache there ever since 'wakening' on the fire escape, but it had been only one of a handful of sore spots from the rough treatment he'd been served by Taylor and the others. His arms and legs were probably black and blue, if he cared to inspect them, but the spot on his lower spine felt grazed, and was weeping plasma. He must have burned the outer dermis when he was struggling with his opponents, probably after his jacket rucked up to bare his back when wrestling on the fire escape.

Passing the mobile phone shop, he paused at the corner and glanced down the service alley. It had grown dark in the backyard, but enough ambient light from the streetlamps lit a path, though it was dappled with shadows cast from the nearby trees. As a breeze danced among the foliage, shapes capered and writhed on the ground and he felt a fresh qualm climb his spine; each of those moving shadows looked like scuttling creatures of nightmare. He shook off the fear and crept into the alley, taking each footstep slowly and silently, listening for any hint his neighbours were outdoors. As he walked, he absently fed a hand into his jacket pocket, digging and finding a hole in the lining, probing deeper, seeking the buckled ring. When his fingertips failed to reach anything, he rucked up his jacket and began feeling along the bottom, seeking a lump in the material: he found none.

He again paused for a few seconds before entering the backyard. A smell of smoke clung to everything, and, beneath it, an unpleasant scent of rot. His apartment didn't smell too good, but this was different, this was stomach-curdling. Gagging slightly, and then spitting out a thin stream of acidic bile, he moved into the yard, wondering at the placement of the old tin bin that had resided under the fire escape for as long as he'd been a resident there. It no longer appeared hot, but he guessed it had recently held a fire and was the source of the stench. What had been burned? He recalled there were old bits and pieces of discarded furniture, junk from the shop that Taylor had deemed too battered and ugly to try selling on, so left to rot under the elements, and deduced that some attempt at cleaning up the yard had been made.

For a brief moment, panic struck him.

What if he'd been forcibly evicted from his apartment and it was his worthless pieces of furniture that had been set ablaze in the yard?

He lurched for the fire escape, digging in his trouser pocket for his door key, and hoping it would still work. Once indoors, he could barricade himself in, claim squatters rights and say fuck to the world!

There was no need. As he thundered up the stairs, all caution forgotten, he saw the door lock was untouched, and somebody had even had the presence of mind to pull his door shut after he had been dragged off in cuffs. Maybe it was Belinda who'd ensured nobody could get in, or better still, maybe she'd returned to his apartment and was inside waiting for him. He hoped so. He didn't exactly love Belinda, he couldn't express his genuine feelings for her in a romantic fashion, but he did like her, and truly felt that they were a couple reliant on each other. Whatever crazy episode had driven him to assault her, he would promise it would never happen again, not ever, and beg her to forgive and forget so they could get back to some sort of normality in their lives.

'They let you go, then?'

Jason spun around sharply, his throat pinching in fear at the unexpected voice. It was pitched low, barely above a whisper, and the accent was sprinkled with gravel.

He couldn't immediately see anyone, but he forced his head to tilt, and he peered up between the metal risers, and could make out a figure limned against the low-hanging clouds, the underbellies of which were uplit from the city lights. It was one of his neighbours, of course; he just couldn't tell which. Most likely one of the couple that regularly came out on the landing to smoke, and therefore most likely one of the lads who had helped wrestle him away from Belinda.

'Uh, about what happened yesterday,' he began by way of apology.

'Forget about it. Shit happens, no?'

'Yeah, well, it does but—'

'I said forget about it. Come here.'

Jason didn't know how to respond. He'd never got on with his neighbours, and continually tried having as little to do with them as possible.

'I just wanted to say I'm sorry, that—' Again Jason was cut off mid-apology.

'Come here. I want to show you something.'

'What is it?'

'A surprise.'

Jason feared that he was walking into some kind of trap, but to disobey an invitation was probably inviting worse trouble further down the line.

'Wh–what kind of surprise?' he asked, but moved to ascend the metal stairs.

'If I tell you, it won't be a surprise,' the lad countered. 'Come, I'll show you.'

Jason mounted the steps. They squeaked beneath him.

He went slowly, trying to see the lad, and to determine if there was any deceit in him.

Overhead the figure was practically a solid silhouette beneath the yellow-tinged clouds. Then he moved forward and it was to flick a spark on his lighter, and he fed a flame to the tip of a cigarette clamped between his lips. Jason got a flash of the face and thought it was the lad who'd called him a wanker yesterday, to whom he'd replied with a two-fingered salute. Unless he was mistaken, this lad was called Caesar, or something like it, and was kind of an unofficial leader of the gang of friends. Mostly he'd been surly towards Jason. His level of wariness sky-rocketed.

'Come,' said the lad, and showed his teeth in a grin. 'Would you like a smoke?'

It was like a magical summons to Jason.

He was gagging for a ciggie. He almost galloped up the remaining stairs and then stood hunched before Caesar-or-whatever on the upper landing. The door to the apartment was shut, but Jason could hear the others inside, all talking and laughing and swearing over the top of each other. He stood, not knowing what to do or say.

'Look at this,' said the lad.

He held out something that Jason first thought was a brick.

It wasn't.

It was that old box thingy he'd seen down in Taylor and King's basement, just before everything went to shit.

'Look closely,' said the lad.

'Uh, you mentioned a ciggie . . .'

'Yeah.' The cigarette in question dangled from the corner of the lad's mouth. He chewed on the butt as he stared at Jason, holding out the box to him.

'There's something about that thing . . .' Jason began, and was rewarded by a nod.

'There is indeed. It's fascinating, no?'

'Fascinating isn't a word I'd use to describe that old piece of junk,' Jason said, aiming for humour.

'Is it not?' Suddenly there was an icy edge to the voice that had not been there before.

'I, uh, don't mean anything by it. Just, well, it's not something I'd put on display in my home.'

'From what I saw yesterday, you live in a shit-hole.'

'Aye, all right then.' Jason turned about, ready to retreat downstairs to the refuge of his shit-hole.

'Wait. I am only joking with you. I made a joke. No, but it went right over your head?'

A joke, Jason thought, *that must have been lost in translation*, because all he heard was a deliberate insult.

Caesar-or-whatshisname juggled the box between both hands, the cigarette dangling still, a single ember at its tip flaring with each inhalation. He again presented it to Jason. 'Look, it holds more mystery than at first sight.'

Despite himself, Jason leaned towards it, and it was so dark and depthless within the box that he felt for a second that he might trip and fall headlong inside. He gasped, stepped back sharply, and was stopped from tumbling down the stairs by a hand that snapped down on his right wrist. He was dragged forward, and the word of gratitude faltered in his mouth as he was greeted by another grin, this time holding no iota of friendliness. In fact, it was the grin of a predator snapping down on bloody meat. The box clattered at their feet. Another hand clasped Jason's throat, and crushed.

He tried to shout in pain, but his windpipe was clamped tight, and immediately he began to black out.

What are you doing? his mind screamed, but all he physically emitted was a warbling squeal that would carry no further than the ears of the one throttling him. He tried to push against his attacker, but had no strength. He attempted to twist away, but was held tight. His vision was filled with bright sparks, one of them the red glow from the tip of the cigarette still clamped between the other's teeth.

Then he was free, and sailing away, and the wind rushed about him as if to lend him flight.

He fell the two storeys headfirst, arcing out from the metal steps from where the lad had launched him, and his head punched the tarmac, cracking open his skull and snapping his neck vertebrae as if they were as insubstantial as papier mâché. He didn't die instantly; he lay on his back, staring up, and his killer leaned over the railing and grinned down at him, cigarette bobbing. The cigarette promised to Jason. Finally the teeth parted and released their captive, and the cigarette tumbled through space as he had before it. Jason reached for it, though his shattered arms did not physically rise, and the red spark faded to nothing as it fell . . .

EIGHTEEN

It was in the hour before the following dawn when Belinda stumbled over the body of her boyfriend, and in her drug-addled state it took a long moment to process what she'd almost tripped over. Perceiving the shape as human, it took another long head-scratching inspection before recognising the form, but even then she wasn't instantly horrified by her find. It was not unknown for Jason to get so inebriated that he failed to crawl up the last remaining stairs to his apartment, and instead bedded down in the yard where he'd slumped. There had been times when they had both sat outdoors together, out of their heads, to be woken hours later when either the cold, heat or rain got to them, or the squawking of the gulls dive-bombing pedestrians, mugging them for their burgers or pasties, got too loud and raucous. Even in an altered state of consciousness, Belinda's instinct was to rouse her lover and encourage him indoors. She crouched over him, hands on her knees as she peered into his lax features. Silly bugger had let a lit ciggie fall out of his open mouth and singe a hole in the front of his jacket; he was lucky that he hadn't burned himself badly. She plucked up the now dead cigarette butt and tossed it away, towards hundreds of others that had formed a drift against the rear wall of Taylor and King's.

'Jace,' she croaked, and gave his chest a soft shove with her fingertips.

He didn't move.

'Jace, you have to get up,' she said, a little more forcefully.

He didn't respond.

In one respect she was relieved that he was so far out of it, because it made her first return home easier than if he was fully cognisant and sober. It could be awkward if they both had to tiptoe around each other's emotions until they could put their fight to rest. This way, she could rouse him enough to get him moving, and help him into their bed. It would be best if they could wake up together, cuddled in and safe, and they could put that horrible incident from two nights ago behind them. She had forgiven Jason, he was not in control of himself, and how could she hold that against him when she too was often so far under the influence that she had no clue about what she said or did? She hoped he wouldn't be too mad about how long she'd taken to pluck up the courage to return home, but thought the fifty quid in her purse would cheer him up a bit.

'Jace,' she tried again, 'c'mon love. Let's get you inside, eh?'

When he didn't respond this time, she straightened up, scratching at the nape of her spotty neck as she studied him. She used her feet to prod Jason. The toe of her trainer dug into his ribs, but again Jason didn't respond, and that was when a ripple of nausea went through her.

'Jason?' she said, more of a demand this time. She prodded him with her trainers, both feet taking turns to dig into his side. His head lolled and his mouth slipped wider open and Belinda *knew*.

Jason's was not the first corpse she'd ever seen. It was she who had found her mother when she had been barely old enough to comprehend what death was, and there was another time, more recently, when a mutual friend of hers and Jason had fallen into an intoxicated sleep, passing away after aspirating his own vomit. In the dimness just before dawn, Jason's face looked so pale that it had luminosity to it, and his open mouth formed a glistening, wet pit. He didn't look anything like the two previous corpses she'd seen; they had died peacefully; there was something about his fixed expression that hinted at terror in his last seconds.

Belinda collapsed on her knees, her hands clasping either side of his head as she tried raising him from whatever hell he'd slipped into. She cried out his name, shook him, and felt how spongy his skull was under her fingertips. His head was broken. It was a wonder that the tarmac wasn't awash with his brains and blood, but she understood that his skull had collapsed and the damage was contained inside. Not only was Jason dead, but it was probably a blessing because there was no possible way he could continue a normal life with such catastrophic injuries. She touched and probed, and her hands went under his neck. His spine was lumpy. He'd broken his neck too. Perhaps if she continued probing, she'd discover his ribs and arms were also broken, because his fall had been a hard one. She followed the track upward to where he must have plunged over the edge of his landing to fall to his crunching death in the yard, and momentarily wondered if the drop was high enough to have caused so much damage. Her gaze tracked higher, following the stairs to their summit and the next landing up; it was more than five metres above her, easily enough to have killed him if he'd fallen that far, but Jason would have had no reason whatsoever to be on that uppermost landing. No, he would have avoided it at all costs. It was more than three metres up to his own landing, and coupled with a topple over the railing, and falling headfirst into the yard, there must have been plenty of force to kill him in his emaciated state.

His face was icy cold and held the consistency of putty. She judged he'd lain there for many hours, perhaps since last evening, undiscovered, waiting for her to return to him. If she'd come home sooner, then perhaps she would have been there for him with a steadying hand and he wouldn't have stumbled and fell. Somehow Belinda felt his demise was totally her fault.

She cried his name again, this time a wail of sheer despondency . . .

Five metres above Belinda, a figure moved to the front of the uppermost landing and leaned out, resting his arms over the low railing. His teeth were set in a shark-like grin, his eyes devoid of life as he stared down at the crying woman. Abruptly, without any warning, his body was wracked with spasms, and then Cezary sank down on his knees, gasping in anguish as whatever had used him like its personal marionette left him, and scurried back to its container, the box left wrapped in plain brown paper on the front step of Taylor and King Curiosities.

NINETEEN

Finding other people's rubbish 'donated' on the front doorstep was not unusual for Ben or Helen. Some people mistook their business for a charity shop, while others used it as somewhere handy to dump their unwanted trash, but if Ben was being totally honest, he didn't do anything to deter the practice. Occasionally there was something of value to him amongst the tat, so he allowed it to continue. Any worthless rubbish just got chucked out back in one of the wheelie bins, while any items of value were added to the shop's inventory, any sale bringing a 100 per cent profit.

Helen, her hand still an impediment, had stayed at home, but Ben turned up for work, and found Rachel patiently waiting for his arrival, having discovered one of those donations in the doorway. She stood clutching a small package wrapped in brown paper, loosely tied with string, and she wore a look of intense sadness. At first he thought her mood was down to the early start at work, but it took him only seconds to dispel the notion. There was no possible way of parking his Range Rover in the backyard with all the emergency services activity going on. There was an ambulance, the coroner's car and a police van all parked across the entrance to the service alley, and a police officer stood guard, ensuring nobody entered the yard without permission or authority. He pulled his Range Rover onto the pedestrianised area adjacent to his shop, and again used the ploy of the handwritten note from yesterday, proclaiming he was busy unloading stock to illegally park. Trudging towards Rachel, he saw her about to walk hurriedly towards him, but she only took a step before deciding against it. She hugged the package tighter to her chest and waited.

'What's going on?' he asked when close enough for her to hear.

She shook her head. 'A terrible accident. There's been a death.'

'Who?' he asked. 'What happened?'

She nodded towards the police officer on guard duty.

'She hasn't said much, but from what I could gather, one of the people living above the shop fell from the fire escape and died.'

'One of the lads from the top floor?'

She shook her head. 'I don't think so.'

'Oh,' said Ben, realising exactly who she meant instead. 'It kind of makes sense, some of the drunken states I've seen Jason come home in.'

'It's so sad,' Rachel croaked, and her eyes grew large and moist behind her spectacles. A fat teardrop rolled down her cheek to the corner of her mouth. She rolled her shoulder, wiping her face on her jacket, her best recourse while holding the package. 'He had his problems, but he didn't deserve to die like that.'

'No. Of course not.' When he thought about it, despite having to ask him to leave the shop on occasion, for no other reason than Ben or Helen suspected he was trying to steal, or to keep the yard clean of his spent ciggie butts, Jason hadn't given Ben any actual trouble. In fact, if the truth be told, the lad had been nothing but respectful most of the time, even when under the influence of drink or drugs. He was, Ben supposed, more to be pitied than despised. 'Was' being the operative word.

Actually, no. Scrub that idea. It was only days ago that Jason had burgled the shop, and then tried murdering his girlfriend Belinda with a copper wire garotte. Karma could be brutal. Maybe those actions were the beginning of a self-destructive spiral that had ended with him tumbling from the fire escape to his death.

As if reading his negativity, Rachel said, 'I told you it was Jason that first came to help when I was trapped in the basement. That side of him just doesn't match with when he later attacked Belinda.'

'That's drugs for you,' Ben grunted. He nodded at the bundle. 'Somebody leave that for us.'

She nodded without expounding.

'I don't know if we're allowed to open the shop,' she said instead.

'I've lost enough trade this week,' he responded, and immediately strode towards the police officer.

The officer drew up to her full height, raising eyebrows in question.

Ben flicked a hand towards the service alley, then nodded towards his shop front. 'Does what's happening here mean I can't trade today?'

'Who are you, sir?' she asked.

'I'm Ben Taylor. I have the antiques shop just there. I was wondering if I am allowed to open for business, y'know, in light of what has happened.'

'I can't see it being a problem, as long as you don't intend to use the service yard or alley for the next few hours. But let me check with my superiors and I'll get back to you.'

'OK,' he said and waited.

She did nothing.

'OK,' he said again, taking the hint, and he backed away, returning to Rachel where she stood in the shop doorway. Once he was out of earshot, the officer keyed her radio and spoke into it. Ben understood her reluctance to speak in front of a civilian, when the subject concerned a fatality, and foul play might not have been ruled out. Perhaps, by presenting himself, he had made himself a suspect in Jason's death.

The officer gestured and, summoned, Ben walked towards her.

She was perfunctory with the facts. 'Once we are done here, you are free to open your shop, sir.'

'Any chance of an approximate time?'

'We can't put a timescale on it. It depends . . .'

In other words, it depended on what the specialists found, and if what at first appeared to be a random accident was suspected to be something more sinister.

'Is it OK to get the shop ready for trade though?' he prompted.

'Yes,' she said, 'but you must stay out of the yard. By the way, do you have CCTV covering the back?'

He shook his head. 'I don't have any cameras.'

She took out a notebook and pen and scribbled down a note, probably a disclaimer showing there was no available footage.

'Can't speak for the phone shop or hairdresser; they might have security cameras,' he suggested.

She acknowledged his words with a squint, and made another note in her pocketbook. He waited. She again fell silent, and Ben took the hint, returning to Rachel. She chewed her bottom lip.

'Let's get things ready for opening,' he said. 'Who knows,

maybe all this activity will draw a few potential customers to this end of the high street.'

Rachel clucked her tongue at his mercenary tactic.

'I'm joking,' he said, but wasn't.

He unlocked the door and silenced the alarm. Rachel carried the package inside and set it on the cashier's counter.

The air was redolent of bleach, proof of the cleaning activities they had carried out before leaving the afternoon before. There was no trace of shattered glass, or of Helen's blood, and Ben had also removed the broken display cabinet. His boiler suit was folded neatly on the counter, and his oversized wellington boots sat atop it. He fully intended to decontaminate both items, suspecting he might need them again. He looked for a bag he could transport them home in: all the bin liners he'd fetched to assist in the clean-up had been used.

Rachel said, 'Want me to put on the kettle?'

'I'd love a cuppa,' he admitted. 'While you're at it, see if there's any of those ginger nuts left over from the other day.'

He found a folded carrier bag, and took it to the cashier's desk. He snapped open the bag, shoved in the boiler suit, but the wellies were too bulky to fit. He set the bag and boots aside, so they wouldn't get in the way while he or Rachel served customers. He drew the parcel towards him, and within a second, snatched his hands away. The brown paper, and several folded sheets of papers under it, couldn't disguise the familiarity of what was inside.

'Rachel,' he croaked.

She had entered the tiny room they used as a staff hideout, so that they could escape for a few minutes' break if needed. In there they kept the kettle and biscuits. She didn't reply.

'Rachel,' he called louder.

She stuck her head around the doorframe, eyebrows arched.

'Where exactly did you get this from?' he asked, aiming a trembling finger at the package.

'Doorstep,' she said.

Her words confirmed exactly as he'd believed.

'Just before I arrived?' he asked.

'Yeah, well, maybe ten minutes or something. I couldn't really say, I was more interested in what was going on with the police and stuff.'

'You didn't realise what this is?' he probed.

'No, Ben. What is it? What's wrong?'

He puffed out his cheeks. 'Hopefully I'm wrong but . . .' He took a pair of scissors from a glass jar next to the till and snipped through the string. Watching him, Rachel approached slowly, carrying with her the empty plastic kettle she had been about to fill when he summoned her.

Ben folded back the sheets of brown paper, and found that underneath, the item inside was further wrapped with pages from a broadsheet newspaper, dated from just before the bank holiday weekend. He teased aside the newspaper and stood back, cursing under his breath.

The box was barely singed at the corners.

'Tell me this isn't some kind of a joke?' Rachel groaned in dismay.

'Not of my doing.' Ben stared at her a moment, aiming the same accusation back at her.

'This has nothing to do with me,' she said, her voice an octave or two higher than normal. 'I don't believe you'd think I'd be capable of—'

'Rache, it's OK. I'm not accusing you of anything. Thing is, though, somebody had to save this from the fire we set and left it for us to find.'

'Wasn't me.'

'I know. Me neither.'

'Cezary?' she wondered, and her face pinched at the idea the young man could be responsible for such a nasty trick.

'Why would he do such a thing?'

'I don't know . . . maybe it was—'

Again he jumped on her words. 'Jason? You think he did it? He came home and found the box in the bin and decided to gift-wrap it and put it where we'd find it? Then he went back and took a dive off his landing?'

'Don't you think we should tell the police, Ben?'

He thought for no more than a heartbeat. 'No. No way. If we suggest Jason left it for us, we might get pulled into whatever happened to him. They might think we had something to do with his death, and this was his way of accusing us . . . no. We don't tell the police about it. I don't know about you, but I think we've had enough drama to last us ages.'

'But what if it *does* have something to do with his death?' she moaned.

'How could it be?' he countered. 'It's just a wooden box with weird crap inside.'

'It is cursed,' she hissed.

Ben's face contorted in incredulity. 'Cursed? You don't believe in that nonsense, do you?'

'I thought that Helen was the sceptical one,' she replied. 'Look at it, Ben. You know there's something wrong about that box, and what those words etched into it mean. It's some kind of curse, I'm telling you.'

'Trust me, Travellers can't really cast curses any more than they can read your future in tea leaves or in the palm of your hand. It's all trickery designed to part fools with their money.'

Rachel nodded at the box. It sat there, almost as if sentient, listening to them debate. 'Explain how that survived the fire then.'

'Could simply be down to the type of wood it's made from,' he said lamely.

'Look inside,' she said.

He shook his head.

'Why not? Afraid?'

'I'm not afraid, it's just—'

'You know there's more to what I'm saying than you'll admit,' she said. 'Come on, Ben. Think about it. When did all the weird stuff start happening?' She aimed a finger at the box. 'It all began after you brought that thing into the shop.'

He exhaled loudly. 'Maybe it's just a coincidence.'

'You know, Ben, maybe you're right. Maybe we don't have to fear the box, but the stuff inside. In hindsight, it wasn't when you brought the box back that everything started going wrong, it was after you opened it.'

DO NOT OPEN.

Yes, now that he thought about it, the warning had been rather implicit.

Tremulously, he reached for the box, and lifted it from its paper shroud.

'What are you doing?' Rachel demanded in a harsh whisper.

'I need to see if the other stuff is still inside. Hopefully the fire turned it to charcoal.'

He gently shook the box, and nausea flipped his stomach contents. He swallowed a mouthful of acidic bile, trying not to choke.

'It feels as if it's still there,' he announced.

The same sensation of something rolling about made the box feel unbalanced in his grasp. He set it down again, and slowly slid the lid open.

'Oh, that's awful!' Rachel reared away from the terrible stench that wafted from the box.

Ben gagged on bile a second time. But he was determined to get to the bottom of things. He tipped the box on end, allowing its contents to spill out. All that slid free from the container was the now charred ribbon and the few strands of brittle hair to resist the heat. Plus, the withered black thing that had confused him since the beginning. 'What is that damn thing?'

'It looks like . . .' Rachel didn't finish her thought.

The front door swung inward, and in strode the police officer Ben had spoken to earlier.

Ben scooped the withered lump and the charred ribbon and stuffed them inside the box. As the woman approached, he slid the lid closed.

Rachel sprayed lavender-scented air freshener from a bottle, but it failed to mask the awful stench.

The police officer grimaced as she got closer. She eyed the box, but appeared unimpressed by the poorly carved object. Ben slid it away under the wrapping paper.

'This is the less glamorous side of my business,' Ben said, forcing laughter. 'One man's trash isn't always another's treasure. Mostly it's just trash.'

'Ugh, you can say that again,' said the officer. She wrinkled her nose, as she doffed her hat, but took the subject no further. 'This is just a quick update. I know from our log that you were involved when Jason Halloran assaulted Belinda Sortwell a couple of days ago, and colleagues took a statement from you. We might need another from you regarding any interaction you've had with Jason since he was released from custody.'

'Well, that's easy,' said Ben, with a glance at Rachel for corroboration. 'I haven't seen hide nor hair of Jason since he was arrested.'

'Oh,' said the officer, taking out her pocketbook again. 'I may as well note that and have you sign it here, if you don't mind.'

'Why do you need anything more from us? I mean, there's no suggestion of foul play, is there?'

'No,' said the officer. 'Not yet. You don't have to say anything, but it will help move along the inquest if we can rule out any anticipated requests from the coroner.'

'Fair enough,' he said.

'I haven't seen or heard from him either, if you'd like me to say so,' Rachel offered.

The officer scribbled down their statements, just a series of brief notes, and allowed them both to read them back and then sign and date them as true records of the facts.

'Jason has been taken away, and CSI have concluded their investigation in the backyard. Feel free to open for business.' The officer plonked her hat on and then left them standing, still engulfed in a cloying cloud of rotten meat and cinders.

TWENTY

'You have to get rid of that awful thing, right away.'

Rachel stood with her sweater pulled up over her nostrils, grimacing at the putrid smell emanating from it. Ben also wore a grimace of disgust, but he shook his head slowly. He grabbed the plastic bag he'd put his soiled boiler suit in minutes ago, and dumped out the garment. Turning the bag inside out, he lowered it over the top of the box and its wrappings and scooped it all inside. He flicked the bag over and tied the handles. 'This,' he said firmly, 'is going back to where the bloody hell it came from.'

Rachel stepped back, wafting her hands, as he turned towards her, holding the bag at arm's length. He marched to the front door, and set the bag on the stoop, up against the wall. He returned to Rachel and they stood staring at the bag through the glass door, Ben expecting it to somehow animate and come crawling back to them.

'Are you just going to leave it there?' asked Rachel.

'Somebody might steal it,' he thought aloud, and wasn't upset at the possibility.

'You intend taking it back to that old lady you bought it from, don't you?' Rachel asked.

'Yeah, and I'll stuff it down her conniving throat for the scam she pulled.'

'Scam?'

'Don't you see? That amulet, for all it is worth a few quid, was actually used as bait, to reel somebody like me in, so she could pass off the box to an unsuspecting person. You believe the box is cursed; well, maybe she didn't curse it, but somebody else did, and she used me to take its effect off her.'

Rachel absorbed his theory and had no argument.

'How do you expect to find her? Was she a regular you knew at the airfield market?'

'Can't say I've ever seen her before but, judging by her set-up, she regularly attends boot sales.'

'You described her as a Traveller,' Rachel pointed out. 'What if she's literally hitched her trailer and gone to the other end of the country?'

'It's a possibility,' he admitted. 'But it's not going to stop me from checking at the market this weekend.'

'So what are you going to do with that until then?' She indicated the bag and its contents.

'It can stay where it's at till the weekend,' he said. 'Like I said, we might be lucky and somebody will steal it and take the bloody curse with them.'

Rachel curled a lip at the idea. 'That's not fair though, Ben. We shouldn't let it pass to somebody else, knowing what it's capable of.'

'We don't know it's capable of anything,' he corrected her.

'You saw my back. I didn't bite myself. Then there's Helen's hand. And the more I think about it, I wonder how much it influenced Jason into attacking Belinda, or to take his own life.'

Ben threw up his hands. 'Rache, for Christ's sake, don't even go there. I admit we've been on the receiving end of some bad luck, but . . . what exactly are you suggesting? That the box, or the thing from inside it, has the power to influence minds?'

'I never believed in demonic possession before but—'

'No! Nope. I'm open-minded, but I'm not prepared to go that far. Next thing you'll want me to bring in a priest to exorcise the bloody shop!'

'It might not be a bad idea.'

'No. Now drop that crazy thinking. Besides, I'm not religious, so I wouldn't know who to go to. Even if I did, what good would a priest be to me?'

Rachel didn't respond. She continued eyeing the bag, as if she could see through the opaque plastic to the thing inside.

'You weren't serious, were you?' Ben asked after a minute's silence. 'About an exorcism, I mean?'

'I swear that something leapt on my back, a spirit of some type, and tried burrowing into me. It felt like it was gnawing a passage into my spine, and the bite mark is proof I didn't imagine it.'

'I've never heard of a spiritual possession happening like that.'

'Know a lot about possession, do you?'

'Only what I've seen in movies,' he admitted.

'Yeah? Green vomit and heads turning back to front?'

She pursed her lips, saying nothing more, and he got the message.

'Those words you searched for online, maybe you should do a little more digging and see what else you can find out,' Ben suggested. 'Do you, uh, need to see the box again?'

'No. Keep that bloody thing far away from me. I already set up a doc on my phone and noted all the words I could read, and I've put translations next to those I already searched for.'

'Good thinking. Keep looking, Rache. Maybe you'll find something useful for putting an end to this madness.'

She nodded and took out her phone, and bent over it.

He put the boiler suit aside, and again stood the wellington boots on top of it. With that done, he was a little lost as to what to do next. He stood, arms folded across his chest, eyes on the bag through the door. Shoppers were out and about by then, but none appeared interested in entering his shop. Rachel kept scrolling, and he began to grow jittery.

'That cuppa isn't going to make itself,' Rachel reminded him, in truth giving an excuse to take his mind off the bag and its contents.

He went into the tiny closet-sized staffroom, and found where Rachel had dumped the empty kettle when he'd summoned her earlier. He filled it at a small washbasin and tap, and plugged it in. Immediately the kettle hissed and groaned as the element began heating. Ben gave it as wide a berth as the small room allowed, fearing that the way his luck was going, the kettle would explode and spray scalding water all over him. He dug in a drawer and found the half-eaten pack of ginger nuts, the wrapper twisted tightly at one end. At least ill-luck hadn't conspired to leave the package open and spoiled the biscuits inside. He dumped tea bags in two clean mugs, added sugar and a splash of milk taken from a small refrigerator in each. Lastly and trepidatiously, he held the container of milk under his nose and sniffed. Thankfully, it had not tainted in the few days since it was opened. He waited, listening to the hissing kettle come to a crescendo, and then click loudly as the fail-safe button shut off. He waited a few seconds for the roiling water to settle, then picked up the kettle and poured water into each mug. He was happy to set down the kettle once more, having safely dealt with a potential hazard, and began stirring the contents of the mugs, encouraging the bags to release their flavour. Briefly he thought how Helen would have scolded him, learning he'd added the milk before the hot water, but hey! He was his own man . . . when his wife wasn't around.

He chuckled at the thought, and picked up the mugs, holding the handles of both in one hand, while grabbing the biscuits with the other. He turned for the shop floor, just as a howl of dismay rang out from Rachel, echoed by a more pained screech from another person. Ben jerked in response, sending a mini tsunami of tea over his hand and up his wrist. Thankfully the milk had taken the scalding heat out of the brew, but it was still painful enough for Ben to drop the mugs and for them to shatter at his feet. More tea splattered up his jeans and over the toes of his shoes. Ben danced to avoid the liquid, but the reaction was an afterthought and too late for any good. He threw the biscuits behind him and plunged out onto the shop floor to witness the latest calamity.

Rachel was already rushing forward to help, almost obscuring the second person. It took several lurching steps for Ben to gain enough of a view past his assistant to see an elderly woman sprawled on her belly on the floor. The woman was immediately inside the shop, and it was apparent what had tripped her: one of her heels had caught in the handles of the plastic bag containing the box. As she struggled to get up, she kicked feebly, and her exertions aided the bag to be drawn further inside the shop. She cried out shrilly, something paining her with each movement, and Ben feared the worst: that she'd done herself some serious injury, for which his injudicious placement of the bag was responsible.

TWENTY-ONE

'Our first potential customer today and the old bird trips flat on her face and breaks her hip!'

Returning home exasperated after another trying day at the shop, Ben dropped wearily onto the sofa alongside Helen. His wife had tucked her legs up beneath her, and sat propped up by large cushions, one of them in her lap to help support her damaged hand. Their large TV dominated the wall opposite, and was currently switched to a bargain hunting programme with two teams pitched against each other as they trawled for goodies around a car boot sale: now he'd have to sit through another televised busman's holiday.

'You could at least show some sympathy for the old lady,' Helen chided him.

'I feel sorry for her, but not as much as I do for *us*.'

'Don't include me.'

'You'll be included if she decides to sue for her injuries,' he retorted. 'Hopefully it doesn't happen, and she doesn't remember what happened to cause the trip.'

He told her about how the woman had caught her heel in the plastic bag containing the box, and lost her footing, causing her to plunge headlong into the shop. Next he told her about how the damned gift-wrapped box had turned up on their doorstep, despite trying to burn it to ashes the evening before. Lastly, the subject of Jason Halloran's untimely death came up and Helen sat slack-jawed as she listened to the sad details. Her eyes grew glossy with unshed tears.

'Do you think that he had something to do with planting the box where you'd find it?' she wondered. 'Then accidentally, or purposefully, fell from the fire escape?'

'I don't know what to believe anymore.'

'Knowing how you and Rachel think, you've probably thrown around some wild theories.'

'You have to admit that there's something weird going on,

Helen. I've lost track of the bad luck that's come our way since I brought back that amulet and the box.' To emphasise his point, he gently touched her bandaged hand. Helen rolled her shoulder, drawing her hand out of reach. 'Sorry, love, I didn't mean to hurt you.'

'You didn't. I was only making sure you couldn't. I'd probably get as little sympathy as that poor old woman.'

Ben blinked in surprise at the accusation. 'Sorry, Helen, but she doesn't mean anything to me. You, however, mean the world to me.'

'The poor soul broke her hip!' Her previously glassy gaze grew sharper.

He rubbed a palm over his mouth, almost as if he could hold back his negativity. He failed. 'Well, maybe not. That's just my prognosis. The way the paramedics treated her was as if she might have broken something, but nothing can be confirmed until they get her to hospital, can it? Before they arrived, I made sure to get the bag and box out of the way. No reason why anyone needs to know what caused her to trip, is there?'

'Where is it, that box?' Helen twisted around to confront him. 'You'd better not have brought it home with you. I don't want that bloody thing in the house.'

'So you do accept there's something weird about it, otherwise why not have it here?'

'Normally I don't believe in that nonsense, but . . .'

'Seeing's believing?'

'I'd rather not see it, thank you very much. Tell me it isn't here, Ben.'

'It isn't here.'

'So where is it?'

'In the car.'

'What, you did bring it home with you?' Helen almost erupted off the sofa, but collapsed back down when he transferred his hand to her shoulder. He patted her gently.

'I didn't bring it indoors. It's in the back of the Range Rover, out on the drive. I locked it inside my old metal toolbox, so it's definitely out of sight, and you don't have to worry about it.'

'I'd rather you left it locked in the shop.'

'I was going to.' In truth, he wanted rid of the evidence in case anyone connected with the elderly woman came to their shop asking how she'd tripped. Initially he'd planned on stopping on the river bridge on the way home and dropping the bag in the water, letting the currents take the damned thing miles downstream. However, the way his luck was going, he didn't trust that he'd be able to carry out his mission without earning a fly-tipping fine from the local council. 'Rache advised against it. We'd probably get a phone call during the night telling us the shop was on fire or something.'

'You're really taking this curse thing seriously, aren't you?' Helen had allowed most of her scepticism to slide, the weight of evidence playing havoc on her usual worldview that normally had no room in it for the weird or whacky. For a moment she appeared bewildered.

'I have to return it to its original owner,' he stated.

'How could you possibly know that?'

'I just sense it's the best thing to do, and Rache agrees. She's going to come with me to find that old traveller witch and—'

'Oh, *Rache* is going with you, is she?'

'Yeah, she's—'

'Getting a little bit above her station, that girl. What next, Ben? Push me out, go full partners? She's going to have you change the shop's name to Taylor and Quinn's?'

He stared at her quizzically, his turn to be truly bewildered.

'She's after you, don't you get it? And I'm pretty sure you have a soft spot for her, too,' Helen said, all traces of sympathy for the injured lady, or for their deceased neighbour, now replaced by suspicion and jealousy.

'Helen, come on. You know it's not like that.'

'Isn't it? I didn't hear you asking me to go with you to find the old hag. No, you'd rather show off in front of your fancy woman!'

'Helen,' Ben sat upright, staring at her in disbelief at where their conversation had taken them. 'What the hell's gotten into you? For God's sake, have you heard what you're saying?'

'I know exactly what I've been thinking!'

'Then you're bloody wrong. Hang on! How long has this been in your mind? You've genuinely thought that there was something going on between Rachel and me?'

'Don't deny it.' Her bandaged hand thrust aside the hand he'd laid on her shoulder. He withdrew it as if he'd been snake-bitten. 'I've seen the way she fawns over you, and how you flirt with her. Neither of you even try to hide your feelings for each other. It's bloody pathetic!'

'Helen, whatever it is you think you're seeing, it's wrong. She looks up to the two of us. For God's sake, Rachel is just a kid, and I'm old enough to be her father.'

'Since when has an age gap ever stopped any dirty old man?'

'Now, hey! That's about far enough. I like Rachel as a person, I do, and I thought you did as well, but that's as far as it goes. I've never as much as entertained a romantic thought about her, or towards any other woman since we've been together.'

'It isn't romantic thoughts that bother me, it's bloody lustful ones.'

'Helen?'

'Get away from me.' She turned abruptly aside, averting her face, swearing under her breath.

'Helen.' He touched her back.

She slashed at him with her injured hand. Before he could dodge far enough, her knuckles cracked painfully against his ribs. He grunted. She howled in agony. 'Now look at what you've made me do!' she cried, and having failed to learn her lesson, struck out a second time with her sore hand. This time she bore the pain in order to apply some to him.

'That's enough! No more hitting!' Ben struggled upright and stood out of reach. He rubbed gingerly at his ribs. 'What are you bloody doing, Helen?'

'Get away from me, then,' she warned. 'In fact, go and do whatever you had in mind with Rachel. It's what you really want to do, isn't it?'

'No, Helen. You know that's not right. What the fucking hell's gotten into you?'

He almost choked on the question. By bringing home the box, despite it being locked in a metal toolbox, could whatever had inflicted itself upon Jason still have enough influence to do the same with Helen? The way that Rachel explained things, she fully believed that some type of spirit, or even demon, had tried possessing her, and when it had failed to gnaw a passage inside her had waited for a second host and found it in Jason. It had caused his madness, and used him to assault Belinda Sortwell, and may well have led to the young man's untimely death. What if it was exerting a similar evil influence over Helen?

'My mum warned me about you,' Helen snapped from her place on the sofa, scattering cushions on the floor.

No. Who was he kidding? The only evil influence over Helen was the vinegar her mother, Gloria, had injected into their marriage. She'd never been happy at Helen's choice of husband, believing he wasn't good enough for her daughter, to a point where she'd forced Helen to retain her family name over his for when they inevitably parted ways. Ben was certain, though it had never been admitted to, that the vicious harridan was also behind Helen's decision to remain childless, so that Ben's spore didn't infect their family tree once Helen saw the light and dumped him.

'I take it she's been here while I was at work?' he challenged.

'Yes. My mum was here. Nobody else cared that I was sitting at home alone, nursing a sore hand.'

'Haven't you taken any painkillers?'

'They haven't helped.'

'Whatever you've had, they sure as hell weren't a couple of paracetamol. What did you take, to send you off the rails like this?'

'What do you mean by that? Off the bloody rails?'

'Have you listened to the way you're acting? Accusing me of cheating, trying to hit me. That's not you, Helen. But I know who it bloody well is!'

'Now who's making up false accusations?'

He forced himself to pause, to physically take a breath. 'I'm glad you think that it's false, same as what you just threw at me. There's nothing but friendship between me and Rachel. She offered to help and I accepted. Not because I don't want to include you; we only wanted to spare you the trouble while you're hurt. Besides, Rachel happens to know more about this weird stuff with the box than I can figure out myself.'

She grunted at his words, but her anger had passed. Whatever had incited her to such quick rage had also disappeared. 'I'm sorry,' she said, though still a little dryly.

He shrugged, trying to downplay things further.

'I'm sore,' Helen went on, cupping her injured hand against her chest, 'and the pills my mum gave me haven't worked. Well, except to send me off the flipping rails, eh?' She looked at him, now wearing a goofy grin, her top teeth protruding, not in an attempt at acting humorous. She genuinely looked out of it.

'What exactly did your mother give you?' he asked, now more concerned that she was having a bad reaction to a drug than that some kind of devil had got a hold on her.

'Couple of her "happy pills",' she said, and her mouth grew slack, and her tongue lolled at one corner. She pinched the bridge of her nose. 'I feel dizzy.'

'Bloody hell, lie down on the sofa, while I try to find out what she gave you.'

Helen flapped a hand, and he understood the gesture. He bent to the end of the sofa and found the waste-paper basket, and the empty pill blisters dumped in it. From what he could tell, she'd mixed several different kinds of medication – Gabapentin, Amitriptyline, Oxycodone, all of them strong doses used to deaden nerve pain – but without knowing how many each blister contained, he'd no idea how much of each.

'Bloody hell, Helen. Do you even know what those pills are for? I think Gloria might have given you an overdose.'

'Quit worrying,' she said, wafting away his concern. 'They're only painkillers. I only had a few of each. I'm sore, Ben. I just needed something to take the edge off, and well . . .' she snorted, and took his advice to stretch out on the sofa. 'They do seem to be finally doing me some good.'

All animosity seemingly fled, she smiled up at him, and he squeezed her a smile of his own. The accusation concerning Rachel was apparently forgotten, but learning that his wife mistrusted them was a bitter pill to swallow and left a bad taste in Ben's mouth. In all likelihood, the effect of the drugs had exacerbated the jealousy in her mind, but a kernel had to have been there to begin with. For a moment he considered aborting his plan to take Rachel on the search for the old traveller woman, but what then? Should he conspire to never be alone alongside her again, maybe only allow her to work when Helen was also at the shop? Should he let her go entirely and look for another assistant less inclined to release the green-eyed monster in Helen? No. Absolutely not. Helen's jealousy was unfounded, and he was damned if he was going to let it ruin their relationship with Rachel: he must simply show her that there was nothing more than mutual respect and friendship involved in their closeness. His decision made, he was taking Rachel with him; whether Helen would accompany them too was down to her.

TWENTY-TWO

It was only a couple of days' wait, but the weekend seemed forever in arriving. After what had happened the last time they had tried opening, and the possibility of a claim for injuries made against their insurance, Ben and Helen had agreed to keep the shop closed, at least until Ben could return the box and its horrible bad luck to its original owner. Shutting shop was only partly due to the elderly woman's accident, but also as a 'mark of respect' to their deceased neighbour; no less, several of his down-at-heel pals had showed up in the backyard, and the last thing they wanted was for any of them to target their shop for a swift shoplifting while they were in the vicinity. Apparently Belinda had organised some kind of starlight vigil for the Friday evening, to be held where Jason fell, and she had extended an invitation to Ben, Helen and Rachel to attend. Suspecting it was simply an excuse to shed crocodile tears, drink cheap plonk, and smoke other people's weed, they had politely declined. Ben had, for a split-second, considered gift-wrapping the box with some shiny new ribbon, and leaving it where one of the mourners couldn't resist stealing it. But conscience nipped him; it was bad enough they'd lost their friend, without him heaping a pile of crap on them that the box was certain to bring. He was yet to check on the yard, to see what kind of mess they'd left after their vigil for him to tidy up.

In the meantime, the box, the item of derision, had been kept locked away in the metal toolbox in the boot of the Range Rover.

Ben and Rachel spent a couple of days remodelling the shop's layout, finishing a deep clean and disinfecting the basement. After her pill-induced jealous rant the other night, Helen had not raised the subject of them cheating since, and hadn't attended the shop to keep a leery eye on them. Ben had begun to grow confident that she'd forgotten her wild allegation altogether, and discretion most definitely being the better part of valour, had decided to keep the subject firmly to himself. Helen had also come to a decision, in that she wanted no part of the box, so gave her blessing for Ben and Rachel to do whatever they must to rid themselves of its horrible effects.

As he drove towards Kirkholme's decommissioned airfield on Sunday morning, Rachel rode shotgun, passing the journey by relating other things she'd discovered about cursed objects. Most facts went in one ear and out of the other, as Ben was ruminating more on how he'd return the box to the old woman, and what he might say when sending the cursed thing back to source. Besides, much of what she talked about was obviously rubbish: as far as he had picked up, different belief systems determined the actions one could take to rid oneself of a curse. The major problem being, Ben didn't exactly have a belief system. Like many raised in a Church of England household, he still practised the traditions of celebrating Easter and Christmas, but was also into Halloween, and as a child had enjoyed Guy Fawkes Night for its fireworks and bonfire; he attended church for weddings, funerals and christenings, but that was his lot. If there was a God, he only believed for fear of how he'd be judged if he didn't when it was his turn to stand before the Pearly Gates. He knew bits and bobs about other religious practices, mainly through his hunts for valuable religious objets de vertu, but nothing that appealed to him more than those of his own part-time faith. The stuff that Rachel referenced was mainly Wiccan, or Shamanism, or daft ideas lifted from online videos and televised paranormal investigations: Ben wouldn't know where to start in sourcing Palo Santo sticks, white sage or sacred resins. He might be able to scoop a bottle of sacramental water out of a font at one of the local churches, but he was damned if he'd try pilfering a blessed cross or crucifix. Perhaps Rachel picked up on his cynicism and didn't appreciate it, because she abruptly stopped talking and stared at a fixed point several car lengths ahead. Her breathing grew shallow.

He knew from when Helen behaved like this to remain silent, so he did so with his assistant too. To help his resolve, he chewed his way through a rubbery Cornish pasty purchased from a filling station.

As they neared the airfield it became apparent that the fair weather had brought out the traders in large numbers, the knock-on effect being that their customers numbered in the hundreds. They were stalled in their journey, tagging on to the back of a queue of cars, buses and campervans waiting to turn off the main road into the airfield. Behind them the queue rapidly elongated.

Rachel unscrewed the cap on a bottle of mineral water and took a sip.

'Could do with a drink myself,' said Ben, finally breaking the silence. His mouth felt gluey with coagulated fat.

Rachel held her water across to him.

'No, no,' he declined politely, 'I don't want to give you any of my bugs.'

'Have you got the lurgy?' she asked, scrunching up her nose.

He thought about it for a second. 'Nah.'

'So take a drink, just don't put any floaters in the bottle.'

He glanced down at a scattering of pastry flakes on the front of his shirt, and used the side of his hand to swipe them into the footwell. 'It's OK, I'll wait and grab a drink once we're parked up.'

'You're choice, boss. It could be a while yet.'

Her prediction proved true. They sat in the slow-moving traffic for a further half an hour before being let through the entrance by a stockily built woman, wearing a high-visibility jacket and rainproof trousers. Her hair was short, dark shot through with silver, and she wore a matching silver stud in one nostril. Ben recognised the woman, was on nodding terms with her and her husband, but for the life of him he couldn't recall her name. He paid the couple of pounds admission that the landowners had levied for the honour of entering the market and looking at other people's cast-offs. To be rid of the box, Ben was willing to pay whatever it cost: by now he was several hundred pounds out of pocket since laying his eyes on that bloody amulet, where the hook had sunk deep and reeled him in like a prize sucker.

He left the Range Rover adjacent to the same teetering red-brick wall as before, within metres of where he'd parked last week. This time his mood was different from when Helen had to cajole him into going to the market; he set off at a determined clip, forcing Rachel to march double-time to keep up. Ben carried the wrapped box, now concealed inside a canvas sack, pulled tight at the neck by a drawstring, slung over his right shoulder.

As before, the air was redolent with the aromas of fried onions and the nearby effluent treatment site; a farmer had also been busy in the nearby fields, spraying something on his crops that smelled bad enough to bring tears to the eyes. Ben was oblivious to the potpourri of competing scents. He sought any dash of canary yellow beyond the meandering crowds of bargain hunters. Rachel tugged at his sleeve and he didn't slow down, merely glanced at her, eyebrows raised.

'Do you want to split up and search separately?' Rachel offered. 'I'll go down one aisle and you can take the other and we'll meet at the bottom.'

'Yeah,' he said, without giving her idea much thought.

'OK. If I find her first, I'll ring you on your mobile.'

'Yeah,' he said, without knowing if he'd actually hear his ringing phone among the babbling crowd.

He kept walking, and Rachel must have taken off down the next aisle of stalls because when he glanced in her direction again, she had disappeared. Ben, slightly taller than average, could see over most heads, and had a view down two adjacent rows of stalls. He could see a few vans but none the vibrant colour he sought. It would be too easy to give up the search and move to the next rows over, because who said that the old travelling woman would use the same vehicle this week; in her culture, buying and selling was de rigueur, so she might have changed vehicles by now. Maybe he should have reminded Rachel—

'Awreet, big lad?'

Ben turned towards his greeter, and saw a familiar face. It was the old man with the creased face that Helen had haggled prices with over the brass poker stand. He had set up his stall more or less on the same plot he'd used the week before. Seeing him raised hope in Ben that he'd also find the old woman at or near the same space she'd utilised. He smiled and nodded at the old man, but kept moving, preferring not to waste time on small talk.

Ben continued walking, having to dance in and out where spaces provided faster passage among the meandering customers. He was stalled briefly by a knot of chortling people when two yapping dogs got their leads tangled and their exuberant owners and the crowd of onlookers thought it the funniest thing ever. Finally, he found an opening and thrust past the bottleneck, and found himself in the vicinity where the old woman had set up her stall the previous weekend. There was no yellow van, no attractive granddaughter, no elderly lady with cataracts turning her eyes blind. Instead there was a huge navy blue van with its side doors open, displaying used tools, some of them so old that they were rusted and misshapen, but Ben knew that some gullible fools would purchase them for their historical value – which really amounted to zero pounds. This van wasn't owned by anyone from the travelling community; Ben knew its owner to be a big displaced Welshman who was as tall as Ben, but built twice the size across the shoulders. Large and jolly most of the time, Ben had heard he could turn dangerous with little provocation, and had once split a man's skull with the rusted wood saw he'd tried nicking from his van without paying. The huge man was inside his van, shifting around his wares. He answered to the clichéd nickname of Big Taffy, but Ben decided not to call him; instead he carried on, seeking the canary yellow van.

Soon he was at the end of the aisles, and he paused a moment to turn in a wide crescent, seeking any stragglers yet to park their vehicles; but except for a converted school bus, there was none to be seen. He looked for Rachel. She was yet to negotiate the entire length of the aisle she was checking, or she had found the yellow van and had stopped to talk. He dug out his mobile phone, checking she had not sent him a message as promised. She hadn't. He was agitated, wanted to continue the search, but decided to give her a minute more before heading for the next rows. He felt certain that he would've spotted such a vibrant yellow colour beyond the stalls he'd already inspected, but again was reminded that the woman might use a different vehicle by now.

Rachel appeared, dancing sideways past a man driving a mobility scooter. She spotted him, raised a hand in greeting, and he moved towards her.

'Any luck?' she asked pointlessly. Her words also confirmed for him that she hadn't discovered their quarry.

'Let's try the next rows.' These were the final rows allotted to the boot-sale traders; beyond them were more traditional mobile market stalls and trucks. Rachel joined him in the search, and he noted that she deliberately kept to his left side, avoiding any accidental contact with the sack containing the box. To ensure her mind was untroubled by it, he unslung it off his shoulder and carried the sack down by his right knee. A couple of times he considered dropping the bag off at one of the other stalls he passed, but again suffered a strange pinch of guilt: he couldn't pass on the cursed item to a total innocent. No, he was determined to send it right back to the one that had caused him all this hellish trouble.

They traversed the full length of the market a second time and, reaching the top end, adjacent to where the customer car park was situated, they turned about and stared out over the bustling crowds. 'I'm not ready to give up yet,' said Ben. 'In case we missed her, we should reverse the aisles we first took and make a second search. What do you say?'

'You're the boss.'

He nodded and, after a brief discussion, he went down the furthest rows that Rachel had originally searched, while she took the one they'd just completed, with the idea of meeting again at the bottom and together checking the central rows.

Five minutes later, Ben still hadn't spotted the woman or any clues to lead him to her. Rachel approached with a nonplussed expression and carrying a small carrier bag. She delved inside and pulled out a bottle of water. 'I bet you still didn't hydrate,' she said.

He hadn't, too engaged in the search to think about his bodily needs.

'Thanks,' he said, accepting the bottle. Now that he thought about it, his mouth was still gluey with fat and also the bitter taste of disappointment. 'I don't think we're going to have any joy here.'

'We should still check those centre rows again.'

He nodded, then Rachel had to wait while he downed two thirds of the bottled water in one long swallow. He offered her the sloshing leftovers.

'Got my own, thanks.'

Ben gulped down the remainder of the water, then dashed his lips dry with the back of his sleeve. 'Sorted.'

They moved up the central aisle, this time checking each stallholder's face as well as their parked vehicles. Once more,

Ben recognised faces that had grown familiar over the years he'd been in the business, but none that hinted at a connection to the woman he sought. Out of options, he paused at Big Taffy's stall. By now the huge Welshman had exited his van and had dropped into a deckchair set in front of the open side doors. He held a large plastic mug of steaming tea in one boxing-glove-sized hand, and a thick cigar in the other. The sweet-smelling smoke drifted overhead.

'All right, Taff?' Ben greeted the man.

'Ah, Ben Taylor. But where's that delectable wife of yours?'

'Left her back home today,' Ben said.

'Shame.' Before his words could be misconstrued, he added, 'She was always the better haggler. You should keep her close for when you're dealing.'

'I'm not dealing today, Taff.'

'No?'

'Actually, I'm hoping to give something back.'

'Aah, you know I don't do refunds,' said Taffy. His eyes glittered, suddenly full of the menace that Ben had been warned about.

Ben waved aside his comment. 'It isn't something I'm returning to you. Last week, there was an old woman parked here and—'

Taffy grimaced, and made to rise from the deckchair; it wasn't a simple task for a bulky fellow, especially while both hands were full. He stuck his cigar between his teeth, and set down the cup of tea on the step of his van, then struggled to stand. Ben held his peace while the big man straightened and approached him. He leaned over the tools piled on the table between them, and his eyes pinched, the menace dissipating, growing softer. He slowly withdrew the cigar from between his teeth. 'Terrible thing, it was.'

Ben frowned.

'I take it you didn't hear, then?' asked Taffy.

'No. I'm a bit lost, mate.'

'Hettie Stewart. This is usually her plot. But – God bless her – she won't need it anymore.'

Ben's gut clenched.

Taff said, 'You didn't hear?'

'No. What happened?'

'That smash on the ring road a few days ago? Some kid high on drugs drove his car on the wrong side, hit Hettie head-on, killed the old girl instantly.'

'No.'

'I'm afraid so, Ben. From what I hear, she didn't stand a chance.' The big man shook his head. 'Bugger was off his head, doing about eighty miles an hour when he hit her van. The sickener is, he survived. Hardly a scratch on him. The bastard.'

Stunned, Ben didn't realise that Rachel had moved up alongside him. He stood open-mouthed, trying to take in the terrible news, and how it impacted his plan to return the bad luck to its original owner. It seemed that he needn't bother now, Hettie had already suffered the worst luck possible.

Rachel asked, 'What about her granddaughter?'

'Leona-Marie?' Taffy wondered for clarity, and caught a stupefied nod from Ben. 'As far as I hear, she was with her and survived too, but the poor girl was hurt. Not sure how badly, but it's bad enough, eh?'

'It's awful,' Rachel moaned.

'Aye,' said Ben, but shaking the sense that this was simply another way for bad luck to mess with him was difficult. He couldn't stir any regret – let alone sympathy – for either woman, when they'd knowingly trapped him into taking the box and its foul contents off their hands.

'Is Leona-Marie in hospital?' he asked, and couldn't help a glance down at the sack by his side.

Big Taffy shrugged expansively. How could he know?

The big dealer puffed out his cheeks, and checked his cigar was still alight. He drew on it several times to reignite it, then blew out a plume of aromatic smoke. He aimed the end of the cigar at the sack. 'What have you got there that you want to return it?'

The temptation was strong to pass the bag to the Welshman, in the hope that he could pass the box off as an antique receptacle of nuts and bolts, perhaps, but he wouldn't fool Big Taffy. Besides, he had no desire to set the curse loose on the big man, not when Taffy might come looking for him the way he had Hettie Stewart. He'd only intended to force the women to take it back; Taffy would more likely smash it over his head. Sadly, he doubted that smashing the box would break the curse when it was already on the loose, otherwise he'd gladly present his head as a target.

'It's nothing important,' he lied, and instead tried diverting Taffy's attention off the bag. 'Didn't take you long to move in on their patch.'

'You don't have a problem with that, do you?' The menace again glittered in the big man's eyes.

'Why would I? You have to strike while the iron's hot.'

'Exactly.' The big man winked, and Ben took the opportunity to tip his head in goodbye.

As they wound their way through the crowd, heading once more for where he'd left the car, Rachel said, 'You don't intend going to the hospital, do you?'

'No. I have no intention of tempting fate. There's a bit of a horrible correlation concerning the hospital and this box . . .'

He continued walking and Rachel waited. Finally, she had to prompt more from him. 'In what way?'

'Don't you remember the other day, when we were at the hospital after Helen cut her hand? When we finally left, we were held up by the traffic that was backed into town because of an accident on the ring road. You know who it was in that accident now. Those flat tyres, it's almost as if they happened by design.'

'What are you implying? The flats were deliberately caused in order to buy whatever resides in that box enough time to cause Hettie's death before returning again?'

He shook his head at the absurdity, but alas, it was the direction his thoughts were leaning.

'The timing was probably a coincidence,' Rachel said.

He halted and looked down at her. He gave the sack a brief shake, causing the box to dance around. 'You have me convinced that there's something evil and sentient in this box – don't try dissuading yourself now. If we're going to put an end to things, we are going to have to stay on the same page.'

'You can count on me, Ben. It's just, well, I'm afraid,' she admitted.

'Yeah,' he said. 'You aren't the only one, Rache.'

TWENTY-THREE

Years ago, finding Leona-Marie could have proved very difficult indeed, her lifestyle meaning she would be constantly on the move, usually following seasonal work wherever it led. But that was then, and in recent decades the travelling community had been forced into changing certain aspects of their lives. Whereas they used to roam free, in this era, many families in the travelling community were semi- or even permanently settled, some living on council-sanctioned camps, whereas others rented or owned ground on which they parked their caravans or built houses. It was possible that her family was staying close by, settled here to benefit from the rural surroundings and land-based work, or to sell their wares in the proliferation of market towns in the region. The fact that Big Taffy knew Hettie Stewart and Leona-Marie by name meant that they had been around long enough for the Welshman to get to know them; meaning, Ben surmised, that they were at least semi-permanent residents in northern Cumbria. Through his networking with other dealers, he'd met other Travellers, and thought that if he approached them correctly, he might get an address where he'd find the young woman. By their nature, not to mention the derisory treatment they'd suffered from the settled communities over the years, they could be very private and secretive people, and anyone asking about a Traveller's whereabouts might be met with suspicion or downright aggression. With the latter thought in mind, he suggested that Rachel return home, where she'd be safe from any repercussions.

'Stuff that, boss,' she said, only half joking, 'whatever happens, I'm in this till the end.'

'That's brave of you.'

'Brave? Selfish more like. It's to make sure you don't just toss that box in the nearest bin. From what we've seen, it has a habit of making its way back to us, and when it does, it seems more dangerous than ever.'

They were seated again in his Range Rover, with Ben behind the steering wheel and Rachel next to him. The sack and its contents were once more in the rear of the four-by-four, securely stuffed into the metal toolbox as before. Ben considered her words. After he'd tried burning the box, a person unknown – who he fully suspected was Jason – had discovered it among the ashes and decided to wrap and leave it where it was bound to be found. He entertained the idea that it was Jason's way of playing a prank, he just couldn't decide to what end. Had the youth felt angry towards Ben after he intervened in his attack on Belinda Sortwell and had decided to mess with him, or was this some alcohol-addled attempt at thanking him for saving his girlfriend's life? However he looked at it, it was a conundrum, especially when he considered the alternative; despite Rachel's assertion there was something supernatural about the situation, and he *kind of* agreed, he couldn't logically entertain the belief that the box's contents had somehow manipulated Jason into returning it to its original target. No more than he could believe that the box had then caused Jason to take a head dive off the fire escape to his death.

'What if it did have something to do with Hettie's death?' Rachel had developed a habit of reading his mind, it seemed. Or maybe she was simply considering things along similar lines to him. Probably the latter.

'Unlikely,' he said, choosing not to totally shut down the conversation. Upon first hearing about Hettie's death, he'd mulled it over, and since spun his first fears on their heads. 'It had to be a coincidence. Think about it. How could it have had anything to do with influencing a drugged-up driver into driving into her van? It would need godlike powers, surely? I mean, to get both of them in the ideal place at the ideal time, how could it possibly do that?'

It would require supernatural powers beyond anything that he could bring himself to believe in.

Rachel wasn't so easily put off. 'We can't rule it out.'

He thumbed in the general direction of the concealed box. 'If that's the case, maybe we should keep it locked in the boot as security against it sending a drunk driver smashing into us.'

'Don't even joke about it,' she croaked.

He didn't, but he paid more attention to the oncoming traffic than before. He also took some pressure off the throttle, driving at a speed where he could react to potential hazards before piling into them. Several vehicles previously behind them overtook, their impatient drivers unhappy at being delayed in their journeys. Ben allowed them room to pass, even slowing further to allow them plenty of time and space to get back on the correct side of the road. Danger on the roads, he realised, was only a split-second away at any time, and it frightened him to think that before now he'd never given it much respect.

There were two established encampments in the north of the county that he knew of. One was about twenty miles away near the neighbouring market town of Penrith, but he chose to visit the nearest first, on the northern outskirts of the city. He could have used the ring road to circle the city, but decided against it. Once off the rural roads and into the suburbs, all traffic slowed to a crawl, so there was less potential for a lethal road traffic collision. He drove past the town centre and over one of the river bridges and took a road to the north-east. It was a few minutes' drive to the dedicated site from there, and the closer they approached, the more he felt nauseous. Saliva flooded his mouth, and he swallowed hard to push down the bilious sensation. A glance over at Rachel showed her blinking wide-eyed behind her spectacles, and she vigorously rubbed the base of her right thumb against her chin.

'Leona-Marie could still be hospitalised,' she reminded him.

'Could be,' he agreed. 'But I only want to find out where she's living, not necessarily to see her in person.'

'You intend on dumping the box there?'

'Yeah. No.' He scrubbed a hand over his own jaw, hearing the prickle of unshaved hair. 'I don't know for certain what I'll do.'

'Her grandma has just been killed,' she cautioned.

Ben puffed out his cheeks.

'She has been hurt too,' Rachel went on.

He glanced at her, and found her staring across at him, her face bereft.

'Don't you think they've suffered enough?' she moaned.

'For passing the curse on to us?' he countered. 'Maybe they deserve everything they have got.'

'Ben! How can you say that?'

'Rather them than us,' he reiterated. 'They tricked me into taking that bloody box off their hands, knowing full well what they were doing. Why should I feel any sympathy for them?'

'I don't think you really believe that, Ben. That's your fear that's speaking. I don't believe for a second that you'd wish death on anybody.'

He deflated slightly, almost flopping over the steering wheel before catching himself and reaffirming his grip. 'Heck, no. I don't wish harm on anyone, but if it's a choice between you and Helen and Hettie and Leona-Marie, I'll always choose your and Helen's safety. I don't know! I only want to give the box back, make Leona-Marie retract the curse, and then she can do whatever the hell she wants with the bloody box and that monstrosity inside.'

'What makes you think Leona-Marie can retract the curse?'

His mouth tugged down.

He felt more nauseous than ever.

Ahead, on the left, was the entrance to the site. He expected that it would be gated, but found it was open to anyone driving their vehicles on and off the camp. He knew from past conversations that the camp had once been a military base, the barracks demolished and retro-fitted as a caravan site several decades ago. Families from the travelling communities had used it as both a temporary or permanent home since, some of them raising their children there and sending them to the nearby schools. Some types of Travellers earned bad reputations, descending upon common ground or moving onto private land, and then leaving behind all manner of waste when forced to move on: not so here. The camp was pristine, well-maintained and obviously kept so through a sense of pride. Either that, or through strict application or enforcement of the rules. There were no burnt-out vehicles, roaming dogs, waif-like children with snotty noses and bare feet, no human excrement; in fact it lacked all the slanderous clichés often levied at the community by ignorant folk. From his interactions with the community, Ben had found most Travellers to be honourable, proud people who maintained respectable and beautiful homes; not all, of course, because there were exceptions in all walks of life.

Rachel sat wide-eyed as he drove a short distance into the camp. Maybe she had been misled by the nasty aspersions often thrown at Travellers, or perhaps she had a romantic vision in mind, of campfires and violins and dancing girls dressed in headscarves, hooped earrings and voluminous skirts. In his experience, for the majority, these people looked no different than any other person seen on the streets of Carlisle. Sure, there was a distinct style to some of the girls with their very long, often plaited hair, and the boys with neatly combed and slicked hairdos, dressed in unbuttoned collared shirts and formal trousers, but otherwise there was nothing to the old clichés seen in movies and books to set them apart. Their caravans, or 'trailers' in their parlance, tended towards huge static caravans, complete with raised porches and fenced flower gardens, to personalised showpiece mobile homes gleaming with chrome and cut glass. Vehicles tended towards vans and SUVs. There was not a horse or wagon in sight, though it was possible some were kept by the residents at other locations.

With no exact destination in mind, Ben drove his car towards what appeared to be the only house on the property. This, he felt certain, was home to a manager, or perhaps private owner, and acted somewhat as an office or hub to the site. As he parked, he waited a moment before getting out. There was no vehicle on the adjacent parking bay, and nobody in sight in the tiny garden alongside. The house itself appeared to be in darkness – it was still daytime, but he expected to see light from a TV or perhaps a lamp within – and felt vacant. He exchanged a glance with Rachel.

'Stay here a mo,' he said.

'Stuff that,' she said, and opened her door.

'OK,' he whispered, and got out also.

Several metres away, a small girl brought a pushbike to a halt. She peered up at Rachel quizzically, and Rachel popped her hand up in greeting, and smiled. The little girl spun the bike around and hurtled away.

'Looking for someone?'

Ben jerked at the vaguely Scottish-accented voice.

A big man approached from the nearest static caravan. He was older, maybe in his early seventies, but still powerfully built.

Some of his strength had submitted to gravity, apparent in the wide downslope of his shoulders, and the manner in which his legs bowed, but he still looked capable of picking them each up, one hand apiece, and throwing them several body lengths. His dark curly hair was shot through with silver, his swarthy skin pockmarked. Brilliant pale blue eyes twinkled with curiosity.

Ben vaguely recognised the man; perhaps he'd even dealt with him in the past. 'You don't happen to know a woman called Leona-Marie, do you?'

The man came to a halt, standing with his left hand across his large belly, the other touching his right earlobe. 'Why do you want to know?'

'I had a little deal with her last weekend at Kirkholme, and was wondering if—'

The big man shook his head, eyes downcast. He said, 'I guarantee you, Leona won't be interested in dealin' with anyone now.'

Ben nodded. 'I heard her grandmother died. It's a terrible shame. I wanted to check on Leona-Marie, to see she was OK, and to pass on my condolences.'

The lies had fallen easily from his lips, but Ben knew instantly that the man wasn't buying his insincerity.

'You had a deal with her, and now you feel like you know her?'

'No. It's not like that. I only—'

'It isn't a good time,' the man said bluntly, and waved off any explanation that Ben might attempt. 'Whatever your true business with Leona, you should let it lie for now. Her family's busy making preparations for Hettie's funeral and could do without any outside distractions. You understand?'

'Yeah, yeah, sure,' said Ben, but he wasn't quite done. 'Ehm, do the Stewarts live here?'

'There are Stewarts that bide all over the country,' he replied, 'most of them up north. But if you mean Hettie's folk, no.'

'You don't mind me asking where I can find them?'

'I just told you this isn't a good time.'

'I only ask so I can send flowers,' Ben said. 'I'd like to pay my respects.'

'Can you read?' the man countered.

'Uh, yeah, of course.'

The man grunted. 'There's a notice in the local paper that says where flowers can be sent. Why don't you go and read it for yourself?'

'Uh, yeah, thanks,' said Ben.

The man turned about and walked away. He didn't enter his caravan though, but stood alongside the step to the door, watching. Ensuring that Ben had understood the message clearly.

Ben checked with Rachel. His assistant arched her eyebrows and whispered, 'Rude.'

Not entirely, thought Ben. The man had spoken quite bluntly, but he was offering Ben a heads-up. Emotions were probably riding high at that time. Poking around the family might not be met with as much politeness as he'd just shown to them.

'Let's go,' said Ben, deciding that trawling around any more caravan parks would only fetch them trouble without any aid from the cursed box. 'You can bring up the local paper on your phone, can't you?'

Rachel was already on it, and before he'd even steered them out of the site and back onto the road, she'd located the local newspaper's webpage and brought up the obituaries. 'It's here,' she announced. 'Henrietta Stewart . . .'

'What does it say about sending flowers?'

'Gives the name of her funeral director.'

'Oh. Bollocks.'

'But it also says when the funeral takes place and where, and we only have a couple of days to wait. We could go, and perhaps get to speak with Leona-Marie afterwards.'

'Not a bad idea,' he agreed. 'But in the meantime, I'm putting the bloody box somewhere it can't cause any mischief.'

TWENTY-FOUR

Hettie Stewart's funeral was not the first to take place in the coming week. A day ahead of her, Jason Halloran's simple funeral was held at the city's crematorium. His parents didn't attend, neither did any siblings, because to a person they had all preceded him to the grave. His only family in attendance was an elderly aunt, and a teenaged female cousin who would clearly rather be elsewhere, anywhere else, than there. A few old school friends turned out to pay their respects. Belinda Sortwell attended, but none of his drinking buddies showed up. Forlorn, weeping, the only person with wet eyes among the small group of supposed mourners, Belinda sat at the head of rows of mostly empty seats, feeling as if her awful life had just grown exponentially worse for her loss of Jason.

On the final row of benches in the room, Ben and Helen sat in silence. Rachel would also have attended, but somebody needed to watch the shop for them, and ensure nobody tampered with the wall safe in which Ben had locked the box and its contents alongside the valuable amulet originally used to entice him. To return the box to its original owner, Ben had thought it only right that he gave back the amulet too. Lost in his own thoughts, Ben barely heard any of the eulogy muttered by the officiant leading the ceremony, and only perked up when a high-pitched wail erupted from Belinda during the committal when the curtains began closing around Jason's simple coffin. For a moment it looked as if Belinda might fling herself bodily over the casket, but she was taken hold of by the officiate, who embraced her consolingly, then led her, staggering in her grief, towards the exit. Music played the attendees out, supposedly a jubilant beginning to Jason's onward journey, but crass in Ben's opinion, with Elton John boasting that he was still standing.

By comparison Hettie Stewart's send-off resembled a state funeral. There were hundreds of mourners, some having travelled from far corners of the country. A cavalcade of vehicles followed the funeral cortege, while a traditional traveller wagon led the way, decked in flowers and ribbons. A tri-coloured horse with magnificent feathers and a flowing mane drew the wagon, stepping regally as it progressed. Hettie's casket rested in the rear of a regular hearse, but immediately behind it there was a second flat-bed wagon piled high with memorial wreaths and flower arrangements. Her immediate family followed in the first four limousines, and then extended family tagged on behind, then came everyone else. The procession stretched out of sight. Her accident had brought the city roads almost to a standstill, but not to the extent that her funeral procession did.

Again joined by Rachel, while Helen guarded the shop, the safe and its captive, Ben stood at the roadside watching the procession as it entered the city's large cemetery. There was a moment of pause whilst it was ensured that the living wagon could pass through the gatehouse without damage and then, once inside the grounds, the hearse followed. Out of respect, Ben lowered his head, his hands clasped at his waist. Only once the hearse and the wagon carrying the floral tributes had passed inside did he raise his head marginally, unable to stop from checking which limousine – if any – contained the grieving granddaughter. Each of the family cars was filled with mourners, and he couldn't determine if any was Leona-Marie. After all the official cars had negotiated the gate, Ben tapped Rachel's elbow, and alongside dozens of others on foot, they entered the burial grounds. The procession of vehicles snaked ahead, following a slope downhill past sculpted trees and ancient leaning tombstones towards a bridge over a stream, then began up the next slope to the current area of the cemetery used for burials. Ben and Rachel strode quickly, for fear the ceremony would begin without them. As they headed uphill again, Ben saw that the hearse and coffin had turned to the left towards where the ground had been opened in preparation. Many cars spread out, parking on the roadsides, and the numbers of people moving to surround the grave was staggering: Ben thought that when his time came, he'd be lucky to have a hundredth of the number of mourners that this one old lady had.

He wasn't interested in any other face than Leona-Marie's, and he finally picked her out, standing close to the tight bunch of mourners gathered around the grave. Several burly men acted as pall-bearers, carrying the coffin on their shoulders, marching solemnly, until they set it on poles astride the open grave. They stepped back, taking up strategically placed ropes, and the closest family members moved tighter together, standing almost at the lip of the grave. Leona-Marie clung to the elbow of a middle-aged woman who looked very similar, and who Ben deduced must be Hettie's daughter, and Leona-Marie's mum. A thickset man with curly blond hair stood at her other side, there for support should she need it, but avoiding grasping the young woman's broken arm. She wore a cast that stretched from her right thumb to her elbow and, despite wearing sunglasses, and hollowed with grief, it was obvious that her face was bruised. Her hair was pulled back sharply, and plaited. A long black overcoat was worn awkwardly, so as not to encumber her slung broken arm, and covered her almost to mid-shin, and her shoes were black. It gave Ben momentary pause that he hadn't dressed for the occasion in similarly dour attire, as he had only the day before for Jason Halloran's cremation service, but it had never been in his original plan to join the mourners at graveside. Then again, there were plenty of others wearing their ordinary attire. At least Rachel had thought ahead and turned out in black jeans and a navy pullover. Her glasses reacted to the sunlight, the lenses turning opaque.

The vicar said a few words. The support poles were removed and, at a signal from the funeral director, the pall-bearers began lowering the coffin into the grave, while the vicar continued delivering the committal in a sonorous voice. Family members, unashamed of displaying their heightened emotions, wailed and howled, and for the briefest moment it looked as if Leona-Marie's mother might lunge headlong into the grave, similarly to how Belinda had lurched towards Jason's coffin the day before. The curly-haired man reached past Leona-Marie to clutch her mother and draw her into his embrace. Leona-Marie also clung to her mum with her one good arm. Tears streaked their faces, as it did dozens of others surrounding the interment. It was obvious that Hettie Stewart was loved and would be missed by far more people than Jason ever had. Regret twinged in Ben's chest and his eyes prickled; it was shameful that he had rarely given the youth more than his disdain when an act of kindness could have made his life more bearable.

A dozen or more fresh-cut roses were dropped on the coffin by family members, and others took the offered dirt and sprinkled that on the casket too. Then, the vicar finished the ceremony and walked slowly away without further comment. For a while longer the mourners sniffled and dabbed at wet eyes, and then began moving away in small clusters. Some went to the closest family members, hugging them and muttering their condolences, and Leona-Marie perked up a little to thank and hug back their friends and relatives. Her mum continued to be inconsolable and had to be led away by the curly-haired man – Ben was yet to decide if he was Leona-Marie's father or an uncle, perhaps even an older brother – and Ben saw an opportunity to speak with Leona-Marie. She had lingered a moment, to say a few personal words to her grandmother perhaps, and the others had moved aside to allow her privacy. Ben stepped forward, but felt Rachel clutch his jacket.

'Give her a minute, Ben,' she cautioned.

He nodded softly, and held his ground.

Leona-Marie whispered something, then screwed her eyes so tightly that lines creased from the edges of her sunglasses almost to her ears. Thick teardrops dripped from her chin. She straightened, and opened her eyes, releasing a sigh. Touching her fingertips to her lips, she then guided a kiss at her grandmother and, with that one small act concluded, she turned away.

Seeing Ben standing several metres away, she jerked to a halt. Her shoulders rounded, and her head lowered as she peered over the rims of her sunglasses at him. 'What are you doing here?'

He held up both hands in surrender. 'I'm not here for trouble,' he promised, 'I only want to speak with you.'

'You shouldn't have come here,' she hissed.

'I had to, and I believe you know *why* I had to come.'

She glanced at Rachel, frowned when she didn't recognise Ben's assistant, and then turned further to hurry away.

Ben took several lunging steps to follow, and before he reached her Leona-Marie spun towards him, throwing out her good arm. She pointed a manicured fingernail directly at his face. 'Not another step.'

'I promise I don't mean any harm, it's just that—'

'It isn't you I'm afraid of!'

Her voice was strident, and drew the attention of a number of other mourners still in earshot. Some of them merely continued on their ways, returning to cars or walking from the cemetery, but not all. Some watched what was happening, while several of Leona-Marie's closest relatives rushed to close ranks around her. A couple of young men immediately went on the offensive, approaching Ben aggressively, and he back-pedalled, holding out his palms to stall them. 'Please, I only want to speak with you,' he directed past them at Leona-Marie.

The men formed fists, one of them throwing out his chest and slashing the air with his arm. 'You'll get yourself away if you know what's bloody good for you,' he snapped. His gesticulations were apparently his way of directing Ben in the opposite direction to Leona-Marie.

Ben shook his head in desperation, aiming his words at her. 'You know what's happening to me, it's why you're so terrified. You know it's what killed your grandmother and—'

Swearing, the nearest young man hurtled at him, face contorted with rage. Ben was a big man, and no weakling, but he'd never describe himself as a fighter. He'd had a few schoolyard scraps, most of which he'd lost, but in adulthood the only genuine physical tussle he'd been involved in was trying to save Belinda from Jason, and even then he'd needed the assistance of Cezary and his cousin in order to control the emaciated youth. The man lurching at him appeared to know what he was doing, though, and before Ben could form any resistance, he'd been struck twice, once at the side of his face, and once in his stomach. His brain almost shut down at the pain flashing inside his skull, and then his lack of wind sent him to his knees on the cinder path next to Hettie's still open grave. His eyes must have closed in reaction, because he was momentarily blind, confused, and felt buffeted by somebody, and then by a second person. It wasn't for a few seconds before he understood the second one had intervened and was protecting him. Rachel screeched like a wildcat as she defended him from any further assault. He grabbed at her for support, and she helped him to stand. Blinking, dazed, voices ringing in his ears, Ben shook some cognisance back into his thoughts.

His attacker had been ushered away by the second male to approach him, plus a couple of the funeral attendants. Also, Leona-Marie had intervened between them, ensuring that her folk could make a hasty retreat rather than protect Ben from further assault. Rachel pawed at some dirt on Ben's jacket, then reached to touch the sore spot on his face. He shied away, more out of fear of Helen hearing how tenderly the girl touched him than from physical discomfort. She was a little hurt by his response, and for a few seconds was unsure how to respond. He put a hand on her shoulder, as if requiring support, and it was enough to reassure her that she was a valued friend. She nodded sagely, and stepped closer again.

'Are you OK, Ben? That was totally uncalled for.'

'My fault probably,' he replied, loud enough for Leona-Marie to also hear. 'This probably wasn't the right time or place to bring up Hettie's death.'

Leona-Marie stabbed a hand towards the retreating men. 'Those are my first cousins. Hettie was their grandma too.'

'I understand. I spoke out of turn and I apologise to you all.'

'You're lucky that they didn't beat you worse,' Leona-Marie warned, and Ben took it as a promise if he again did anything to displease her.

'If anyone comes near us, I'll have them arrested for assault,' Rachel responded.

'It was you that came here, you weren't invited,' Leona-Marie reminded them dryly.

'We won't need the police,' Ben said, his way of reassuring her he'd no intention of having her cousin charged. His recent attacker had joined others from the family in unloading the floral memorials and wreaths off the flat-bed wagon, as if nothing untoward had just occurred.

Leona-Marie stared at him a few seconds over the rims of her sunglasses, before she pushed them up a little. She didn't turn away.

The funeral director approached. Her nearest and dearest expected Leona-Marie to return to the lead car, to be ushered to a traditional wake elsewhere, no doubt. The director had missed the brief scuffle, but easily picked up on the tense atmosphere. He coughed politely, and whispered something to Leona-Marie while casting a suspicious eye over Ben and Rachel.

'I'll be along in a minute,' she promised. 'I just need a quick word with these folk.'

'Would you like me to wait and accompany you to the car?'

'That won't be necessary,' said Leona-Marie. The man nodded and retreated, glancing back several times.

Ben dug in his jacket pocket and pulled out his wallet. He opened it, flicked through various cards and random pieces of paper stuffed inside and then found what he was looking for. He held it out towards the young woman. 'I need your help to put an end to what's happening. You can choose not to help, but I think you've realised the frightening truth: that the curse didn't end when your grandma passed it on to me.'

At the word curse, he saw her features tighten, but it was followed by a deep sigh of resignation. 'I can't promise that I'll be able to help.'

'I think you know more about what's going on than we do. Please, Leona-Marie. Take my card and please call me on that number. We can meet somewhere of your choosing and talk. That's all. Just talk . . . OK?'

She paused for a moment longer, and then moved forward a few feet. Ben matched her step for step, still with his business card outstretched towards her. They remained at arm's length, but the young woman took his card, briefly glanced at it, and then tucked it into one of her coat pockets.

'I'm genuinely sorry,' he said, barely above a whisper.

'You needn't be. You didn't even know my granny.'

Ben meant he was sorry for causing the disruption at the ceremony, but now that he thought about her response, maybe his condolences should've been directed towards losing her grandmother. Except there was a tightly wound spot in his chest, a reminder that his bad luck and woes were the fault of Henrietta Stewart, which denied him any feelings of sympathy towards her.

He smiled, a tight line of his mouth only, and Leona-Marie turned sharply and strode away, taking high steps over the spongy turf. Beyond her the living wagon was once more being driven away, and she picked up her pace to join the caravan of vehicles ready to fall in its wake.

'Do you think she'll call you?' Rachel wondered.

He didn't give it a moment's thought. 'She'll call. She's more frightened than we are after that crash. She escaped with a broken arm and a few abrasions last time, but I'd say she's terrified that the curse isn't done with her yet.'

'Yeah,' said Rachel. 'The way she reacted when she recognised you proves she thinks it's still following her.'

Knowing so was disturbing. Apparently, pawning the box and its horrible contents onto him hadn't proved enough to save Hettie Stewart from it, and if Leona-Marie had experienced further proof that it still stalked her, then what hope was there for him, Helen or Rachel to escape the insidious hex?

TWENTY-FIVE

Through the window of the antiques and curios shop, Cezary Nowak watched Helen King as she kept busy during a lull in customers. The glass was beaded with drizzling rain that had recently started, but not enough to cover any detail yet. She had one hand bandaged, and was conscious of keeping it from further damage, holding it across her belly and relying solely on her other hand to complete tasks. She was unaware of his perusal, distracted by something else that caused her to frown and mutter to herself. Her attention kept going to what was some kind of safe or strongbox located on the wall behind the service counter.

He'd gone there hoping to find Rachel, but instead had seen her boss was watching the shop for a change. Cezary felt like a creep, spying on her like that.

Yesterday, he had spied on Jason Halloran's committal to the flames too, through a gap in the doors at the very back of the room. He had stayed at the door so that he could easily slip out again, though the necessity hadn't arisen, because other than the officiant, who had glanced at him on a couple of occasions, nobody else had noticed his presence. He might have entered and taken a seat on the back row of benches, except Ben and Helen huddled on it, watching in silence. Cezary hadn't wanted the shopkeepers to note his presence, because they might wonder at his reason for attending the cremation; it wasn't as if he'd shown any interest or any fondness towards Jason before. He could lie, of course, and claim to be simply paying his respects to their mutual neighbour out of duty to the dead, but knew he wouldn't be able to. His real reason for attending was to try to convince himself that he was not somehow responsible for Jason's death. He couldn't; his memories of that day were riddled with deep, dark holes he couldn't fill. When Belinda hurled her frail body at the coffin, clutching as if about to tug down the curtains closing slowly around it, her wail of grief stabbed his heart sharper than a dagger, and he'd fled the crematory, leaving quickly by the front rather than following the other attendees out through the designated exit. He had run, not stopping until he was fully clear of the grounds, and then collapsed on his backside on the low wall encircling the cemetery. Iron railings dug into his backside and shoulder blades, but he paid the discomfort no mind. He had scrubbed the balls of his thumbs in his eye sockets, and moaned in a different, more soul-wrenching torment.

For several days Tymon had tried to get Cezary talking, but he'd remained silent and refused his cousin's attempts at engaging him. They were first cousins, workmates and smoking buddies, but Cezary had refused to hand over his cigarettes and finally swore at Tymon, instructing him in no uncertain terms to spierdalaj and buy his own cigarettes in future. Tymon had called him a dupek, which he supposed was fair, because he probably was acting like an arsehole for telling him to fuck off. Rather than apologise, Cezary had thrown his pack of cigarettes at Tymon and told him to choke on them, and had refused to speak to him or their friends, Patryk and Oskar, since. He knew that – should his friends press him for answers over his behaviour – they would probably guess what was troubling him, because they must have some inkling that he was outside smoking on the fire escape around about the time that Jason had returned home and fallen to his death. If they pressed him, he was unsure what he would admit to: he hoped that the flashes of tricking him to the upper balcony and then pushing Jason to his death were lies conjured in his overwrought mind. The last thing he recalled clearly from that evening was when he'd rescued that crazy old box from the ashes and opened it on the fire escape . . . no, he also had an inkling of wrapping it in brown paper and delivering it like a cherished gift to the front door of Taylor and King's, his reason for now spying on Helen.

He thought the box was inside that safe, and that it should be. If not there, then somewhere even more secure.

An uneasy compulsion forced him to open the door and enter.

He lingered in the entrance, unsure what to do next. He used the blade of a hand to wipe the drizzle from his forehead and cheeks.

Helen darted a glance at him, offered a strained smile but didn't move towards him.

He feigned interest in some baubles on a shelf.

He was probably acting as shiftily as Jason or Belinda had during one of their frequent shoplifting sprees.

'Can I help you?' Helen offered.

He shrugged, and said what the majority of her customers probably did too: 'I'm only looking.'

'You are one of the boys from upstairs,' she said, a statement rather than a question.

He nodded, but didn't expound. Entering the shop had been a bad idea. Why had he come inside when he had already guessed the location of the box? In fact, why was it important to him that he knew where it was, and that it was being prevented from doing him or anyone else further harm?

'You're Cezary, right?' said Helen.

Cezary felt like running again.

'Ben told me you helped Rachel get free when she got stuck down in the cellar, and that you also helped him when Jason attacked Belinda.'

He shrugged again, and looked down, almost introspective as he searched for where her questioning was leading.

In the next second, he discovered that she wasn't checking his helpfulness in order to thank or praise him.

'You're a nosy fucker, aren't you?'

Startled, he looked up.

Helen sneered at him.

'You're here now, poking around, sticking your nose where it isn't welcome.'

'What are you talking about?' Stunned, he couldn't conjure a more erudite response.

'What are you looking for?'

'Nothing. I'm not looking for anything.'

'Liar! Looking for this?' From behind the counter, she used her good hand to lift the wooden box. The lid had slid open several inches along the twin grooves. Within was a darkness so deep it drew his gaze, and vertigo assailed him so sharply that he staggered towards it. He grabbed at shelves of curios, trying to halt from pitching headlong, as if he was about to fall into an open pit. His grasping fingers knocked vases and trinkets to the floor, and he couldn't avoid stepping on them. Porcelain shattered underfoot.

Helen leered. Her eyes were as sharp and as dark as the box's interior. Her mouth stretched in a jack-o'-lantern grin. 'I knew it,' she crowed.

He managed to catch his balance. Forcibly he pushed backwards, grabbing at the shelves again.

'Run,' she said.

He stood a moment more, indecision causing his mind to falter.

'You have the mark of Cain upon you,' she whispered, and the manic grin reappeared.

Cezary's English was good, but for that moment he was thinking totally in his mother tongue: he had no idea what she meant.

'Murderer,' she enunciated, as if reading his mind, and she licked her lips lasciviously.

His head shook in denial, but he knew. He couldn't deny what his mind had refused to show him clearly before. His memory was filled with holes because those were the memories of something else, the same thing now residing within Helen King. This mark of Cain she spoke of, the murderer's mark, was not on him, but on the devil that had used him, as it had Jason Halloran previously.

As before, it was as if Helen, or the thing compelling her to do its bidding, could read his mind.

Still clutching the open box, Helen advanced through the shop. 'Nobody will believe you, Cezary Nowak. Nobody. They'll try you for murder and your only excuse will prove your insanity. Your only hope is to run. Run, Cezary.' She lunged, mouth opening as wide as an attack dog's. Within the open maw writhed something black and withered. 'Run.'

Cezary ran.

He slammed into the door. Rebounded. Grabbed at the handle and tore open the door towards him, even as Helen, or the devil within, screeched at him to run again. He slipped and staggered through the opening, out into the street, almost colliding with two passersby huddling under a single umbrella. He jerked to one side, then the other, and they responded in surprise, crying out, almost colliding with each other. He darted around them, and was positive that Helen's laughter pursued him as he fled along the street. He aimed away from the alley that led to the backyard and the stairs to his shared apartment, hurtling along the high street, heading away from his home, his cousin and friends. He couldn't return to them. Not now. His only recourse was to get far away, as far away as he could. In his panic, he knew a single recourse: he must flee home to Poland. It was his only chance to escape his guilt, and to avoid spending the rest of his life in an English jail cell.

He ran as if his feet would carry him across the country, across the North Sea and half of Europe. He barely reached the end of the pedestrianised section of the high street. One heel skidded on a scrap of greasy brown paper. Trying to catch his balance, his feet tangled together, and he pitched forward to skid along the rain-dampened paving. His face impacted a raised brick flower bed, erected there in the 1990s to both prettify the city centre, and to thwart desperate thieves from driving stolen cars through shop windows. His neck bent sickeningly, even as his spine arched torturously and flipped his heels upward like he was a contortionist. When his body unfurled and slapped the paving, it didn't move again.

TWENTY-SIX

Helen slumped on an office chair in the tiny closet designated as their staffroom. Her knees were drawn up so that her feet hovered above the floor, while her upper body had collapsed over the small table in front, pushing aside the electric kettle and a few softened gingernut biscuits abandoned there, days ago, on a saucer. As she grew aware of her position, she tried rising up and inadvertently used her sore hand for support. The pain helped bring some clarity to her thoughts, but refused to tell her anything about the recent past events. She had no recollection of going to the staffroom, none whatsoever of Cezary Nowak's visit to the shop, or how she had forced the young man to flee in panic; neither had she any memory of returning the box and its contents to the wall safe.

Settling her soles on the floor, she tensed her thighs and buttocks, and stood erect, cradling her painful hand against her abdomen. She blinked around, trying to wring form out of a kaleidoscopic whirl of memories that must have led to her retreating to the staffroom. She could picture herself working, moving around, but rarely straying far from the service counter. She thought that at one point she must have rung up a sale or two, because there had been a few customers in the shop prior to the rain starting. Yes, she even recalled that, after a brief spell of sunshine, it had begun to drizzle, turning to sharper showers for a while, and then settling into a prolonged spell of fine rain. Not good weather for a funeral, she thought randomly, and it jolted her into recalling where Ben and Rachel had gone, while she'd stayed behind to stand guard over the box.

Spotting that the kettle teetered at the edge of the table, she righted it in a safer position, and then dragged the saucer and biscuits alongside it. Turning, she could immediately see through the door and into the shop's interior. Thankfully there were no customers. A flutter of panic climbed her chest. What if she'd been asleep for ages and customers had come and gone, some of them helping themselves rather than paying? What if any of them had rifled the till and stolen what little cash they had made in the better part of a week and a half now? Worse again, what if somebody had gained access to the safe?

The latter thought caused her to lunge towards the service counter. The safe was closed, and the cash register appeared unmolested. However, a quick check showed that some porcelain lay shattered on the floor near the entrance and some of the items displayed on the nearby shelves were in disarray.

She wondered if she was responsible for causing the mess. It had to have been, who else could be responsible?

Had she come over faint, staggered and clutched at the shelves for support? Had her fumbling knocked down the vase that had been broken into fragments? Had her dizziness caused her to claw a darkening path to the staffroom and collapse unconscious in the chair?

Other than her confusion, and the holes in her memory, she didn't feel weak or even faintly ill. On reflection, the only lingering effect from her collapse was a horrible taste that was like she'd consumed mouldy bread and sour milk. She didn't feel sick as such, not until she concentrated on the rotten taste and found that it grew worse. Clamping her good hand over her mouth, she swallowed until she was confident she wasn't about to projectile vomit all over the shop.

Returning to the staffroom, she looked for a dustpan and brush, but there wasn't one in its usual place. Recalling that Ben and Rachel had done a substantial clean-up a few days ago, she realised that the brush and pan must've been placed elsewhere. A wave of unease flooded through her when she thought that they must be downstairs in the basement, but in the next moment she gathered her resolve. If the cleaning utensils were downstairs, she must go and fetch them: what was she afraid of? The box and its contents were locked safely away upstairs, so logically the basement should be safe from their effect now. Not only that, but she was still of the opinion that there was nothing to this silly curse stuff that Rachel had convinced Ben into believing. She had given Ben leeway to follow his plan of giving back the goods originally purchased – or practically tricked from the old woman – by way of an unspoken apology for accusing him of enjoying an affair with their assistant. She had been out of order, and only partially through the lowering of her inhibitions brought on by the concoction of drugs fed to her by her mum. She had wondered on occasion if Ben fancied trading her in for a younger model. He'd never given her genuine cause to believe he had eyes for Rachel, or for any other woman for that matter, but she couldn't help feeling twinges of jealousy when watching how close they'd grown of late. As well as showing him leeway, his freedom to roam with Rachel was a personal test of her self-control; up until then she'd managed not to ring Ben's mobile and check *just what the bloody hell was keeping him.*

She shook off the idea, and the fresh twinge of jealousy, and returned to the shop floor. The door to the basement was shut, but hardly a substantial barrier. It would open at her lightest touch, and she could be down the stairs in seconds to retrieve the cleaning tools she needed. The box was locked in the safe. She didn't really believe that it was responsible for their run of terrible luck. And yet . . .

She turned away from the basement door and approached the broken vases and began delicately picking at the shards and setting them on a clear space on the nearest display shelf. Who needed a brush and pan when she could collect the shards on the shelf, then scoop them all together into the waste basket fetched from behind the service counter?

She glanced up from her work. The rain had grown harder, now making a faint drumming on the shop's windows. From where she stood, she could see how the rain pattered the already wet pavement outside, causing tiny splashes and expanding concentric rings in the puddles caught in the dips and hollows. She sighed wearily. A shower could often assist a day's takings in that it pushed customers indoors, whereas continuous rain only served to send them scurrying for home. Today was going to become a literal washout, she thought, pun frigging intended. A few shoppers scuttled past, their collars pulled up against the sudden downpour. None approached her shop. She walked to the front door and pushed outside, standing out of the rain's reach in the recessed doorway. She looked both ways, and saw that the town square was practically devoid of humanity, as everyone had either taken shelter in doorways or within shops. No, that was not true: there was some human activity, though it was at the far end of the pedestrianised shopping area, only she couldn't tell exactly what was going on. There were people dressed in green, another person wearing a high-visibility jacket and cap, as well as a couple of concerned women standing wringing their hands from several metres away. Two of those dressed in green crouched low over another figure on the ground. It took a moment longer for the scene to make sense to Helen, helped when the green-clad people stood and lifted the person off the floor on a stretcher. She had to crane further, risking a drenching, to spot the ambulance that the paramedics delivered their patient to. Some unlucky soul was having a worse day than hers.

She grunted.

'Do you see, Ben?' she posed the question into the ether. 'It doesn't take a cursed hoodoo box to mess up somebody's day; sometimes all it takes is a splash of rain and a slippery pavement.'

TWENTY-SEVEN

Counting the minutes was not healthy for Ben, but he couldn't help dwelling on each. Every sixty seconds that passed felt like an eternity. Every hour felt as it had as a child when waiting for Christmas, but with nervous excitement replaced by a sense of dread in this case. His trepidation was that Leona-Marie might never call, and that he'd be left trying to fathom how to deal with the box alone. When confronting her at the graveside yesterday, he'd handed over his business card, but it hadn't escaped him that she had shoved it into a coat pocket, and very likely it was her coat saved for specific occasions, probably to be taken off and hung away in a closet until the next funeral called it back into service. He wondered if she even recalled accepting the card from him, and barely registering what was printed on it during a cursory glance, or if she'd only done so in order to brush him off at the time. Whilst at the grave, he'd assured Rachel that she would ring him, but the more minutes that ticked past, the more his confidence wavered.

He tried keeping his mind off the silence from his mobile phone by restacking stock on the shelves and guarding the wall safe. After holding down the shop yesterday, Helen had taken a day off, and Ben had given Rachel a day's paid holiday in lieu of her work over the recent bank holiday period. He suspected that Rachel would prefer to be at work too, because he knew that she was equally on tenterhooks awaiting Leona-Marie's response. Ben had promised to call his assistant immediately following any communication from the woman, while Rachel had promised that she would continue researching cursed objects and the method for dealing with them. Telling her not to, and encouraging her to enjoy a rest from the madness was pointless, because he knew that she was as desperate to put an end to it as he was.

Upstairs somebody moved about. The sounds of footfalls filtered through the ceiling, a slow and measured tread. He wondered if a stranger had already taken over the tenancy after

Jason Halloran's untimely death, or if it was Belinda he could hear, sadly plodding around the apartment in her grief. Earlier, he'd spotted some of the lads from the uppermost apartment outside the shop, caught in a three-way huddle as they discussed something. He recognised their faces, if not their individual names, and saw that Cezary was not among them. The other day he'd gained the impression that Cezary had shown interest in their burning of the box more to be close to Rachel than to be helpful. Rachel had been shy around him, but Ben had caught her watching the young man when she thought he wasn't looking, equally as often as he'd caught Cezary eyeing her up. It surprised him that Cezary had not shown his face at the shop since, or that Ben hadn't met him in the backyard where he often liked to smoke. Briefly he'd considered asking his friends about him, but the moment passed and the trio of lads had wandered away into the town centre. Seeing the lads out and about during a weekday was uncommon; as far as he knew, they worked shifts at a nearby seafood-processing factory, and usually weren't around until late evening or weekends. Perhaps they had scheduled a holiday off together, he couldn't say. He wasn't really that bothered, but thinking about it helped pass a few more interminable seconds.

His mobile phone rang.

The ringing was so sudden and loud in the silence of the shop that he started, swearing aloud while grabbing at his chest.

He dug for his phone, drawing it from his trouser pocket.

Hoping for an unknown caller, he swallowed a second curse when he saw Helen's name on the screen.

He accepted the call.

'Something happened, Ben,' she said. Her voice sounded distant, weak.

'What do you mean? Are you OK? Are you hurt?'

'I'm OK,' she assured him. 'At least, I'm not physically hurt or anything. That's discounting this bloody hand, of course.'

'So what's up?'

'Yesterday,' she said.

'I don't follow. What do you mean?'

'When you were with Rachel . . .'

'Oh, come off it, Helen. Not this again?'

'No, I don't mean . . .' She must've held the phone aside,

because her voice grew muffled, and then he heard a series of three sharp coughs. She returned the phone to her mouth: 'Something happened to me when you were out.'

'What? Why didn't you say something when I got back?'

'I had convinced myself that secrecy was my best policy. But it never is, is it?'

'I've never kept a secret from you,' he said, before guilt nipped him. 'Well, nothing too important, anyway. I swear to you that I've never cheated, and never wanted to, let alone—'

'I'm sorry for accusing you and Rachel the other day. I was wrong. Let's put it behind us, eh? Anyway, that's not what I'm talking about. Something happened when I was in the shop alone.'

He snapped a glance at the safe. 'Something *weird*?'

'Something concerning,' she corrected him.

She didn't immediately expound. For the first time that day, the worry about Leona-Marie's failure to call him was forgotten. 'What is it, love? You've got me worried now . . .'

'I think I blacked out.'

'You fainted?'

'I didn't fall down or anything, I must've made it to the staff-room in a daze because I woke up with no idea how I'd got there.'

'How? I mean, did you take anything from—'

'If you're asking if Mum called by and gave me another of her Mickey Finns, then the answer is no.'

'I was going to ask if you'd taken anything from the safe.'

'I'm not that stupid,' she sniffed.

'You know not to touch that bloody box, but it's not the only thing in there. Maybe you had to fetch something else and you—'

'I didn't take anything from the safe,' she said, but she sounded strained. A warble in her voice told the lie, doubt in her own memory, perhaps.

'It's important that you don't go near that bloody thing, Helen.'

'I didn't.'

'OK. I believe you.' He actually didn't. 'But it doesn't make me feel any better about you blacking out. How do you feel otherwise?'

'Right now I'm fine. Yesterday, I didn't feel any illness as such, just had this horrible taste in my mouth.'

'Burnt toast?'

'Eh?'

'Did you taste burnt toast? It's supposedly a sign you're having a stroke. Or is it that you're supposed to smell burning toast?'

'You're not being very helpful by making me worry like this, Ben. I'm pretty confident that I didn't have a stroke.'

'How's that hand feeling? Still painful?'

'A little. But it doesn't feel swollen or infected, if that's what's worrying you.'

'You probably haven't got sepsis, but we should keep a close eye on your wound. It's been a stressful week or two,' he suggested as an alternative explanation for her collapse. 'Maybe it all caught up with you and you had to shut down for a little while.'

'Maybe,' she said, sounding unconvinced.

'Make an appointment to see your doctor. It's probably nothing, but best we get you checked out, eh?'

'I'll see. Chances of getting a doctor's appointment these days are slim. Not unless I'm prepared to wait a week or two.'

'Don't you have to go back tomorrow to have your dressing changed or the stitches removed?'

'Yeah, but I won't see a doctor, only the practice nurse.'

'Try to get an appointment at any rate,' he pushed. 'For peace of mind, if nothing else. Or if you want, I'll try for you. Uh, in a bit.'

He'd recalled that he was waiting for an important call back from Leona-Marie, and was tying up his phone too long as it was.

'Anyway, you should get some rest,' he said. 'You aren't missing much here, there's hardly anyone around and the takings are kind of slow today. I'm keeping busy moving stuff around a bit, trying to make things look more appetising.'

She expelled air. 'Ugh, you just reminded me of that horrible taste. I'm going to get a strong coffee . . .'

'Yeah, good idea. I'll speak with you later, OK?'

'So she hasn't rung yet, your wild gypsy girl?'

'No.'

'Best that I free up the line, then . . .' Without further comment, she ended the call.

Ben looked for a slow beat at the screen, then returned his

mobile to his pocket. What the hell was going on in Helen's head? He had hoped that her momentary spike of jealousy had been heightened by the effects of the concoction of medication fed to her by her mother, Gloria, and that it had since faded away. But reading between the lines, it was still there, festering in her mind. When she'd asked for her accusation towards Rachel to be put behind them, he suspected she'd lacked genuine sincerity. And just now, calling Leona-Marie '*your* wild gypsy girl', her words had dripped with unspoken incrimination, as though she'd already judged and found him guilty of infidelity. Plus, there was her assertion that she had blacked out while alone at the shop yesterday; why the hell hadn't she told him that when he'd returned from the cemetery? Her sudden blackout could be a sign of something hidden, an illness, and possibly connected to whatever was feeding her jealous streak. She'd probably blown off his suggestion of ringing the doctor because she was afraid of what she might learn, some people preferring ignorance over discovering that they are suffering an insidious illness. She was a strong-willed woman, meaning that Helen could be difficult at times, and once she put her mind to something she was difficult to shift. She had already decided not to bother trying to get an appointment with her GP, so he supposed it was his duty as her husband to ensure that it happened for her. He dug for his phone again, worming it out of his pocket, wondering if he had a number for their doctor's surgery saved in his contacts list.

His phone rang, and in his surprise he juggled it for a few breathless seconds, waiting for it to fly from his grasp and shatter on the floor. He chased the phone, battling gravity for a couple of steps, and then once he had control of it, he read the screen: Unknown caller.

'Hello?' he said, then thought it prudent to add, 'Ben Taylor speaking.'

'It's me. Lee,' said a woman, her accent faintly Scottish.

'Lee? Is that you . . . Leona-Marie?'

'You keep using my double-barrelled name. Please, just call me Leona, OK?'

'Uh, I'm sorry. It's just that I heard you called by your full . . .'

'Yes. My granny was adamant in giving me my full name, whether or not I liked it. I was named after her mother, my great-grandmother, as are several of my cousins and nieces. To everyone else I'm just Lee or Leona.'

'I understand. Uh, call me Ben.'

'I think we might already have established that.'

'Yeah. Uhm, just a second.' Momentarily stuck for what to say next, Ben took a steadying breath, and walked quickly to the front door. He threw the lock, so that their call wouldn't be disturbed. He moved towards the service counter, chin raised to get a clear view of the wall safe. He had kept it resolutely shut all day. 'OK, I'm back.'

'You wanted to meet. To speak.'

'That's right.'

'Where and when?'

'I, uh, haven't really thought it through. I hoped you'd have an idea, one suitable to you. My only hope is that it's sooner rather than later.'

'Is one hour too soon?'

'Well, yeah, it's a little short notice. I've a shop to watch and . . . oh, stuff it! Yeah, an hour will be perfect. Where?'

'Do you know Hawkins' Green?'

'No, I—'

'Of course. It has a different name to country hantle; a country gadjé like you will call it Potters' Lonning. It's a few miles west of the city on the . . . hang on, I'll text you a location.'

Hearing the locals' name for the location, he was ashamed to admit that he had used the derogatory term for a Traveller before, so let her believe he had no idea where the old lonning and swathe of common land was situated. In decades previous it had been a well-known stop for transient Travellers, until it had more recently been blocked off with large concrete barriers set astride the entrance to the lonning to thwart overnight camping.

'Are you there now?' he wondered. 'I could be there in less than an hour . . . if it's not too far.'

'Take the hour. You'll need it to pick up your lassie.'

'Do you mean my wife?'

'If that's the young lassie that was with you at the cemetery.'

'Uh, no. That's Rachel, she's just my assistant.'

'Just your assistant, eh?' For a second she sounded almost as suspicious as Helen had concerning his relationship with Rachel. 'I think she might think better of you than you do of her.'

'I like and respect Rachel. She's a lovely girl.'

'You don't need a lovely girl. You need one that's prepared to follow you to hell and back, and from what I saw when she came to your defence yesterday, she's the girl for the job.'

'Those cousins of yours aren't going to start roughing me up again?'

'They won't be with me, so you needn't worry.'

'You'll be alone?'

She didn't immediately answer, and he worried that he might have given her pause for thought.

'I'll make sure that Rachel is with me,' he assured her.

'I won't be alone,' she finally admitted. 'I'll have someone with me too.'

'Should I, uh, bring the box?'

'No.'

'I hoped you'd be able to translate the words on the box and tell us about it.'

'Why would you assume I'd understand what those words say?' she asked sniffily. 'I'm not Romany, I'm a Traveller.'

She said it as if he should have known there were distinct differences. 'I'm sorry, I didn't mean to offend you.'

'I'm not offended. I'm used to it,' she said, with little conviction, before softening a little. 'Besides, a couple of them are in cant, and my granny was able to translate some of the Roma words, and I'm hoping my friend will be able to shine a bit more light on what we're up against. I already took photos of the box while my granny had it, so, no, wherever you've stashed it, leave it there and don't tempt the ruffie.'

'Can I just ask about those words . . . is it some kind of curse?'

'What, as if some Roma witch has given it the *evil eye* or something? Don't believe everything you see in the movies, Ben.' She ended the call abruptly, and he stood a moment waiting, and as promised a text arrived with a screenshot of a map attached; he raced to close down the shop even as he pulled up Rachel's number and asked her to get ready. She didn't give the slightest argument, meaning she'd probably been on standby all day.

TWENTY-EIGHT

Hawkins' Green sat at the edge of a B road west of Carlisle. Ben had memories of the location going back to his childhood. Back then the greensward had looked huge, and a lay-by practically encircling the grassy area had seemed big enough to allow a train of lorries to park up overnight. Now the green patch was barely large enough to erect a couple of tents on, and the lay-by had been abandoned to nature, so that the tarmac had become rutted and split and weeds and bushes had punched through, clawing towards the nearest light. A stand of hawthorn trees, thick with foliage, threw the area into dense shadows for the most part. Barely ten paces along what was still recognisable as the lay-by, huge concrete barriers had been erected. Beyond the graffiti-scarred concrete, the ancient lonning was barely discernible from the landscape, overgrown with bushes and shrubs. Thirty-odd years ago, Ben and another couple of kids from the nearby city had ventured out that way, in search of adventure, and come across the green and adjacent lonning, and there Ben had seen his first and only living snake in the wild. When one of his friends tried pinning down the adder with a forked stick, it had squirmed free, and struck at Ben with its venomous fangs – luckily missing him by a fraction – and they'd fled the lonning, expecting a thousand serpents to come boiling out of the earth in defence of their kin. Because the episode with the snake had creeped him out, it had stuck in his memory, a mini-trauma of sorts, and to this day he retained an abiding fear of slithering things. As he stood at the verge, chunks of perished tarmac underfoot, he avoided the untended grass where he was concerned that a nest of adders might lurk to the present day.

He'd briefly mentioned his youthful misadventure to Rachel on the drive there, but she was untroubled by the thought of any serpent wriggling from the grass, and stood at ease with the unruly grasses tickling her ankles. She waited with her hands in her jacket pockets, occasionally feeding out one hand to settle her spectacles on the bridge of her nose, a habit more than necessity, before tucking it away again. Ben held his mobile phone, checking the time every few minutes, and also half expecting Leona-Marie – no, he must remember to call her Leona – to ring with an excuse not to meet. The B road was busier with traffic than expected, and he watched the approach from Carlisle, wondering if the next vehicle would contain the young woman.

'Hey, there!'

Leona arrived on foot, and not from the expected direction.

Ben and Rachel turned in joint surprise as Leona emerged from the lonning. She was dressed in jeans, trainers and a sweatshirt, her white-blonde hair tucked back behind her ears and pulled into a braid. She'd lost the sling from her broken arm, but had it supported in the front of her partially zipped-up jacket. Another woman accompanied her, about the same age as Leona, and darker. Her hair was cut short, almost pixie-like, and feathered across her forehead. A silver stud twinkled in her left nostril, and dark eyeliner encircled jade green eyes. She wore a long black cardigan, beneath a sheer black throw that was held in place with thumb loops. Her black leggings terminated in black boots, embellished with silver. At the front, where her cardigan hung open over an equally dark T-shirt, a silver belt buckle glimmered in the mottled light.

'This is Shay Connolly,' Leona announced as the women approached.

Rachel hailed them both, raising a palm in greeting. Ben failed to conceal a grimace of confusion. Had Leona and her friend been lurking out of sight in the lonning, checking that he had brought Rachel before emerging? Leona misconstrued his initial response to their arrival.

'Maybe you expected me to fetch a wizened auld chovihani with me?'

Ben shrugged, and offered an embarrassed smile. 'I couldn't say. I mean . . . what's a chohavanee?'

'Chovihani,' she corrected him. 'It's a Roma witch woman. A healer and dukkerer.'

Again Ben didn't understand her meaning.

'Dukkering is what you non-travellers think of as fortune telling, among other things.'

The women came to a halt before them.

Ben gave his name, and Rachel also introduced herself to Shay. The young woman nodded in greeting but didn't speak. She'd obviously heard about them from Leona and was understandably guarded.

'No offence,' said Ben, 'but part of me was hoping that you'd bring a Roma wise woman . . . a chovihani. Those are Romany words scratched into that box, aren't they?'

'Mostly,' said Leona. 'But they've proved ineffective as warnings. They were etched into the box over the years, by superstitious people who didn't fully comprehend what they were dealing with. It's time that we reached out and got help from somebody that knows what they are doing.' She waved a hand in Shay's direction.

'Are you a Traveller?' Ben asked the newcomer.

'Not in the same sense that Leona is,' Shay said enigmatically.

'Wiccan?' asked Rachel.

Shay only offered a tight smile, but again didn't expound. She aimed a hand towards the lonning. 'Please,' she said, and turned abruptly, and it was only when Leona followed, urging them to join her, that Ben understood they were being invited to follow the young woman.

Ben looked back at his Range Rover.

'Your car will be safe enough where it is,' said Leona.

It wasn't the security of his car that he was concerned about. Despite Leona's instruction to keep the box far away from her, he wouldn't leave it unguarded in the shop, and had brought it with him, again secreted in the toolbox in the rear of his car. Briefly he wondered if he should own up, and bring the box with them to wherever Shay was leading. Apparently the young Goth-looking woman was some type of expert, whose assistance Leona had reached out for. But there was the probability that Leona would react badly if he brought out the box, and refuse to deal with him. Better that he stay quiet and not rock the boat, now that she seemed willing to work with him to end their shared problem. He took out his key fob, aiming it and pressing the button to ensure that the car was locked.

They passed the concrete barricade, and entered the ancient

lonning. There was not a viper in sight, but Ben still swallowed in trepidation. He saw how three decades had altered the landscape. The lonning had felt long and narrow when he was a child, a dappled tunnel of shadow and light beneath the arching boughs of the trees, disappearing into the undefined hazy distance. Now he saw that it was not as long as he'd thought back then, and actually terminated within a hundred and fifty metres at a couple of five-bar gates, entrances to a meadow, and a field recently ploughed. The two young women agilely scaled the gate to the right and, after a slight hesitation, Rachel followed, equally spry. Ben was less fluid, clambering awkwardly, and scraping a shin on one of the rusty crossbars. He settled his feet on hard-packed earth on the far side of the gate, but saw that they must traverse the ploughed field if the twin row of footprints made by the women on their approach was to go by. His footwear was not exactly appropriate for crossing a mucky field, and for a moment he regretted not bringing his wellington boots from the shop. However, a swift glance at the women's shoes showed them free of mud, so the earth must be dry enough not to adhere. He followed them into the field, heading towards a cluster of agriculture buildings on the far side.

'The farm used to belong to Shay's parents, and she inherited it from them when they retired,' Leona explained over her shoulder as they walked. 'We met when we were little girls. My family camped on Hawkins' Green, working for Shay's dad over the tattie harvest, and me and Shay became, and have stayed, good friends since. I wish I'd gone to her for help the first time, instead of obeying my granny . . .'

Leona turned away, but not before Ben watched her eyes sparkle with unshed tears. He gave the woman a few beats to gather herself before lowering his voice and asking, 'Is Rachel correct, is Shay a Wiccan or something?'

'She's an occultist,' Leona corrected him. 'She specialises in demonology.'

'Oh.' He glimpsed at Rachel, but saw that she was unperturbed by the idea.

Several paces ahead, Shay had still overheard and announced in a surprisingly deep voice: 'Demonology isn't about demon worship, it's about studying and gaining knowledge on how to combat evil. There are resident demonologists in the Vatican, for example. I'm also a student and practitioner of Thelema, a system of ritualistic magick, and before you ask, no, it isn't black magic, nor is it white; spell casting is determined purely by intent, so can be either.'

Stomach acid fizzed in Ben's trachea, and he had to forcibly swallow to avoid being sick. As much as he'd attempted to deny it, or at least pop his head in and out of the sand rather than fully embrace the idea, the truth that they were dealing with something uncanny was becoming clearer to him with every passing event. He stole a quick glance over his shoulder, but the lonning, let alone the thing hidden in his car parked at its far end, was out of sight. He returned his gaze to the front, and the buildings that they approached. At first he had made out large agricultural sheds but, as they neared them, other structures became apparent, and they were the original buildings comprising a working farm. There stood a couple of red-brick barns, some squat slate-roofed outbuildings and a large family-sized home. An olive-green Citroën Berlingo van and a larger Mercedes-Benz Sprinter van took up space on the courtyard to the front of the house, while a tractor stood partially reversed under a tin-roofed shed almost overflowing with baled straw.

Shay let them in her family home. Earlier, Leona had explained that the young woman had inherited the farm from her retired parents, but there'd been no mention if her mother or father still lived in the property. Neither had there been mention of a husband, or any partner for that matter, or children. Ben thought that the house lacked the atmosphere he'd expect if it were inhabited by a bunch of kids, or by an older couple. In fact, the place felt rather sterile. It certainly didn't strike him as the home of an occultist!

There were no black candles, no pentacles or pentagrams or any other stars or magical symbols inscribed on the floor as far as he could tell, and no Ouija boards, tarot cards or crystal balls on display, and more importantly the air was redolent of freshly baked scones, rather than of sulphur. In fact, he would have to admit that all his preconceived notions of an occultist's lair had been shattered, not that he'd ever given it much thought in the past. Only Shay's gothic appearance gave a hint that she was into weird practices. She offered them a seat in her living room, and Ben and Rachel sat with their shoulders touching, squeezed close together on a two-seater couch loaded with extra cushions. Leona assisted Shay to bring a pot of tea, milk and cups, carrying the stacked tray propped upon her plaster cast, while the occultist carried a second tray of freshly buttered scones and saucers. They set them down on a coffee table in front of their guests, and then took seats on a second couch that sat perpendicular to the first. Shay was positioned so that she was nearest to Ben, while Leona took on the task of pouring tea into each cup, and then offering milk and sugar. Apparently she was at home in Shay's house, and it took a moment or two before Ben realised he'd deduced she was *literally* at home. He wondered how long the women had lived together, and if it had only been a reality since after Hettie perished: hadn't she claimed to have wished she'd gone to Shay for help the first time, instead of listening to her granny?

They sat in relative silence. Only the puttering around as cups were served with dashes of milk or sugar could be heard, and then Ben accepted one of the scones, still warm from the oven and dripping melted butter. It was all very nice and cosy, in total contradiction to why they had met. He was desperate to get on with things and put the horrible matter behind them. However, this show of hospitality was important, especially to Leona, so he took his time to enjoy the scone and allow the meeting to proceed naturally.

Around a mouthful of buttered scone, Shay asked, 'Who else has been in contact with the box since you took possession of it?'

'Only my wife,' said Ben.

Shay briefly glanced at Rachel, but apparently she had already been briefed on their professional relationship. The occultist nodded, swallowed, and said, 'You should have brought her here too.'

'She's not in the best of health at the moment,' Ben said.

'I bet.'

'No. Not because of the box . . . well, not that I know of. She cut her hand badly on some glass and has had a bit of a bad reaction to some medication. It was better that she stayed home and rested today.'

'All who have come into contact with the box need to fight its effect together,' said Shay. She chose a second buttered scone, but only went as far as putting it on a saucer on her knee.

Rachel shifted uncomfortably, as if asking permission to speak. Ben raised his eyebrows, and she almost mirrored the expression. 'What about Jason Halloran?'

'Who is he?' asked Shay.

'He was a neighbour . . .' Rachel again looked at Ben, perhaps for his input.

'Was?' Shay prompted.

'He died,' said Ben bluntly. 'He was a troubled lad. He tried burglarising my shop and ended up stealing a gold ring from the box. Shortly afterwards we had to drag him off his girlfriend after he tried choking her to death with a wire garotte.'

'Oh . . .'

'We tried burning the box,' Rachel added, 'but it mysteriously turned up again, mostly undamaged. Why wouldn't it burn when it can be easily scratched?'

'I suppose it can only be damaged when the box is sealed, not when the chipe is loose and able to protect it,' Shay offered in explanation. 'You said it turned up again?'

'Yes, in the shop doorway,' Rachel continued. 'We think Jason returned it to us after digging it out of the ashes. Soon after, he jumped to his death from a fire escape.'

Shay exhaled. Beside her, Leona's good hand had crept up to cover her mouth; her eyes looked round and sparkled with tears. Ben suspected that she was experiencing a rush of guilt; if she and her grandmother hadn't tricked him into taking the box off their hands, Jason would have been safe from it and would still be alive. He supposed, by that token, he was equally guilty of the youth's untimely death.

Shay had a different opinion. 'His sinfulness brought the curse on himself.'

'That's how it works, through targeting sinfulness?' Rachel frowned hard.

'Can't be that,' Ben was quick to interject. 'What wrong have you ever done?'

Rachel shook her head, a bit dismayed by the question.

Leona said, 'It only takes one sinful act to ignite the hinjiri muktar, and then it attacks all those that subsequently come into its radius. Rachel didn't need to do a thing, other than be around it after you set the chovanó's chipe free.'

Rachel's fingers crept to her mouth, and she plucked her bottom lip with her thumb and index finger. Behind her glasses, her eyes were stark as she took in the woman's words. After a few seconds, she grew aware of abusing her lip, and dropped her hand into her lap. She croaked, 'I've done some research into the words on the box, and also learned others from the Rom language. Chovanó means a sorcerer, doesn't it? But what's a chipe? You've mentioned that word a few times now. Is it some kind of witch's familiar?'

Leona glanced at Shay, and the occultist only shrugged, giving her the opportunity to continue. After all, they were speaking about words used by a travelling community closely aligned to Leona's, so the young woman would regularly mix with them and know more about it than any of them.

'Chipe isn't Rom, it's Scottish Traveller cant and means "tongue".' Leona switched her attention to Ben. 'When I called the entity you freed the "sorcerer's tongue", I wasn't referring to how they'd call out an incantation or spell or anything like it, I was being literal.'

'What?' Ben again tasted acid in his throat. 'That black withered thing that . . . ugh, you're saying . . .'

Leona nodded, glanced quickly at Shay, and said, 'Yes, that's right. It is the actual tongue torn from the mouth of an evil man.'

TWENTY-NINE

Ben wouldn't readily accept the idea that the thing in the box was the desiccated remnant of a man's tongue; he'd seen it move and roll of its own volition, an impossibility for any dead flesh . . . surely? He shook his head, exhaled sharply, and began to stand. Rachel grabbed at him to stop him.

'This is bloody nonsense!' he proclaimed, while trying to pull free.

Rachel kept hold of him. 'Please, Ben. Don't leave. Listen to them, we have to learn everything we can—'

'Learn what? What kind of bloody scam they've got going here?' he demanded angrily. 'They're feeding us stories that are supposed to frighten the lives out of us, and then what? We pay to put an end to the curse?' He switched his ire on to the two young women, who only stared back at him, unsurprised by his overreaction. He dug sharply in his back pocket and pulled out some loose change. 'Whose palm must I cross with silver? Oh, a few quid is not enough for you, eh . . . do you accept credit cards?'

'It's hard to believe,' Shay agreed with him, pacing her words steadily, 'but it's also the truth.'

'Like fuck it is.' Ben yanked free and began to stride away, aiming for the exit. Rachel didn't rise to follow. He stopped. 'Rache? Come on.'

She shook her head. 'I want to hear everything.'

'They're scamming us!'

Leona frowned at him, nose wrinkling up as if at a foul stench. Her eyes were wet, but this time with the strength of her conviction. 'You asked for my help.'

'Yeah, but I didn't think you were going to try to rob me.'

'Have I asked *you* for anything?'

'No. But only because I sussed your game first. You were in on the trick with Hettie, why would things be any different this time?'

'I tried warning you, Ben. Remember?'

He did recall her words about doing Hettie fair.

Also how she'd accepted his payment on Hettie's behalf, by snapping her fingers around his, and refusing to release him while delivering her next words at a whisper. *It's yours now, and remember I told you to play my grandmother fair.*

I was fair, he had lied, and then added insult to injury. *I even gave her more than she was asking.*

Leona had been full of scorn then, perhaps rightly so: *And you country hantle call us Travellers thieves.*

'Why did you let me take the damned thing, knowing what would happen?' he challenged. 'And you were happy pawning the cursed thing onto me, then, so why should I believe you want to help now?'

'I was never happy about it. That was my granny's idea . . . she was frightened, and thought she could pass the curse on, but only to a person of low virtue.'

Ben almost choked.

'You did try tricking her in turn,' Leona reminded him. 'You knew the true value of the amulet, and you consciously lied so you could swindle her, telling her it was costume jewellery and practically worthless. Are those the acts of a virtuous man?'

'They're the acts of a dealer!'

Exhaling noisily, Leona scoffed at his words. She turned her face aside, unable to meet his gaze for a moment.

'Ben,' Rachel said timidly, 'please don't argue. You know there's truth in what Shay and Leona are telling us. Don't let fear get the better of you and spoil things, when they're the only ones who can help.'

He rocked on his heels for a moment, thinking, chewing his inner cheek.

Shay smiled up at him, and nodded at the tray of buttered scones. 'Those won't eat themselves,' she said, and it was a sly way of inviting him to sit again without actually instructing him to.

He grumbled, shook his head at his own apparent stupidity for staying, but again settled down next to Rachel on the couch. She held firmly on to his sleeve, using it as a support crutch this time rather than a restraint. After a few awkward seconds, Ben reached for the saucer he'd placed aside, and fed another scone on to it. Shay caught Rachel's eye, and winked, as Ben began to eat mechanically.

Rachel asked, 'Leona mentioned something – the hinjri muktra, I think – is that the name for some type of demonic entity?'

'Hinjiri muktar,' Leona whispered, emphasising the correct pronunciation.

Shay translated. 'A muktar is quite simply a box, any box, it's the hinjiri part that makes it rather unique, and, well, concerning. Hinjiri was a term used as far back as the medieval period by travelling folk, and its literal meaning is "executioner". It doesn't necessarily translate as executioner box, meaning a hangman's or headsman's box; it's more likely to mean a murderous box . . . as in a container of death.'

It was as if the scone that Ben chewed had taken on the taste and consistency of wet concrete. He dropped the remaining chunk of baked dough on his saucer, and set both on the coffee table. The mulched scone in his mouth was the only thing to ensure his jaw didn't hang open as he attempted to absorb Shay's words. Until that moment, he'd thought that the box had brought him bad luck, and Hettie worse; he hadn't realised that instead of that single extreme example, the purpose of the cursed box was to direct death at all who fell within its radius. It added a sinister layer to Jason Halloran's manner of death, too, because until then he'd assumed that the youth had taken his own life, but what if he'd been forced into plunging from the fire escape? He blinked at the young traveller woman, then turned to appraise Rachel. His assistant gnawed her bottom lip, also contemplating the horrifying purpose behind the box. Ben shivered, and turned his attention back to Leona. He pointed. 'None of us are safe?'

'I told you before. Anyone that has been in contact with it since the chipe was released is in terrible danger.'

'Maybe when Hettie tricked me into taking it off your hands, things should have been written more implicitly. I mean, I'm assuming it was her, but Hettie's poorly handwritten warning saying "do not open" doesn't really cut it. And the words scratched onto the box weren't really helpful either. In fact, combined with her note piquing my curiosity, they practically ensured I'd want to see what was inside. Why even use Rom words when few people would understand them?'

'As I explained, those words weren't put there by me, nor by my granny. They were there when it came into our keeping, and had been added to by previous keepers over the last eighty-odd years since the box was first constructed.'

'What do you know about its origin? How could you possibly know that the horrible thing inside is the tongue of a wizard?'

'Sorcerer,' she corrected him.

'Same difference,' he said, childishly.

'Don't get ideas about some white bearded, genial old man in a pointy hat,' she warned him. 'If your impressions of sorcerers are taken from kids' cartoons, you're in for quite a shock.'

'What do you know about Aleister Crowley?' Shay interjected.

Ben thought for a few seconds, felt Rachel's grasp on his sleeve tighten, and he turned to her for help.

'The self-styled "Beast",' she croaked. 'Six, six, six. Surely you've heard about him?'

Now that she'd reminded him, yes, he had heard. He simply hadn't given any credibility to the occultist before, had never really given him or his alleged status as a black magician much more than passing notice before discarding the idea as rubbish. Many cult leaders had claimed divine or unearthly powers when, in his opinion, they were charlatans and grifters, whose single genuine claim was an ability to control weaker-minded and gullible marks. 'Don't tell me that's Crowley's tongue or I'm bloody out of here.'

Shay chuckled.

Leona remained deadly serious. 'Don't be daft.'

Rachel asked, 'Why bring up Crowley, then?'

Shay said, 'He was a genuine sorcerer of historical note, and progenitor of the magickal system that I practise. There were many others who moved in the shadows who did not enjoy the fame or notoriety of, as you said, the self-styled Beast. The tongue was allegedly taken from one of them.'

'By whom?' Rachel challenged.

Shay indicated Leona, so that her friend could take up the story.

'According to the woman that passed the box to my granny, the sorcerer was executed by Nazis with the express purpose of empowering the box with an evil entity.'

'Nazis? Are you kidding me?' Ben blurted.

Shay said, 'You're obviously unaware of Hitler's connection to the Thule Society, and how he had an intense interest in the supernatural, more so how it could be weaponised.'

'The tool society? Never heard of them.'

'Thule,' Shay corrected him, and spelled out the name, to another incredulous shake of Ben's head. 'I'm not going to give you a history lesson. All you need to understand is that some Thule Society members, most notably Heinrich Himmler, became leading voices in Nazi Germany, and in the Ahnenerbe section of the Schutzstaffel.'

'The what?' asked Ben.

'You know of the SS, and the atrocities they were responsible for, but this is more specifically their pseudo-scientific branch, tasked with finding and securing religious icons and magical tokens and suchlike.'

'I've heard about them,' said Rachel.

'Me too,' admitted Ben. 'Who hasn't watched *Raiders of the Lost Ark*? Aren't they supposed to have invented flying saucers and escaped to a hidden base in Antarctica after the war ended?'

'You may laugh,' said Shay, unoffended, 'but there's sometimes a grain of truth in every conspiracy theory. It is alleged that they searched for and discovered the lost secret of vril, an ancient source of great energy or power, and used it to build their flying craft. Haven't you heard of Die Glocke, or The Bell, their supposed gravity-defying, vril-powered, technological craft resembling a UFO?' She shrugged at his blank look. 'It's unimportant in your case, but don't be too quick to discount things without first checking where they originated from. The point is, the Ahnenerbe SS were heavily into occultism, black magic and sorcery, and it is no surprise to me that they weren't only interested in the building of Wunderwaffen – wonder weapons – but also smaller versions of magically weaponised objects for use against individual targets. What is more innocuous or less threatening than a gift that appears to be a simple trinket box? Whose interest wouldn't be piqued, encouraging them into sliding open the lid and releasing the chipe?'

'Nazi soldiers slew a sorcerer, tore out his tongue and used it as a magical token to empower their killer box? What's not to believe?' Ben aimed an insincere smile at the women, but it felt more like the rictus grin of a skull. 'I mean, come on, how could anyone know that?'

'The story was passed down by keeper to keeper. If only the bare bones of the tale are true, then the hinjiri muktar *is* still something to be treated with fear and great care.'

'If it was made by Nazis, why has it got a Romany or traveller name?' Rachel pondered.

Shay said, 'Most people are under the wrong impression that it was only the Jews who were persecuted and killed by the Nazis during the Holocaust; all kinds of Travellers were also rounded up and held in concentration camps, where they too were tortured or blatantly slaughtered. After one particular camp was liberated at the end of the war, the box fell into the hands of a prisoner, a Romany, who later used the box in a revenge attack against a rival, a Nazi sympathiser responsible for betraying him and causing the subsequent murder of his entire family. From then, the chipe sealed safely within, the box was passed down through several generations of Travellers, where it found its name, until it was sent to Hettie.'

'Jesus,' Ben croaked. 'Who hated your grandmother enough to target her for death?'

Leona didn't answer immediately. She sat, hands in her lap, her knees bouncing, in total disregard of the discomfort she must have felt in her broken arm.

Shay searched her friend's face for an answer first. 'Should I tell them?'

Leona finally raised her chin, and her eyes grew flint hard. 'I have nothing to be ashamed of, I'll tell them.'

Ben waited. Rachel tensed, bending forward at the waist, as if the few extra inches closer would help clarify what was coming next.

'Hettie wasn't the target. She requested the box, and was sent it from its previous keeper.' Leona paused, swallowed with difficulty at some painful memory, and then added, 'to set the chipe against my gorger husband, Keiron . . . and kill him.'

THIRTY

Beforehand, only Ben had launched out of the couch, but was joined this time by Rachel. Last time his reaction was in disbelief, this time theirs was at the enormity of Leona's admission.

Leona jerked up a split-second behind them, reaching for Rachel across the coffee table. 'Wait, lassie. Wait. Don't run before you hear the reason why Hettie took such drastic measures to protect me.'

Rachel dodged her groping hands. 'Protect you? By all accounts she was a murderer!'

'No! It wasn't like that,' Leona cried. 'She was only interested in saving my life.'

'She's telling the truth,' Shay insisted, standing alongside her friend. 'Please hear her out.'

'She knowingly sent that terrible thing after your husband, the same way she later tricked me into taking it off her hands,' Ben snapped. 'And she had the cheek to say that I was of low virtue. Fucking charming or what?'

Leona dragged down the collar of her sweater, displaying a puckered scar immediately above her collar bone. 'Do you see this? It's where my husband stabbed me with a broken bottle. I've got more wounds. Do you want to see them? I've also got internal scars – you can't see those.' She began yanking at her clothing, but Shay got between them and blocked her, protecting her modesty. Leona rattled her broken arm. 'This is nothing compared to what I suffered when I was with him.'

'Your husband was that abusive towards you?' Rachel croaked.

'Yes. More than abusive.'

'And Hettie's only recourse was to send some fuckin' Nazi wonder weapon at him?' Ben scoffed. 'Why didn't your cousins step in to protect you? They were pretty hands-on when it came to sticking up for you at the funeral. I've still got the bruises to prove it.'

'You have no idea about how things sometimes work in my community,' Leona replied. 'You've heard the expression "You've made your bed, now lie in it", I'm sure. Well, it's pretty much the way things are with some travelling families. What goes on between a man and his wife is private, kept between them and not for anybody else to interfere in. My parents guessed that I was being systematically abused, but wouldn't intervene, while my granny, God love her, wouldn't stand by and watch me being battered, day in and day out.'

'Why not just leave him, or call the cops?' Ben asked.

Leona stared at him as if he was an imbecile. In hindsight, he felt stupid having asked those questions.

'I suffered years of torture at his hands,' Leona continued. 'We lived in town, in *his* house, and he controlled me, kept me away from my family and friends as much as he could, so his secret wouldn't come out. There are only so many times you can claim to have blackened an eye on a cupboard door before people begin to suspect, though. He made me dress a certain way, and controlled our spending. He forbade me from carrying a mobile phone, and systematically checked the bills to make sure I hadn't been using the house phone behind his back. He'd regularly hit me, beat and kick me, but that wasn't the worst of it. You can heal from cuts, bruises, even broken bones. It's the other stuff that . . . lingers.' She looked up and nodded gently at their horrified expressions. 'He demanded sex, and if I refused – hell, it didn't matter whether or not I refused – he'd force me . . . he'd rape me.'

Rachel knuckled her mouth in horror.

'Hettie knew it was Keiron or me,' Leona continued after a moment. 'Either he'd kill me, or I'd snap and stick a knife in him while he slept. She chose to help me get rid of him, but in a way that wouldn't directly implicate either of us . . . neither would it end with my cousins being sent to prison for getting *handy* with him. She knew of an old dukkering woman, who once admitted possessing a hinjiri muktar, and reached out to her. Before you ask, I'll stress again, this has nothing to do with gypsy curses; it came about through the ritualistic murder of a sorcerer, and entrapment of his spirit by Nazi occultists. The woman had inherited the sorcerer's chipe and kept it locked away, safe from doing harm, and resisted allowing Hettie to use it at first, until she heard how Keiron was hurting me. It was this old chovihani that warned Hettie that there could be repercussions, and afterwards she must pass it on to somebody of low virtue, or else the chipe would turn on us and continue its evil ways.' Leona paused for a second, assessing if Ben and Rachel were following and coming to accept her explanation. The fact they had both halted their escape confirmed it. They now stood, wide-eyed and loose-jawed, waiting for her to continue. Beside her, Shay placed a palm at Leona's lower back, gently patting her in encouragement. Leona sighed and sat down heavily.

Following her lead, the others returned to their seated positions, though this time the food and beverages were left untouched. Rachel asked, 'How is the box targeted?'

'When you opened it,' said Leona, her attention on Ben, 'you found a gold ring and a hank of hair inside.'

'Yes,' he confirmed, 'but the ring has since been lost.'

'It doesn't matter now as its target has changed. The ring was mine, my wedding band. After Keiron died, I gave it to Hettie and she twisted it, breaking the covenant made upon it when I married him, and she placed it inside the box alongside the chipe, so that the spirit would know its task was done. The hair was tied with a magic ribbon, an ancient traveller relic called a mulengi dori, or dead man's string, and is supposedly used to call on and control the spirits of the dead.'

'Magic . . . supposedly?' Ben wondered.

'Only supposedly because it doesn't seem to have done its job and controlled the chipe. We can't be certain that it was responsible for killing my granny – maybe that crash was just a coincidence – but I'm not prepared to take the chance. I also came into contact with the horrible thing and am afraid it will return for me once it's finished with you.'

'Perhaps it did help subdue it, but I took it out of the box, and that's when the tongue-thingee got loose.' Ben shook his head morosely.

'How does it work?' Rachel asked. 'I felt as if I was assaulted by a living presence, something tangible that left scratches on me, and a bite mark on my lower spine.'

Shay nodded knowingly. 'Most evil spirits will try to possess the living by entering at an energy point on your lower back. Spiritual mediums and psychics often report a sensation of something invading them via an energy point called a chakra on the lower spine when channelling a spirit.'

'It seems like the bloody thing tried chewing its way into me!'

'The visible wounds are a good thing. You were fortunate that it was freshly released from the box and not too strong yet; it meant it had trouble getting to you and the scratches and bite marks are signs of its frustration. It's a good job you had the strength of will to fight it off. Had it found an easy way inside, then it would have taken control of you and had you carry out who knows what.' She eyed Ben steadily, adding import to her next claim. 'Perhaps it would have made you murder Ben, or his wife.'

'The way in which it had Jason attack Belinda,' Rachel croaked to Ben.

He didn't reply. Thinking instead of how he'd dodged a bullet when first releasing the damned thing and it had still been weakened from its confinement. He wondered at Helen's overreaction the other day, and if they'd wrongly judged her behaviour a response to whatever concoction of drugs Gloria King had fed her. His stomach had curdled so many times now that he'd grown used to the taste of acid in his throat.

'Jason killed himself,' he muttered, 'suicide.'

'Or he was forced into killing himself.' Shay shrugged, not knowing the full details about their neighbour's untimely death. 'Tell me again who else has been in contact with the box.'

'Us,' said Ben, with a nod to include Rachel, 'and my wife Helen.'

Shay checked with Rachel. 'You mentioned Belinda . . .'

'Yes. Jason's girlfriend.'

Ben added, 'She never got near the box. She was attacked in Jason's apartment after he broke into my shop's basement and stole the ring from it.'

'And Jason subsequently killed himself?'

'That's right. Suicide,' Ben confirmed.

'Likely she's safe from it then, but can we take that chance? You need to go and find Helen and Belinda, and they must join us to finally take back control of the chovanó's chipe.'

'Belinda's a druggie and alcoholic. I'm not convinced she'll be interested in helping, when her priority is getting her next fix.'

Rachel clucked her tongue at Ben's opinion of the young woman. 'If she's in danger from the chipe, it's our responsibility to protect her. If we explain what happened to Jason, she will probably—'

'Ask for cash to buy her silence?' he grumbled.

'She will probably want to help us,' Rachel replied firmly.

Ben rolled his neck. 'Aye. Maybe, you're right.'

'It's settled then,' said Shay. 'Fetch Helen and Belinda, and I will perform the ritual, and with Nuit's grace I will put an end to this.'

'What about the executioner box and tongue?' Ben asked, barely able to believe the words coming out of his mouth.

'Yes. I'll need them, too, but whatever you do, keep the lid firmly sealed and the tongue inside.'

'You'll do the ritual here?'

'No chance,' Shay coughed. 'No. We'll need someplace remote, where we can do the ritual without any interference from anyone else; someplace we can walk away from and never have to return. Leona has your phone number, but before you leave I'll give you both mine so you recognise it when I call. Let me have a think and I'll be in touch once I come up with an appropriate location. You were warned earlier that it would take everyone who has come into contact with the box to fight it together, and I wasn't being dramatic. Once we commit to this, there's no turning back. We must all go through with the binding ritual, or else the cursed thing will continue to follow us all until there's not one of us left alive.'

THIRTY-ONE

She had felt unwell for days, and the recent blackout troubled Helen greatly. Fear assaulted her in waves, almost consuming her one moment only to ebb away the next, replaced by a burning anger in her chest that felt almost physical, like the worst case of indigestion ever. She knew that something was wrong, and that she should reach out to a doctor for expert help, rather than to her overbearing and occasionally caustic mother. It pained her to think of her in those terms; she loved her mum, but it was true that Gloria could be a difficult woman to like. When she wasn't enraged, Helen wanted nothing more than gentle contact, a hug, something which a clinician or GP would not offer in these days of finger-pointing and fear of accusations of impropriety. Not that she could expect an embrace from Gloria; it just was not her manner to show affection or enact any intimacy. Gloria's way of support was through what used to be called 'tough love', but was often in actuality an unsentimental, metaphorical kick in the backside. Ha! When she was a child, the kick to the bum from Mum had not always been a metaphor. And when Gloria took it upon herself to help Ben along to a decision attractive to her, it was usually by way of an acerbic tongue-lashing. Ben didn't love Gloria, so finding anything to like about her was almost impossible for him, but then the feeling was mutual. It added heat to her opinion of Helen's husband, whenever the opportunity to judge him arose.

'Where is the useless idiot?' Gloria demanded. 'He knows you're not well but has gone off gallivanting with Rachel instead of staying home with you?'

Helen had not explained the real reason for his absence, only that he was out on an errand with their assistant. 'He couldn't help me if he was here. What's he going to do, mop my brow with a dampened cloth?'

'He should be around to fetch and carry for you. You need to rest, and getting up and down isn't helping with those dizzy spells you're having.'

'I haven't had one in a while.'

'No. But you know why, don't you? It's because I'm doing the getting up and down for you.'

'There's no need for that, Mum. I've got everything I need right here.'

Helen had formed a nest out of a duvet and several plump pillows on the settee in her living room. The TV played, the sound muted, after Gloria had taken charge of the remote control the instant she'd entered the house. Several packets of pills and a bottle of gin dominated a small occasional table pulled up to the settee in hand's reach. Helen snorted at the half-empty bottle. 'It's probably too much of that which has made me dizzy. Drinking at this time of day doesn't do me any good.'

As it happened, Gloria had polished off two large tumblers of gin and tonic water, and was onto her third by then, so the actual amount of alcohol Helen had imbibed was minimal. 'It will help you to relax,' Gloria contended. 'That's half your problem, you're too stressed. What trouble has that man got himself into this time that's got you all messed up?'

Helen didn't respond to yet another barb aimed at Ben. Instead, she leaned forward and pushed her gin glass to the far end of the table. 'I shouldn't drink any more in case I do need to go somewhere.'

'And how do you expect to do that? By driving? Didn't you say your car's still in the garage?'

She had fully expected to have her car returned from the garage by now, but apparently her mistake in misfuelling it had cost her more than simple inconvenience; trying to start and drive the car off the forecourt had caused damage to its fuel pump, injectors and filters, and her mechanic had been waiting for the delivery of parts before attempting to fix the problems. She found it hard to believe that so much damage had been done so rapidly, but apparently their back-alley mechanic knew better: he had also warned that the catalytic converter, used to filter exhaust emissions, might need to be replaced as well. Typically, instead of taking her car to the appropriate car dealership, Ben had sought help from a friend of a friend in a luckless attempt at saving a few pennies, and now the repairs were mounting up and taking a hell of a time to put right.

'If I do go anywhere, it will probably be in the back of an ambulance,' she said, and a sudden burst of illogical anger flared in her chest. She pressed her bandaged hand against her sternum, groaning, until the pain in her hand outdid that in her lungs.

'I'm beginning to worry about you,' said Gloria, sounding unperturbed by her daughter's discomfort.

'I'm not having a heart attack, if that's what's concerning you,' said Helen.

'That's not what I mean. I'm talking about Ben. I warned you he was no good for you when you first met, and time has only gone to show that I was right about him . . . abandoning you in your moment of need. He's such a—'

'Stop it, Mum.' Helen glared, and for a moment Gloria must have recognised a reflection of her own harsh spirit in the set of Helen's rigid features and flat eyes.

'He should be here, not out living the life of Riley.'

'He's on an important errand. He's working, Mum. Doing his best to earn enough to keep me in a manner expected by you, as he said he would when we married.'

Gloria peered around the living room, her mouth set in a lopsided sneer. 'Yes, he has really lived up to *that* promise, hasn't he?'

It was easier to drop the subject than continue trying to defend Ben.

'I might have to go to the doctor's,' she said. 'Ben said he'd try to get me an appointment and I'm waiting for his call back. If he isn't home and I must go, I'll have to call a taxi, unless—'

'I can't take you,' stated Gloria.

With Gloria having three large gin and tonics onboard, and probably planning on drinking more before she was finished, Helen wouldn't trust her to drive without them ending up in a ditch or worse. But her mother's swift rebuttal wasn't because she refused to drive under the influence, she simply planned on going to other places than a GP's surgery that day.

'I was about to say "walk",' Helen added.

Gloria almost spat at the notion. 'You will fall on your backside before you reach the end of the street. If it comes to it, then you must call a taxi, or one of those Uber-thingamajigs.'

'I will,' said Helen, because expecting Gloria to change her mind was futile.

'Then you can have another drink,' said Gloria, and approached the table, intending refilling Helen's glass, as well as her own.

'I couldn't touch any more gin.'

'A glass of wine, then, and if you're worried about getting drunk, I'll drown it with soda water.'

Helen pinched the bridge of her nose with her good hand.

'Headache?' Gloria asked.

'It's the spirits. Like I said, I'm not an afternoon drinker.'

'I'll go fetch the wine.'

'There's some in the—'

'I'm a lush, I don't need directions to the wine rack,' Gloria said with a smile, which was the most self-aware truth she'd admitted in a long while.

While Gloria plundered what was left of the wine from when Ben and Helen had celebrated his purchase of the amulet at the market, Helen dug her fingertips into her hairline, with enough force to feel the nip of her fingernails in her skin. She worked downward, kneading her forehead and cheeks, and again gripped the bridge of her nose. She groaned, but was unsure why. She had no headache, despite claiming to have one and blaming it on drinking the gin, she suffered instead from a strange sensation, as if her consciousness was about to float out of the shell of her cranium, so she must hold it in. Releasing her nose, she exhaled sharply, took several deep breaths, and threw her head and shoulders against the back of the settee.

'Hey,' Gloria's call sounded from the kitchen, 'where's your corkscrew?'

Helen screwed her eyelids, thinking . . . no, only trying to think. A fog had invaded her thoughts.

'Never mind, I found it,' Gloria called.

She opened her eyes, looking around, frightened by flitting shadows on the walls. More darkness edged Helen's vision. She was on the verge of another blackout.

A raw panic assailed her, and she lunged forward, driving her feet down into the pile of the carpet, ready to thrust up and run. Where should she run to? She didn't know where, or why running would help, so she collapsed backwards again, mouth open, moaning as if in fake ecstasy. The panic retreated, and instead she felt a rush of seething heat throughout her body that she couldn't properly find words to define, causing her blood to tingle and her flesh to sting. She barked in delight and this time there was nothing false about the euphoria.

'What?' Gloria asked from the opposite side of the house.

Helen didn't respond, and Gloria didn't ask again. She carried a set of matching wine glasses, a bottle of white wine and the corkscrew she'd found, each striking against the other items, announcing a tinkling progress.

Helen turned and observed her mother's return to the living room. Gloria pursed her lips, her mind working on an unspoken idea or query. She frowned slightly at Helen's intense perusal. She held up the bottle. 'This one do?'

Helen didn't answer.

She looked at the bottle, but could not recognise it or its purpose, and an upward tilt of her chin returned her gaze to Gloria's face. She didn't recognise her either. The fog had turned black, and through it swarmed motes of red, as if she had blundered through the smouldering cinders of a bonfire, kicking free a cloud of sparks.

'Are you OK?' Gloria wondered.

Helen screwed her eyelids again, then snapped them open and clarity returned to her vision, if not her thoughts. There was concern on Gloria's face, an uncommon sight, and yet Helen couldn't comprehend its meaning. Her mother approached, setting down the glasses on the occasional table, and then turning her attention to opening the bottle. Helen rocked forward, and thrust her bandaged hand behind her, scrubbing at her skin.

'Why do you keep rubbing your back?' Gloria wondered as she twisted the corkscrew into the stopper. 'You've been at it off and on since I arrived.'

Helen didn't respond. She rubbed furiously at a spot on her lower spine.

Gloria set down the wine bottle on the table, the corkscrew twisted hardly more than a finger's width into the cork. She bent around Helen, lifting up her daughter's shirt, but was unable to see what was troubling Helen so much. Helen shoved away her mother's hand. Gloria tapped her bandaged wrist, scolding her with a pinched expression. 'I'm trying to help. Now let me see.'

'See?'

'Yes. Let me take a look at what's wrong.'

'See,' Helen repeated, her voice strangely flat.

Gloria couldn't see. Instead she moved a step to one side, attempting to find a better angle of approach. Helen leaned forward, and Gloria contorted around her, and saw what appeared to be a faded pink welt just above the waistband of Helen's trousers. More livid scratch marks showed where Helen had clawed at the itching brand. 'What is that? Did something bite you . . . an insect perhaps?'

'See, see, see,' said Helen, in monotone.

'What?' Gloria moved back, still bent at the waist, and Helen turned towards her to meet her gaze. 'What is wrong with you, Helen?'

Opening her mouth, Helen displayed only darkness where something equally black was hunched atop the place a moist, pink tongue should've sat.

Gloria croaked in disgust.

Helen lifted her bandaged fist, displaying the corkscrew she'd snatched from the neck of the bottle. Tiny flakes still adhered to the sharp, curved tip, from where she'd yanked it out of the cork.

'Not see,' Helen stated.

Her meaning never dawned on Gloria. She only concluded that perhaps a glass of wine wouldn't be enough to heal whatever was wrong with her daughter, and then Helen jabbed sharply. Helen snapped her hand away, empty once more.

Gloria cried out in horror, and reeled backwards, the corkscrew embedded deep in her left eye socket. The orb was skewered through, leaking blood and a jelly-like liquid down her cheek. She grabbed at the handle of the corkscrew and, her mind exploding at the enormity of the horror, she dragged it out. Her eyeball was a ruined mess, and the blood gushed. She staggered backwards, and Helen rose up, grabbed her mother by each shoulder, and showed no mercy whatsoever. She dragged Gloria onto her raised knee, knocking the wind out of the older woman, and then swivelled to her side. Transferring her bandaged hand to the back of Gloria's neck, she thrust down, and powered her face into the table. The wine glasses shattered into twinkling shards; the wine and gin bottles, though, were made of tougher stuff. They flew off the table to land unscathed on the carpet, the gin spilling from the open neck. Helen's gin tumbler broke under the pressure and a jagged shard speared into Gloria's throat. Her hand spasmed, and the bloodied corkscrew flew free. She clutched instead at her throat, but the spurting blood couldn't be dammed. Helen stood over her mother, observing dispassionately while Gloria sank fully to her knees, and then spilled over sideways, too weak to try stemming the blood again, her fingers fluttering like hummingbird wings in her death throes.

THIRTY-TWO

Ben and Rachel detoured to the shop before returning to either of their homes, but didn't enter. It was paramount that they found and convinced Belinda Sortwell to join their group before they were summoned to the appropriately remote location decided upon by Shay Connolly for the binding ritual the occultist had in mind. On the drive back from the young woman's farm, silence had dominated for the best part, because each was again tumbling over the revelations about the executioner box in their own minds, trying to make sense of what they'd learned, and, especially in Ben's case, trying to come to terms with whether or not he should believe them. He wasn't a fool – there was no question that something was decidedly uncanny about the box and its horrible contents – but he wasn't totally, 100 per cent convinced that they had become the target of an assassination weapon summoned into being by sorcery. How could he without admitting to insanity? All that stuff told to them about Nazi occultists ripping out the tongue of a wicked sorcerer and then binding his demented essence to the box to enact their murderous bidding was the stuff of pure fantasy, surely? It was not the type of claim he would normally give any credence to, and would actually more than likely laugh at anyone for speaking such ridiculous nonsense, but how could he ignore the evidence he, or those close to him, had personally witnessed?

A part of him warned him not to go along with the madness. After all, everything that had happened could simply have been a sequence of bad luck and timing. He could be fitting the events to suit the crazy narrative he'd been fed, only using evidence that strengthened the story while discarding anything else through – what was that term that scientists were fond of? – confirmation bias. He only had Rachel's assertion that she had been assaulted by some evil, tangible force down in the basement; her 'bite mark', those scratches, all could be self-inflicted, or even self-induced if there was any truth in psychosomatic wounding. Helen's cut hand could very well be explained through clumsiness, her recent behaviour down to jealousy, aggravation, the drugs pushed onto her by Gloria or all together. Hettie's death could have been a tragic accident. After all, the drunk driver who had driven into her van had not come into contact with the box – as far as any of them knew; and, as for Jason Halloran, well, maybe he should expect nothing from a messed-up drug addict other than occasional irrational violence or self-destructive behaviour.

All that being said, there he was, peering up at Jason's apartment, hoping that his grieving partner was home.

'Looks deserted,' he muttered. But he switched off his engine, and climbed out the Range Rover.

Rachel followed as he led the way down the service alley into the rear yard. At the foot of the fire escape, he paused a second, and Rachel sidestepped him, eager to get past. If he was reluctant to check, she had no qualms.

'Rache,' he cautioned her, and she halted, looking at him from the first step. She was still several inches below his eye level. 'Are we doing the right thing?' he asked.

'I gave it a lot of thought on the way over here. I bet you did too. I wondered if we were being sucked into some ridiculous delusion, or whether you were right earlier and we were being played by some kind of scam, but I can't deny what happened to me, Ben. Being locked in the basement, and then getting physically assaulted by something unseen, was not a figment of my imagination. It happened before we knew anything about the box's background, and even before I began researching what those words meant, so I wasn't just letting fear get the better of me. That crazy stuff about Nazis and occultists and whatever . . . it doesn't matter if we believe it or not, because our doubt doesn't negate what's happening, or the lives already lost. The way I look at it, we have to go through with Shay's ritual, because what if we were wrong, and to brush it off sees more deaths? Betting on our lives, or those of Helen and Belinda? I don't know about you, but going against Shay's plan isn't a chance I'm willing to take.'

He puffed out his cheeks. She had made quite a statement. He'd have made do with a simple yes. His hope now was that Belinda would believe enough that she'd answer in the affirmative too.

Rachel began a steady climb up the stairs. Ben watched her for a moment, and then gritted his teeth and mounted the steps. As they climbed, the metal staircase groaned and creaked under their combined weight.

Rachel waited at the first landing.

Ben moved alongside her, seeing what had given her pause.

The door to Jason's apartment stood ajar by a few centimetres. The lock had been forced out of its bracket, and there were definite scuff marks at the door's base where somebody had kicked it free of the frame. As far as Ben knew, the apartment had been let to Jason, and had probably been reclaimed by his landlord after the youth's demise. He wouldn't have thought Belinda capable of kicking open the door, but on a slightly longer examination he saw that the lock and the door were both cheap quality and relatively flimsy.

Rachel raised a hand to knock, but Ben caught and held her wrist.

'We don't know who is inside,' he cautioned her.

She shrugged, unafraid at the prospect of a squatter having moved in. 'If Belinda isn't here, maybe they can tell us where to find her.'

'Probably on the nearest scuzzy street corner,' he said cynically.

Rachel clucked her tongue.

She rapped her knuckles on the door, and the simple action caused it to shut, though it gently rebounded a second after, the busted lock unable to secure it.

Nobody answered.

A gentle rain began falling. It was barely heavy enough to stir Ben's hair, but the chill it brought caused him to shudder and step closer to the door where the building offered more shelter. His action brought him up close to Rachel. His front touched her backside, and she merely glanced up and back at him, but it was enough to jolt him away, as if he'd done something deliberately lewd and uninvited.

'Uh, eh, I'm sorry. Excuse me,' he blurted.

Rachel only frowned slightly, probably wondering what all the fuss was about.

She didn't know how he'd suffered accusations of impropriety towards her from Helen; if his wife had witnessed what he just did—

Rachel drew open the door, and her action was enough to still his concern over accidentally touching her bottom.

'What are you doing?' he asked in a tight whisper.

'Going inside,' she said.

'But nobody answered,' he said.

'Exactly.'

About to touch her uninvited again, he consciously dropped his hands by his sides. 'You can't . . . it'll be . . . uh, burglary, won't it?'

'Trespass at the most,' she corrected him. 'I don't intend to steal or do any damage. Besides, what if Belinda's inside and needs our help?'

He glanced around, checking they were unobserved. Discounting any of the lads being out on the balcony above them, the chances of being seen in the enclosed yard were nil. Had Cezary or any of his three pals been around, he doubted they would raise any complaint. In fact, in hindsight, he had to consider that one of them could have been responsible for forcing entry into the apartment to check for anything they could appropriate before Jason's meagre belongings were cleared out.

Ben bit his lip at the thought. There he was again, casting aspersions on people's characters without any proof. Maybe there was something of low virtue about his character that he was only recently being made aware of. Was this entire sequence of events a life lesson in morality for him? If it was, the answer would have to wait, because Rachel had entered the apartment, and had glanced back to ensure he was still with her. He ducked inside, and immediately set his back against a wall. When no frothing-at-the-mouth crazy person came charging out of the adjacent room, he relaxed a little. Rachel seemed less troubled by the possibility of squatters than him; she continued on, gently calling Belinda's name, as if hoping the girl wasn't really at home. Ben followed.

It took less than half a minute to check the apartment for life and find none. There were hints that whoever had broken in had treated Jason's home with more respect once inside, and had not turned the place upside down. His large-screen smart TV, the only thing of obvious street value in the apartment, was still where it had stood before. The bedclothes had been smoothed down, and some blankets that had made a comfortable nest on the settee in the living room had been folded and stacked at one end. The small kitchenette showed recent usage, with a single cereal bowl and spoon, a mug ringed with tea stains and a side plate stacked in the sink, but looked as if they'd been placed there in the last few hours rather than days. Rachel approached the kettle and touched it tentatively with the back of her hand: she smiled knowingly, and said, 'It's still warm. I think we might've missed Belinda by an hour or less, but I bet she plans on coming back to do the washing up.'

'I don't fancy waiting here for her,' Ben said quickly. 'Let's just go out and have a look around the town centre. Chances are she isn't far away.'

Rachel heard his suggestion but didn't respond. She had discovered a small, untidy stack of envelopes at the far end of the settee. They appeared to have been collected over a period of time, and brought to Jason's apartment where they could be opened in private. 'Without digging into these, which would be an invasion of privacy I'm unwilling to take, I can still see where Belinda actually calls home.'

'You know the address?' Ben asked, faintly impressed by her detective skills.

'Yeah. I can read.' She held up the topmost envelope and, through a translucent window, she read Belinda Sortwell's home address. 'Her street's on the same estate that I live on.'

'Great,' said Ben, relieved to have a good reason to leave the apartment. To him it felt like a haunted crypt, almost as if it was still home to Jason Halloran's restless ghost. 'Let's be off, then.'

Setting down the envelope, Rachel turned towards him, and halted. Her features elongated slightly as she momentarily took stock of what she was looking at. Ben followed her gaze, tensing, expecting to be greeted by one of Jason's down-and-out pals, or worse, the police alerted to their unlawful entering of the apartment.

Instead he was greeted by the slight figure he'd last seen being escorted away from Jason's coffin accompanied by the inappropriate jaunty soundtrack. If anything, Belinda looked more frail than she had at the cemetery, a veritable washed-out rack of skin and bones fading into nothingness, and for the first time he felt a genuine pang of pity towards her. Belinda shivered as she peered back at them, her eyes wet ovals, her mouth hanging open, showing gaps between her caramel-tinged teeth. Her limbs jerked as if she wished to flee, but didn't have the strength to get moving. She bleated, 'I don't live here, I'm only visiting!'

'Belinda,' Rachel said, palms out to calm the girl, 'it's us. Ben and Rachel from the shop downstairs. You recognise us, right?'

Ben touched his chest. 'I helped you last week when Jason, uh . . .'

'You were at his funeral,' Belinda finally said, after squinting to bring their faces into relief. Apparently the drugs, or drink, had kept her from regular eyesight tests and she hadn't been dispensed the spectacles she required. Her exclamation from a moment before must have been her natural response to a police raid, or debt collectors.

'I was there,' Ben confirmed.

Maybe she didn't know that Helen and Rachel were different people. Not that it mattered for the moment. As well as having poor eyesight, she also looked to him as if she was under the influence of one chemical or another.

'But why are you here?' she countered. She nodded sharply at the envelopes that Rachel had put down. 'What business are those to you?'

Rachel pushed fingers through her short hair, a nervous tic of sorts. 'I wasn't snooping. Not at what was inside the envelopes. I promise I only looked to get an address where we could find you.'

'You'd have found nothing but a fat, nasty pig there,' Belinda said, and hiccuped out a laugh at the description. 'I moved out, took over Jason's letting here. The only one there now's my fat, nasty pig of a stepdad, and he's not too welcoming.'

'I'm pleased you came back when you did,' said Ben.

'You don't look pleased,' Belinda said, 'you look like a little kid who's just been caught with his hand in the biscuit barrel.'

'Trust us, we aren't here to steal,' he said.

Belinda shrugged, and then pushed her hand deep into her jeans pocket. Her forearm was scarred and mottled, and painfully thin. She grunted a little as she dug down into the deepest part of the pocket. Finally she extracted her hand, and the thing she'd winkled free. She offered it to Ben. 'Looking for this?'

He had forgotten about ever seeing it again. He had thought that the small, twisted gold ring stolen by Jason had been discarded along with the clothes most likely cut from his corpse after it was delivered to the morgue, or had possibly gone with him into the crematory fires. Leona had explained that the ring – her wedding band – was an offering of sorts, given to appease the demonic thing used to rid her of her abusive husband, a reminder that its task had ended with the bully's demise.

Ben raised his fingers, but held off a few seconds, peering at the ring as if weighing not its value but its power. As far as he knew, the ring had been worthless as a ward, and taking it back from Belinda would be a pointless exercise, but he couldn't be totally certain. He had cut the head off the silver nail, removed the lid from the box, and taken out the twisted ring and the mulengi dori – the dead man's string – so perhaps all had been performing their respective jobs until his meddling had broken their collective potency.

'I found it,' she went on, again offering it to Ben, 'stuck in the lining of Jason's jacket pocket. It'd fallen through a hole into the lining. I kind of assumed it was what he took when he broke into your basement.'

This actually was confirmation that it had been Jason who had burgled the shop and set off the PIR alarm. It went to show that Ben's instincts about the lad had been correct, and that it was Jason's thieving nature that had led to him being influenced by the sorcerer's chipe into attacking Belinda, and perhaps taking his own life. Ben felt some relief: the lad's death was not his fault.

He accepted Leona's ring from Belinda.

Rather than calculate its scrap value as he normally would, he decided it should be returned to Leona, so that Shay could incorporate it back into the resealing of the executioner box during the upcoming ritual, despite its target now allegedly having been changed. He wondered if the ribbon and lock of hair needed to be replaced, seeing as he'd charred the last one to cinders when trying to destroy the box.

He tucked the ring away in his pocket, and then looked at Rachel, hoping for guidance. How did he hope to convince Belinda that she was in dire peril unless she joined them in some magical ritual, when he wasn't totally convinced by the supernatural nature of what had happened?

'I wish you'd stop dithering,' Rachel proclaimed, and he wondered again if his assistant was so in tune with him that she could read his thoughts. However, it grew apparent she wasn't referring to how he continually straddled the fence between belief and disbelief, hopping from one side to the other as his mood took him. He'd never persuade Belinda to join them unless he put some commitment into it.

He nodded, pointed a finger at Belinda and said, 'Unless you come with us, you're going to die horribly.'

Belinda's expression went instantly from sad to stupefied to terror, and she again jerked as if about to flee.

'Flaming hell, Ben!' Rachel again placated Belinda with her raised hands. She stepped forward slowly and controlled, so as not to alarm the girl any further. 'We aren't going to hurt you, or force you into anything you don't wish to do. What he means is, you are in danger, but we can help.'

'In danger from who?'

'Not who . . . what,' said Ben, with equal vigour to his previous statement.

Rachel frowned at him. 'Maybe I should speak with Belinda alone,' she suggested.

Yes, he decided, that would suit him, and probably she wouldn't feel as intimidated if she was allowed to communicate privately with Rachel.

'Fine by me,' he announced. He edged around Belinda, who sidestepped him. The exit was clear, and he moved more swiftly. He emerged onto the fire escape, feeling it shudder under his feet, and then, after a moment, he quickly descended and stood at the bottom. The rain had continued to fall but he waited, distracted, barely noticing as his hair and forehead grew slick and his clothing darkened under the drenching. It took a moment to realise that he was standing within a metre of where Jason had died, and again he was assailed by a sense that he was under the gaze of Jason's unseen spectre. Moments ago, he'd shed the notion that he'd been responsible for the youth's death due to bringing home the executioner box, but Jason's spook might be more judgemental.

'Yeah,' he croaked in self-admonishment, 'you'll believe in Jason's vengeful ghost but not one trapped by Nazi occultists? You're going to have to draw a line in the sand, Benny-boy.'

His mobile phone rang. Dread clutched him afresh.

It wasn't Shay calling with directions to the ritualistic site.

'Hey, Helen, are you OK, my love?'

'I need you to come home,' she replied.

'Something the matter? Have you—'

'Ben, I need you here.'

He darted a look upward, wondering how far Rachel had managed in convincing Belinda that they weren't a pair of nutters. 'It shouldn't be long until I get back. Uh, you know that I was going to meet Leona-Marie, well—'

'I need you now! Never mind your fucking wild gypsy girl, get home to *meeeee* . . .'

Helen's final word was an enraged screech.

'Helen, for crying out loud!'

'Are you . . . deaf . . . or is it . . . that . . . you don't care . . . about me . . . any . . . more?' A second after her angry scream, and now her voice was a broken crackle of barely whispered syllables.

'Helen. I love you to the moon and back. You know that, surely?'

'Prove it. Forget all those other bitches. Come home to me. Me!' Now her voice was filled with venom.

'I am coming back, but I'll have Rachel and—'

'No. Come alone. I don't want any of them near us.'

'Helen, love, what's going on? Has Gloria been again—'

'She was here. Ha! Now she's gone.'

'Yeah, but did she give you anything,' he asked, 'like she did the last time?'

'No. Ben. Come home to meeeee.'

'Are you sure you haven't taken anything? You don't sound right.'

'I'm not right.'

'Stuff getting you a doctor's appointment, I'm coming to collect you and we're going straight to the hospital. Do you hear me?'

'I don't need to go to hospital, I only need you.'

He searched the fire escape, hoping to spot Rachel and Belinda on their way down. It was empty. The rain chose that second to grow heavier, and a breeze caught it, splattering his face. He turned his face away from the wet squall, back to his phone, and saw that the screen was dead. He hadn't ended the call, Helen must have. Either that or his battery had just dropped out without warning. He tapped at it, hoping to bring up the call screen, but it opened to the home one, as if he had only that second wakened it. He dabbed at that, bringing up his recent calls. Oddly, Helen's number was not the most recent: the first one listed was Rachel's, when he'd informed her he was coming to collect her from home; the previous showed the incoming call from Leona, when she'd summoned him to meet at Hawkins' Green.

'What the fu—'

He didn't know Helen's number by heart, but it was listed by name third down the call list from when he'd spoken to her from the shop and he'd promised to make her an appointment to visit her GP: so what about the call they'd just shared a minute ago? He hit her number, and heard the corresponding ringtone. It rang a number of times before an electronic voice told him to leave a message after the tone. He ended the call, and instead immediately rang their home landline number. Again, he received an instruction to leave a message.

What was wrong with her? What was she up to? What if she had taken something she shouldn't have, like the last time, maybe not given by, but left for her by Gloria? According to Helen, his shrewish mother-in-law, had been and gone, but he wouldn't put it past her to have bombarded Helen with who-knew-what from her personal stash of meds, to be washed down with litres of alcohol.

'Shit.'

More than anything, Helen's welfare took priority.

He again visually searched the fire escape, but saw nobody.

He should hail Rachel, whether or not she'd convinced Belinda to join them yet, but he couldn't waste any time on explanations, when every passing second could mean further harm coming to his wife. He rushed out along the alley, heading for his car, intent on calling Rachel – once he was on the move – and informing her he'd had to make an emergency dash home.

THIRTY-THREE

Where the heck had Ben disappeared to? Rachel stood on the fire escape, peering down into the yard, while Belinda made an effort to secure the door, despite its busted lock. Thankfully, Belinda was of the opinion that Jason was not himself when attacking her, ergo he was being controlled by some weird external force, so didn't take as much convincing into joining their gang as she had feared. Perhaps the fact that Belinda was under the influence of an illegal substance helped her thoughts to go places most people would never entertain. Whatever the case, she had agreed to accompany Rachel and Ben to the as yet unspecified location where Shay would try binding the chipe inside the executioner box. Guilt stung Rachel; if the young woman was of her right mind, she might run a mile to escape them. However, she'd take the sense of guilt over what might happen to them all if Belinda failed to join them. She urged Belinda to join them in the Range Rover before second thoughts could set in.

'Where has your boss buggered off to?' asked Belinda, echoing Rachel's own unspoken question, only with more colourful language.

'I don't know. Probably in the car already.'

The rain pattered down, striking the fire escape and nearby rooftops, causing a hiss of white noise.

'Makes sense, under these circumstances,' she added as she dashed raindrops off her spectacles.

Rachel wasn't dressed for the downturn in the weather. Belinda had on her coat, and she yanked up a hood that framed her narrow features and lank hair. Rachel waited a heartbeat longer, ensuring that Belinda was on her way down too, before she began a swift descent.

The metal stairs thrummed under their feet. A heavier clang sounded, and Rachel paused a moment to glance upward. Her gaze travelled beyond Jason's – no, Belinda's – level to the topmost floor. Her view was blocked of the upper landing, but she detected shadows and movement through drainage holes in the metal plate. For a moment she wondered if Cezary had exited his apartment, and she was stung afresh, this time with regret that she had not followed up on the brief time they'd spent together. She had sensed he was as interested in her as she had been in him. Never mind that, she scolded herself, there'd be time for romance after this was over, if she got to survive the day. That said, she kept on glancing upward, hoping to catch sight of his face. It wasn't until they reached ground level, and Rachel was able to move out several metres into the yard that she spotted who was above them. It wasn't Cezary, but one of the other lads who stared back at her, his expression empty of any joy. He held a cigarette, but didn't appear to be benefiting from the nicotine-laden smoke, if his glum aspect was anything to go by. Whatever troubled him, she believed it was worse than the falling rain he was forced to endure while outdoors feeding his habit.

She acknowledged him with a tight smile, but his features, and eyes, remained flat as they stared back at her. She raised a hand to wave, thought better of it, and used it to again wipe raindrops off her glasses. Belinda had gone ahead. Rachel sped up to catch the woman before she decided to avoid Ben's car and run for the hills instead.

The Range Rover was gone.

'Awww, come on, Ben. What are you playing at?' Rachel stood, peering past the end of the pedestrianised area to the turning circle where Ben had parked his car on their arrival. What did she expect from staring? It wouldn't make the car suddenly materialise out of the ether.

She took out her mobile and brought up his number.

He didn't answer.

She rang his house, although it was probably too soon for him to have made it back there already. He didn't answer, but neither did Helen, who had supposedly stayed home that day, being unwell. A qualm swept through her; what if Helen had been taken seriously ill and Ben had been summoned urgently to the hospital? No, she cautioned herself, it wouldn't be as extreme as that, surely? If Ben had rushed to be at her side in hospital, he would have told Rachel where he was going. Wouldn't he?

'It's pissing down.' Belinda stated the obvious.

What she actually meant was that they were needlessly standing out in the rain instead of seeking shelter in Ben's shop doorway.

Distracted, Rachel only nodded.

Belinda walked away and huddled against the wall in the shallow alcove. Rachel again tried to call Ben's mobile, but this time the call fell out before it had established a connection. She finally realised she was soaked, and lunged for cover. She had a spare set of keys to unlock the shop, but having no expectation of visiting the shop again today, they'd been left on the small sideboard in her bedroom.

'What now?' asked Belinda.

Rachel wasn't exactly sure, so didn't answer immediately. She shook raindrops off her shoulders, and swept them from her hair and face with the blade of her left hand, while holding her mobile in the other. After a few seconds, she determined a course of action that might work. Before leaving Shay's farmhouse, the occultist had given them her mobile number. Rachel brought it up and then paused another moment, her finger hovering over the call symbol.

'Who you gonna call?' Belinda wondered, then chuckled as she announced the well-known movie tagline.

Rachel tapped the call symbol.

Belinda began humming the movie's theme tune, and chuckling, again repeating the same question and response at an exaggerated whisper. How high was she?

'Shay?' Rachel asked, holding up an index finger to Belinda for silence. 'Hello, yes. It's Rachel. I was the one with Ben Taylor . . . uh, yes, of course you do.'

After confirming that she knew who was calling, Shay asked, 'Are you having trouble convincing the others?'

'No. We've spoken with Belinda Sortwell and' – Rachel checked out the young woman, who had sunk to her backside in the doorway, and pulled up her knees so that she could hug them, while grinning up at Rachel like an enthusiastic puppy – 'she's happy to join us.'

'I'm very happy!' Belinda chimed in, her voice a squeal of delight.

'Does she understand the gravitas of the ritual?'

The 'how' had never fully been described to Rachel or Ben. It stood to reason that they must take the proceedings seriously, and there was no room for doubt, cynicism or frivolities. Rachel turned her back on Belinda, leaned into the phone to whisper. 'I don't know what she has taken, but hopefully she'll have come down by the time you're ready to perform the rite.'

'If the worst comes to the worst, Ben will have to hold her down,' Shay said conspiratorially.

'Yeah. That's the problem and why I called you. Ben's gone, and he isn't answering his phone.'

'What?' Shay had heard, and understood, Rachel realised, but her response was more to the ramifications his disappearance might signify. She heard Shay turn to Leona, and the two had a brief, urgent discussion. When she came back on, there was concern in Shay's tone. 'How was he acting before he left?'

'Normal,' Rachel said. 'He waited outside while I convinced Belinda to join us. We've come out and he has disappeared. As I said, I tried phoning but—'

'Where are you?' Shay cut in.

'Currently? In the doorway of Taylor and King Curiosities on the high street, taking shelter from the rain.'

'Wait there. We can be with you in a quarter of an hour.'

'What if Ben comes back for us in the meantime?'

'My advice? Don't get in his car with him.'

A second shiver ran the length of Rachel's spine. 'You think that the sorcerer's chipe has a hold of him?'

'I don't know for certain, but are you willing to bet against it? I can tell from your voice that you've sensed something wrong in the way he disappeared; would you disagree?'

'No, but—'

'Fifteen minutes, Rachel. Don't go anywhere, especially not with Ben after he's acted weird.'

'OK. I won't.' They ended the call and Rachel checked on Belinda. The woman was still hugging her knees in the shop's doorway, now wearing a dreamy smile. Rachel again wondered what it was that Belinda had taken, and thought that by the way it had suddenly kicked in, she must have palmed it to her mouth when pretending to struggle to secure the door. Rachel's knowledge of street drugs was as limited as her social life, but she thought it must have been an amphetamine of some sort to make her euphoric: perhaps she needed uppers to get her through this horrible period of heart-rending grief; perhaps she needed them simply to continue to exist.

'When did you last eat?'

Belinda shrugged, the action barely making an impression on her padded coat.

'There's a coffee shop just up the street – let's go and grab something.'

'It's raining,' said Belinda. 'Peeing it down.'

'I'm wet already and you have a coat,' said Rachel, fatalistically.

'I'll wait here,' said Belinda.

'It is for your benefit,' Rachel pointed out. Loath to leave Belinda unguarded, she dithered a moment longer, then sank down next to her in the doorway. 'I've an energy bar in my bag, if you'd like it?'

Belinda declined.

Rachel dug out the protein bar, broke off half of it and spent minutes munching it. She didn't know what else to do. Finally, dabbing a few stray crumbs off her chin and licking them from her fingertip, she wondered how she might pass the remaining minutes until Leona and Shay's arrival. She bolted upright. Face pressed to the door, she peered inside the shop. From her position she had a clear view of the service counter, but couldn't see the safe in the wall beyond. How were they going to hold the ritual to seal the chipe back in its prison unless they could access the box? She was trusted by Ben and Helen; she knew the code to open the electronic lock, but she had no way inside.

She cursed under her breath.

'Something wrong?' asked Belinda, looking marginally less like a grinning loon.

'I left my keys to the shop back home,' she replied.

'Why don't you go in the same way that Jason did?'

'You know about him breaking in via the chute around the back?'

'Yeah. Can't remember who told me, but . . . anyway, I gave back the ring he took, so . . .'

'Nobody is judging him, Belinda. Nobody is judging you.'

'Yeah, right. You just think I'm a worthless prossie.'

'No, that's not what I think.' Rachel was unaware of the girl's activities as a sex worker. She knew that Belinda had problems with addictions, but hadn't given much thought to how she financed them. She had believed most of Belinda's illicit income came from stealing and selling on the loot.

'Don't judge me,' Belinda warned.

'I swear to you I'm not.' Rachel's cheeks glowed with the lie.

'You've thrown me out of the shop a dozen times,' Belinda reminded her. 'Called me a thief, too.'

'I've never accused you of anything. I only asked you to leave because I was instructed to by my bosses. I've never physically thrown you out . . . I mean, there's a bit of a difference.'

'Same difference,' Belinda snorted, using a phrase that Rachel had always found both contradictory and ridiculous.

Rachel didn't argue the point. Ben and Helen both believed the policy that deterrent was preferable to chasing shoplifters up the high street, and wrestling with them to get their goods back, and Rachel had bought into the strategy too. Never before had she imagined that the same act couldn't be recognised as a good thing by Belinda, despite the fact it saved her being arrested and put in a cell until she could be interviewed and charged. If she saw things the same way that Rachel did, being asked to leave was actually a kindness.

'We live in different worlds,' Belinda commented, losing all trace of the burgeoning anger of a moment before.

'Despite that, we're not so different, really. Right now, we are both in the same boat.'

'Yeah.' Belinda chuckled again. 'Up shit creek without a paddle.'

Rachel laughed.

Belinda laughed.

'Do you have any of that energy bar left?' Belinda asked after a few seconds of reflection.

Rachel handed over the half she'd saved.

She sank down alongside Belinda. The young woman munched silently, then licked the crumbs from her fingertips. They were not so different, at all.

An olive-green Citroën Berlingo van pulled onto the turning

circle. Recognising it as one of the vehicles she'd seen parked outside Shay's house earlier, Rachel bolted up again, stepping out into the rain to indicate their presence in the doorway. Through the rain-washed windscreen, she saw Shay behind the steering wheel, and Leona seated next to her. It stood to reason, having a broken arm, that Leona would give up the driving duty to her friend. Leona powered down her window and gestured for them to join them in the van.

Rachel offered a hand to Belinda, feeling how insignificant and bird-like her fragile bones were. She rested back on her heels, and allowed the counter-balancing effect to bring Belinda to her feet. Belinda was still chewing on the last of the energy bar. 'This your friends?' she asked pointlessly.

They rushed to the small van.

'Sorry, but there's no more room in the front, you're going to have to jump in the back,' said Shay, leaning across Leona to speak out of the open window.

'What's the plan?' Rachel asked.

'We have to find Ben, and make sure he isn't a danger to anyone,' said Shay.

'What about the executioner box?' she asked.

Rachel looked back at the shop and had second thoughts. Ben had taken to securing it in an old metal toolbox he carried in the rear of his Range Rover; what if he'd had it with them the entire time? 'I'm not quite sure where it is.'

'Do you know where Ben lives?' asked Shay.

'Yes.'

Leona thumbed towards the back of the van. 'Jump in, then, and show us the way.'

The rear interior of the van had been cladded with sheets of plywood, and the wheel arches adapted to form practical, though uncomfortable, seats. A spare tyre and jack were stored in a rack. The only other item inside was a large holdall bag. They had to crouch to climb inside, and they each took a wheel arch. Rachel reached forward, supporting her weight on the back of Shay's seat, and sang out the location of Ben and Helen's home in one of the leafy, upscale suburbs of the city.

THIRTY-FOUR

Ben staggered from his car, leaving the door hanging wide open. Red flashed in his vision, and a pain numbed his reactions, so that his steps felt leaden and ungainly. He grabbed at the bonnet of his car, steadying himself, and blinked down at the road ahead. The red in his vision greyed out, then cleared, but he had to shake his head and rub his eyes vigorously to bring everything into clarity. He swore, but more in disbelief, than regret, because no one lay in his path. There was no sign whatsoever of the stumbling figure that had lurched out in front of him, causing him to stamp the brake so savagely that his head cracked against the steering wheel, almost knocking him unconscious. Why the airbag had failed to deploy, he couldn't say, and at that time was unimportant: all that mattered was that he had not killed an innocent, and that he too had survived his injury. His forehead more than smarted: it felt as if he'd been struck with a steel bar, which, in actuality, he had, albeit one sheathed in a thin layer of leather.

This was the latest, but definitely the most worrying delay he'd suffered since fleeing Belinda's apartment for home. He had been caught up in heavy traffic, then the flow had stalled completely for the best part of five minutes while emergency services responded to a two-vehicle smash on a major roundabout on the city centre's outskirts. Moving again, he'd been held up a third time by a school bus dropping off its charges every few hundred feet, before pulling into his neighbourhood, and now this! He had been so intent on getting home, he'd been driving too fast for the roads and wet conditions; how he had not struck a pedestrian or other road user before he couldn't say, but his luck might have changed for the worse again.

After rubbing his eyes once more, he checked under the car. It rode high enough on large wheels that he could see all the way beneath the chassis, and no figure lay there either. He looked all around, wondering if somehow they had been thrown into the air by the collision, and lay out of sight in one of the nearby gardens. Yet, there was no hint on the front of the car that he'd struck anything of significance, let alone a grown person. It took him another moment to realise that there never had been a person in his path. It was a spectre, a figment placed into his mind, and had to be a weapon of the executioner box. He thought how Rachel had claimed that a darker-than-dark figure had clambered on her back, to scratch and claw her when she was first assailed by the box's occupant, and he had to wonder now if she'd conjured the image or if it had been cast into her mind in the same manner. Figments, he had to remember, were incapable of causing physical harm, but maybe it had worked in tandem with the more substantial spirit attached to the sorcerer's tongue.

Had a similar figment been sent to shock the mind of the inebriated driver who'd swerved head-on into their van, killing Hettie and injuring Leona?

Whatever!

The hows and whys were not important to him.

All that concerned him was that it had acted to stop him from reaching his wife.

Meaning, more than ever, he must race to her rescue.

He stumbled on his return to the driver's seat. He fumbled the ignition: the Range Rover had stalled when coming to such an immediate and violent halt. Then he had the car moving again, and he rocketed along streets lined with privet hedges, cherry-blossom-laden trees and rhododendron bushes. Gardens beyond the perimeter hedges were expansive and well-tended. Houses were predominantly grand, and expensive. Despite Gloria's misgivings about him, Ben had – in partnership with Helen – done better than his mother-in-law had imagined when they first met.

Yes, he'd shown the sniffy old witch.

Or had he?

'If it were objets de vertu then at least *that* would be something,' Gloria had sneered about his business leanings, and maybe it had been some kind of precursor to this current nightmare, as Hettie Stewart had deemed him lacking in virtue too.

What in this modern era counted as virtuous?

Surely racing to save his wife from a supernatural terror was worth mentioning?

Or it was a misguided act of madness?

His Range Rover sped along streets never designed for anything faster than a coach and horses, bouncing on the uneven surface, and then he again hit the brakes. The large car skidded on rain-slick cobbles, but he miraculously controlled the skid, and it even aided him in taking the corner into his driveway. He gave the car more throttle and hurtled towards the house at the end of the drive.

It was the afternoon, still light, but the low-hanging rain clouds had brought gloom to the day. The house looked as if it was caught in a skein of shadow, with only pinpricks of light behind the windows showing any hint of warmth within. He jumped out of the car, again leaving the door hanging open, and he charged for the front door. Ordinarily he would have parked alongside the house, under an extended canopy, and entered via the side entrance, once reserved for servants, but speed was of the essence. He turned his key in the lock and shouldered the heavy front door inward. He stumbled again, his brain not fully functioning after hitting his head, and again his limbs felt disconnected from his body. He slapped hands on the entrance hall wall, as he charged towards the sitting room, where he and Helen usually spent their leisure time together. He had left her there earlier, tucked up on the settee, and had imagined her there when speaking with her earlier on the phone.

Helen was not there.

He called for her, even as he stepped further into the sitting room.

Her blankets and pillows lay scattered across the settee.

He smelled coffee and spilled alcohol.

And something else: a coppery tang.

His heart felt as if it was clutched by an iron hand.

He lunged towards the far end of the settee, where a small table had been swept clear of the glasses and bottles it had recently held. Shards of glass gleaned wetly, some darkened with a liquid redder than wine. A corkscrew lay on the carpet, a dot of bloody jelly at its tip. There were scuff marks in the carpet pile, and more droplets of blood. There, he spotted another stain, and this one was large; a pool of darkness on the fireside rug.

'Helen?' he hollered, and spun on his heel.

His wife had suffered some kind of accident, and cut herself worse than when she'd broken the cabinet door at the shop. The amount of blood spilled on the rug was terrifying.

In his pocket, Ben's mobile phone rang, but he didn't register it, the same way he hadn't registered any of the previous calls made to it during his hasty drive home. He lurched around the sitting room, spotting the signs of bloody violence, but misinterpreting their meaning.

He bolted from the room.

Where would Helen have gone, bleeding so heavily?

He thought she might have rushed for the kitchen, where she might find tea towels to use as impromptu bandages, or to the upstairs bathroom, where they kept medical supplies in a wall cabinet. There were no drips along the hallway carpet, but there was a ribbon of blood, a smear, as if her foot had bled and she'd been dragging it.

'Helen?' he hollered again. 'Where are you?'

She didn't reply.

The bloody trail avoided the stairs, so he did too, racing for the kitchen instead. In the kitchen he saw that the track grew wider, more smeared, and wound a path beyond the food preparation counter, past the central island where they usually ate breakfast before heading out to work. Helen had left the prints of her bare feet in the gore.

He shouted her name a third time, with as little response.

Had she succumbed to blood loss and collapsed? Had she hailed an ambulance and been taken to hospital? He didn't think there'd been time for the latter scenario, so he feared the first. He darted past the bloody prints, towards a door from the kitchen that accessed a vestibule and a couple of adjacent utility rooms. The first contained a washing machine and dryer. The next was a large store closet. That's where the blood smears led.

'Helen?'

He bashed up against the door.

In his haste he fumbled with the door handle.

His hand came away tacky with blood.

He glanced at the gore on his hand, and a small quarter of his mind warned him that something was *very* wrong.

Why had Helen fled to the store closet when bleeding so heavily?

There were items she could have used to staunch the blood long before accessing the closet.

Maybe she simply was not thinking straight and had gone there in her panic.

It didn't matter!

If she had gone inside, perhaps sinking down into unconsciousness, he wasn't helping her by dithering.

He grabbed the handle and practically tore it loose, before he managed to drag open the closet door.

Inside was in darkness.

He leaned in, calling for Helen again.

She didn't reply.

He spotted a tarp that he occasionally used to conceal expensive goods transported in the rear of his car. Green plastic, with a thin blue nylon rope fed through eyelets. It was draped over a slumped shape, the ropes pulled taut around the bottom.

'Oh, my god!' he squawked.

Before he'd believed Helen had injured herself, now he understood that a third party had been involved, and that she'd been hurt deliberately, then dragged and hidden in the closet to perish out of sight.

He tore at the tarp, trying to free it from his wife.

A foot was released, and it poked from the bottom. It was shod.

It never occurred to him that the footprints he'd followed had been made by bare feet.

He continued to yank and pull at the plastic sheet, and finally was able to haul upward on the loosened rope, the figure inside spilling free. He collapsed backwards, his back hitting the opposite wall, and he slid to an almost sitting position. He stared, in a mixture of horror and mild relief, not at Helen, but her shrewish mother. In the next second he felt a wave of guilt assail him; he held no love for Gloria, but he would never wish her real harm. And she'd suffered badly. She had lost an eye, gore leaking down a cheek drained of lifeblood. Her throat was gashed open, her clothing soaked with the blood that had first spurted, then later welled from the wound as life fled her.

He shook his head in disbelief, then slapped palms against the wall, trying to climb back to his feet.

Gloria's one remaining eye was fixed on him, filled with her normal reproof even in death.

He screamed for Helen.

Where was she?

Why didn't she answer?

If the blood was Gloria's, then . . .

No. Both women could have been hurt, Helen dragged elsewhere by—

He recalled her words from earlier when he'd asked if Gloria had visited: 'She was here. Ha! Now she's gone.'

Those were not words spoken by his wife under duress; now that he thought about it, they had a faintly boastful quality to them.

Gloria's murder was not down to an intruder, but to the person closest to her in her entire life.

'Oh, no, no, no, noooo . . .'

'Why are you upset?'

The voice snapped his head around, and there in the narrow vestibule stood a figure, cast in silhouette by the light spilling from the kitchen behind it.

'You never liked Gloria,' said the voice, which was Helen's and yet not Helen's. Likewise the figure that stood slightly bent as if her spine was afflicted with agony was Helen, and yet *not her*. 'You should be happy that she is dead. You've wished her dead so many times before, probably as often as she wished you dead too.'

'No, that's . . . that's untrue. I never wished—'

'Liar.' The word was sharp, almost spat out, and incredibly loud in the enclosed space. Ben recoiled as if physically jabbed between the eyes.

'Helen,' he began with a croak, 'what have you done?'

'Only what you wished to do to her all these years.'

'No . . . you're the one who's lying. I never—'

'Liar!'

'I admit we didn't get on, but I never wanted anything bad to happen to Gloria, or to anyone. Helen?' he gasped. 'This isn't you speaking. It's whatever has got a hold of you. It's—'

'She can't hear you.' The thing puppeting his wife sounded almost flippant.

'I don't believe you. Helen. It's me, it's Ben. I love you, and it doesn't matter what this thing says or does, I know it isn't you. Please, fight it, don't let it make you do anything you don't want to do.'

'Ha!' it snapped. 'She can't resist me. Besides, what makes you think that she hasn't dreamed of taking your life before? There have been times when you argued, and when she was unhappy, and she pondered about putting a pillow over your face while you slept and—'

'No! Now who's the damn liar?' he barked. 'Helen would never deliberately harm me.'

'Wouldn't she?'

The thing that was Helen and yet not Helen raised her bandaged right hand. Something glinted dully; a knife drawn from the wooden chopping block in their kitchen. This was no huge cleaver, or even a chef's knife; it was one of the smaller, extremely sharp paring knives. She held it between them, drawing Ben's gaze along its wickedly sharp edge. He shied back, but was checked by the corner of the vestibule. He glanced at her as Helen matched his step, and her silhouette was broken by the uninhibited light washing in from the kitchen doorway. Her front was almost as sodden with blood as Gloria's. There was no corresponding wound, though, so it had all transferred from her victim when she'd bundled the older lady in the tarp and then dragged her from the sitting room. The whites of her eyes almost glowed in the dim light, and her teeth glistened redly, as if she'd perhaps sucked some of the gore from her fingers.

'Wh–what are you going to do with that?' Ben croaked, his gaze fixed on the knife again.

'What do you think, genius?'

'Keep back,' he commanded.

'Ha!'

'I'm warning you . . .'

'What are you going to do, hurt your beloved Helen?'

Her hand with the knife darted forward.

Ben cried out, tried to snatch her wrist but missed. The sharp point jabbed his abdomen, and he knew it had pierced his flesh, not through pain but from a rush of wet heat that spilled down into the waistband of his trousers.

She grinned, took another jab at him.

'Don't,' he cried, and again tried grabbing her wrist. The knife jab found his palm. He snapped his hand away, this time feeling an instant burn of steel in his flesh. He slapped with his other hand, and batted aside a third strike. 'Don't make me hurt you, Helen!'

'Hurting her won't stop me,' the Helen-thing crowed.

'I won't let you kill me,' he hollered, and lunged forward.

He grabbed her bandaged hand, clenching his fist over hers, so that he had control of hand and knife. His right hand caught her other arm by the bicep. He drove at her, pushing from both braced feet. He was taller and outweighed Helen by a third. Yet she resisted him. It was as if the entity possessing her added an otherworldly density to her. He shouted with effort, wrenching her knife hand down to one side, and forced her back through the vestibule, until he reached the open doorway to the kitchen. There he dropped his weight and thrust in with his left shoulder, catching and lifting her bodily in the air, and together they hurtled into the kitchen.

They checked up against the central island. Ben regretted hurting his wife, but the alternative was to allow the knife to sink repeatedly into his flesh. He doubted he'd take as much punishment as the entity-driven thing could. He forced her backwards, her spine arching painfully over the edge of the counter. Her bare feet kicked, and then clambered up his legs, and their momentum sent Helen fully backwards onto the counter. She skidded, thrust away by Ben, and somersaulted off the far side. Her skull rang hollow as it struck the floor. Her landing was ungainly, and impactful, and it occurred to him that if his wife survived this possession, she might be disabled for life. He staggered away, his own spine smacking against the food preparation counter under the large kitchen window. He gasped for air, and his brain was again assailed by a whirl of crimson, as if his head had struck the steering wheel anew. Shadows invaded his peripheral vision.

'Noooo!' he shouted in denial. He couldn't allow himself to pass out.

Opposite, the Helen-thing popped up from behind the island, grinning wickedly.

'Yessss,' it hissed in direct contradiction.

It seemed untroubled by the abuse to its host's body.

'Stay back,' Ben warned.

She ignored him, hopping toad-like onto the central island, and waving the knife at him.

He cast about for something defensive.

There was nothing to hand.

He jerked to the right, and she followed, almost going on her belly on the counter to cut off his escape back through the door into the vestibule. He immediately darted in the other direction. There were dirty breakfast dishes still soaking in the sink. Next to it, a metal drying rack. Ben snatched it up and swung it as Helen reversed direction and cut at his buttocks with the blade. The rack smacked the knife out of her hand, and it clattered across the floor. Undeterred, she slinked from the counter, head-first, landing on the palms of both hands and then dropping down into a compressed crouch between him and the dislodged weapon. She grinned, and from her mouth wriggled something withered and inky black: the sorcerer's chipe.

How? He wondered in that chaotic moment. He believed the severed tongue was safely in the box, contained within the metal toolbox in the rear of his car.

Obviously he had been deliberately misinformed following the events that occurred in the shop when Helen reported first passing out. She'd lied, saying she had not removed the box from the wall safe; she must have taken it out, released the chipe, and it had taken hold of her, perhaps controlling her on and off since. It was the devilish thing that had caused those jealous accusations towards him and Rachel, an effort at throwing a wedge between them all. When speaking with her earlier, that first time when he'd promised to get her a doctor's appointment, he'd fully believed that had been his wife he was speaking with, but the next time? Her words had been to gloat about murdering Gloria, but more so a lure to fetch him running to his own gory death. That shade that stepped out in front of his car? He must now consider it a different phenomenon entirely; that it was a harbinger, a warning spirit, the shade of Gloria trying to halt his headlong rush towards his murder? In life the woman had hated him; in death she might have tried saving his life.

Helen rushed him. One instant she squatted like an animal, next she flew for his throat, her fingers hooked like talons to rip and tear at his flesh. Ben smashed down with the drying rack, again and again, the metal rungs bending almost double with the force of the beating over her head. It didn't stop her, but it knocked her to her knees, and a kick to her belly sent her sprawling. She grappled him as he lunged past, aiming to grab the knife first, but he tore loose and snatched up the knife. He could easily have turned it on her then, but it was never his intention; he threw the blade through the open doorway into the vestibule and slammed shut the door, denying its retrieval.

He stood with his back pressed to the door, facing her as the Helen-thing again rose to its feet.

'Get out of my wife,' he warned.

'This does not end until you are dead,' it replied.

'Why? Why are you doing this to us?'

'It's what I do, I kill, it's my only purpose to exist.'

The entity probably had no more power over the necromancy that had trapped it, turning it into a weapon of brutal vengeance, than Helen had over her actions right now, but Ben could feel no pity for it.

'Let my wife go,' he said.

The thing inside her reflected for no more than a few seconds before its face split again in an open-mouthed grin. 'I've touched her. She will die, but you won't be around to witness her demise. You die first.'

'Not if I tear that bloody tongue out of her first.'

A bandaged hand, stained pink with Gloria's blood, touched Helen's breastbone over her heart. 'Your threat hurts me *here*,' it mocked petulantly. Then it hooked its fingers into wicked talons again and its voice lowered to a rough growl. 'For that I shall rip out your heart.'

He sidestepped away, even as it began a steady pace towards him.

Distantly, fists hammered on the front door, and voices urgently called their names.

THIRTY-FIVE

The drive from the shop to Ben and Helen's house took Shay a measurably shorter time to complete than Ben had endured. The traffic had spread out now that the collision had been dealt with and the roundabout cleared, and it was as if she timed the lights to perfection, so each was on the turn to green as they approached. The school bus that had slowed Ben in the latter part of the journey had continued on to an adjacent housing scheme, and no shade of a deceased old lady tried to thwart their forward momentum: if in reality Gloria's ghost had tried to slow Ben's return to the house, she'd have no such intentions for them.

In the cladded rear of the van, Rachel and Belinda found it difficult staying upright on their seats, and both slid off several times when Shay took corners without slowing. Finding it easier to kneel in the back, with her hands clutching Shay's seat, Rachel leaned over the woman's shoulder, giving directions. Leona was pale with expectation, but Shay was flushed with excitement. On the rare occasion she took her attention off the road, it was to offer a feverish grin to Leona, and her dark eyes sparkled. Rachel also caught herself grinning, though hers would probably be described as a rictus.

In the exclusive suburb they found the roads almost empty, with only a few pedestrians braving the inclement weather, coat collars turned up, and hems of trousers splashed. There, some of the roads were private, and still consisted predominantly of cobblestone surfaces, as they'd been when built in the years between the two great wars. Kerbstones were large and made of red sandstone. Some of the pavements had buckled as trees outgrew the gardens they'd originally been planted within and had sent roots questing under the paving. Inhabitants on the estate were reasonably well off. Rachel had been impressed the first few times she'd visited her employers' home, but through familiarity she hadn't given it much thought since: it hadn't occurred until she directed Shay through the twin gateposts and onto the drive that, set in its own grounds, the house was possibly the ideal remote location Shay had sought where she could perform the binding ritual.

As the small van continued up the drive, heavy droplets fell from the trees to either side, drumming on its roof and bonnet. It was like a drumroll, building anticipation at an execution.

Ben's Range Rover sat abandoned in front of the house, its driver's door wide open, rain invading the interior. The speed and lack of care shown by Ben when evacuating it spoke volumes to them.

'This doesn't look good,' Shay said.

'You're no' wrang,' Leona replied, her Scottish accent having grown thicker.

Shay brought the Berlingo to a stop, and Rachel immediately released her grip on the seat and lunged for the back door. There was no release on the inside of the doors. 'Quickly,' she called to the two in the front, 'let me out.'

Shay hollered back. 'One of you grab my holdall for me.'

Belinda was nearest to it, but she looked slightly bewildered; as the effect of her pills had waned, so had her understanding and appetite for the situation. She cringed, as if something in the bag might bite her.

Rachel snorted, and lunged the way she'd just come to grab the bag. By then Shay had got out, and she ran to the back. The doors opened, one after the other, and Rachel spilled out. Her feet sank in loose wet pebbles. She passed the holdall to Shay without comment, then leaned back in. 'Belinda. Come on.'

Belinda shook her head. 'I'll wait here.'

'We can't split up.' Without waiting for an answer, Rachel reached for Belinda, snagged her coat and dragged the waif-like woman off the wheel arch. She practically lifted Belinda and set her on her feet, and was rewarded by a gust of overly sweet breath as Belinda exhaled at the indignity.

Leona appeared alongside them. Despite her arm being covered in a plaster cast from thumb to elbow, she took hold of Belinda and dragged the woman with them as they all headed for the house. Shay threw her holdall over one shoulder, and darted for the steps to the front door. Rachel made it there before her, and she didn't rest on decorum; she thrust both hands against the door, hoping that it would open under the pressure. It didn't.

'Listen,' said Shay.

From somewhere deep inside the house came the sounds of crashing and banging, and muffled voices.

'Oh, no! What's going on in there?' Rachel moaned.

Shay battered the door with the heel of her left hand, shouting Ben's name.

Rachel called for Helen.

Inside, the ruckus fell instantly silent.

Then a scream rang out, Helen screeching at the top of her lungs. 'Heeeelp meee! He's going to kill meeee!'

The announcement set Rachel back on her heels. Yes, they'd driven there in fear that Ben had been overtaken by the entity from the box, but she had hoped against hope that they were wrong and his reason for abandoning her at Belinda's apartment had a more prosaic explanation.

'What do we do?' Leona demanded, her face as colourless as glacial melt.

Shay gritted her teeth, but excitement rather than fear was her overriding emotion. She gripped the straps on her holdall tighter, keeping the bag close to her body. 'We need to find a way inside.'

'Round the side,' Rachel announced. Most times that she had visited, she had used the entrance adjacent to the car porch, and on one other occasion, accompanying Helen from the garden, they'd used another door that accessed the utility area, and entered the house proper through the kitchen. 'Follow me.'

She had only taken a few steps when Helen screamed again from deep inside the large house. Something crashed down, and shattered. Ben shouted angrily, but his voice was muffled. Biting her bottom lip, Rachel led the group past the front of the house, about to take the corner towards the awning. A glance at Ben's car halted her in her tracks. The others bunched up against her, and Rachel was almost knocked flying. She staggered, but spun to face the car, a realisation striking her. She signalled the others to wait for her, and in the confusion they did the opposite, following instead as she raced to the Range Rover. She ignored the open front door, instead going immediately to the rear and throwing up the hatch door. She dug in the back, lifting up a cover and exposing the well where the spare wheel was stored. There, nestled in the wheel hub, was the metal toolbox. She grabbed it and hauled it out, then tore open the twin flaps. The toolbox was empty except for the executioner box.

'I thought this was locked in the safe at the shop,' she croaked, 'but it had to have been here with Ben in order to affect him . . .'

Skin crawling, she looked at the box, suddenly averse to the idea of touching it.

Leona reached past her and grabbed the box, unafraid now, or perhaps simply determined to be shot of the cursed thing for ever. With the box clutched under her good arm, she continued to haul Belinda with her broken arm, a definite sign of her determination to end the horror. Shay jogged ahead, the holdall bouncing on her shoulder. After a moment Rachel gave a mental shake and rushed after them.

Shay tried the side door. It was locked.

From the side of the house, the sounds of conflict rising from inside could be heard louder than before, but it was unlikely that it would travel beyond the boundary of the property. Besides, the houses on each side and opposite were the dwellings of professionals, more than likely out at work at that hour of the afternoon. Nobody was going to hear the commotion.

Shay threw her shoulder against the door. It didn't budge. She looked at Leona, eyebrows raised almost to her spiky hairline: what did they do now?

'Give me a go,' said Belinda, and aimed a kick at the door, before Leona moved her aside.

Rachel grabbed the handle, and set her shoulder to the door, but it wouldn't budge.

'We'll have to go around the back,' she announced and set off, confident the others would follow.

At the rear of the house there was a large patio, a wooden deck, an arched pergola and a summer house sitting at the centre of an expansive lawn. While the others sought a way around onto the patio, Rachel didn't wait, scaling the low brick wall that encompassed it. She hurried to the back door and again found it locked. She cast around. To her left there were large French windows that could be opened during nicer weather to fetch some of the outdoor ambience inside. Already Shay had headed towards them, but rattling the handles achieved nothing. Inside the house, Ben shouted something and Helen cried out. A clatter and crash were so loud they rattled the glass in the French windows.

'Can you see them?' Rachel called, but Shay shook her head.

Rachel stooped down, lurching towards a large terracotta pot containing an exotic palm, and she tried picking it up.

'Shay, help me,' she called, and immediately the woman got the same idea. But she didn't join Rachel at the huge pot – which was probably too heavy for them to lift still – and instead yanked the holdall off her shoulder. Approaching the door, she swung it by its handles, and whatever was inside was heavy enough to crack the door pane. Shay struck twice more, and then a huge chunk of glass shattered, leaving a gap through which she could reach. A thumb-turn lock was all that secured the door, and she had it open in a second. She pushed the door and Rachel darted inside the house. Shay only checked on Leona and Belinda, and seeing they were tight behind her, she followed Rachel in . . . to the sound of another blood-curdling scream from Helen, and then a pained cry from Ben.

Rachel had already disappeared within the house, but it didn't matter, because the sounds of commotion were easily followed. Shay, Leona and Belinda all moved in a bunch to where Rachel yelled at the top of her voice, 'No, Ben. Don't do it. You're going to kill Helen!'

THIRTY-SIX

The last thing that Ben ever wanted to do was to hurt Helen, but it was getting to a point where he would have no choice over the matter if he wished to see another day. By disarming her and throwing the knife into the vestibule where she couldn't reach it, he'd hoped to diffuse her murderous intent long enough to subdue her, even going so far as knocking her unconscious if he must, but when he had been distracted by the banging and calling from the front door, she had capitalised on the moment, and upended a cutlery drawer, so had the pick of a number of sharp objects to throw at him.

'Helen, fight it! Come back to me!' he begged.

Dancing to avoid the hurled missiles, he'd batted aside others with the metal drying rack. A thrown fork became caught between the rungs, and the tines scraped his knuckles raw with each fresh swing of his impromptu shield. Helen – or the thing mobilising her – laughed at his feeble attempt at calling his Helen forward, in the hope she'd once more claim her corporeal shell. He swore at it, not her. But it galvanised a different response: it screamed.

Ben was stricken by the sound, for a second thinking he'd somehow reached his wife and she'd responded by screaming in abject terror. He blinked, mouth gaping open in expectation.

Then the facsimile of Helen's mouth turned up in a sneer, and she yelled: 'Heeeelp meee! He's going to kill meeee!'

Ben was equally set back, this time at the enormity of the accusation.

'I'd never hurt her, and everyone knows it.'

'Really? Let's test that theory, shall we?'

She leapt, thrusting down on the central island with both hands, and used it almost like a vaulting horse. She sailed towards him, and Ben had no recourse except to throw the rack over his head. Helen landed on top of him, latching her bare feet around his torso, simian-like in the way they clutched him. Her hands scrambled about and came away once more with the previously trapped fork now held in her bandaged hand. She struck repeatedly at him, the sharp prongs digging painfully into his shoulders and the back of his neck. Blood ran in rivulets from tiny stinging holes. Ben hurled her off him, and she crashed among some breakfast stools. As he lunged in, trying to control her, she stabbed at his face with the fork, and he fell back to avoid being blinded.

Helen screamed again, then taunted him with a waggle of the blackened tongue, the entity somehow aware of his fear of wriggling things. She scrambled up to her feet, and darted around the island, towards where she'd dumped out the cutlery. She cast more items at him; forks, spoons, blunt butter knives. When she found nothing more dangerous, she grabbed another drawer from the counter, and flipped it over. More utensils clattered, and some kind of jug was sent spinning off the counter to shatter on the floor.

Next, she lunged for the wooden block, and this time snatched a knife more dangerous to him than the paring knife she'd used earlier.

She showed him the chef's knife like it was a winning prize.

He'd withstood several jabs from sharp objects already, but they'd been insubstantial by comparison.

If she got that blade into him, he would not survive.

Ben shouted in dismay.

She charged, and he had no other response than to try to escape. He leapt away, and barely avoided a slash across his shoulders. He threw the metal rack backwards and it bounced off her with little effect. He jumped over the downed breakfast stools, and then he was at the opposite side of the central island, near the sink again. He grabbed a handful of the spilled cutlery, and mimicked her attack from a minute earlier by throwing them at her. She swatted them aside with the flat of the wide-bladed knife. As she advanced on him, he heard somebody kicking or beating on the side door, but to reach it he'd have to get past Helen, and he doubted he could do so without being stabbed. He snatched one of the overturned drawers, and threw it at her. She was being used as a puppet, but she was still his wife and he loved her and didn't want to do her any harm. He threw the drawer to distract rather than bash in her skull. It hit her thighs, momentarily halting her lunge after him, and gave him a second's grace to dart around the central island again, to fetch up once more at the door to the utility vestibule. He threw open the door and scanned the floor rapidly. His gaze alighted on the paring knife, and in his desperation he went for it. Helen slashed his hip. He cried out, but got fingers on the smaller blade and snatched it off the floor. He spun, cutting at throat level. Thankfully, there was some form of self-preservation instilled in the thing possessing Helen, and its reaction was to rear back. Ben followed the cut by spinning and aiming a kick at her legs. She back-pedalled into the kitchen, and he followed, encouraged by his small victories.

Helen was on the defensive now, cutting in wide swathes, and he lunged, using the smaller blade to jab and to force her back. Her grin was set, with no trace of the wicked humour of before: he genuinely had the thing in retreat!

He grabbed the metal rack he'd thrown at her earlier. Using it as a shield, he continued jabbing with the paring knife. She stumbled, caught her feet in the fallen breakfast stools and fell on her backside, the chef's knife flying free and skidding under the central island, momentarily out of reach.

It was Ben's opportunity to control her. If he could subdue her, somehow restrain her until help could arrive—

Somewhere behind him glass tinkled.

Another couple of smashes followed and more glass fell to the floor. He hunched over Helen, who for the moment lay on her back, legs splayed, hands up to ward off the metal rack that he forced down on her. He threatened her with the knife, although it pained him to do so.

He sensed a rush of bodies behind him, and a voice howling his name. Helen cringed up at him, her eyes wide and wet, mouth a wet hollow, now devoid of the black withered thing. He realised Helen's blackened tongue was only ever a visual manifestation caused by the spirit, intended to cause terror, and not the actual mummified flesh. It was obvious to him why it had ended the charade, seeing it had a new audience to deceive.

Rachel screeched words that he couldn't fathom, though her next were crystal clear. 'You're going to kill Helen!'

He turned feverish eyes on his assistant. He was flushed, his hair in disarray, hip weeping blood, face and hands dotted with gore, and probably looked like a maniac.

'Help meee!' Helen warbled.

More figures crowded into the kitchen, Shay leading Leona and Belinda. The four women all stared at Ben as if he was the devil himself.

'No,' he croaked, 'it's not me.'

'Please, Ben,' Rachel said, 'just drop the knife.'

'No, Rache. We have to stop her. Don't believe her lies, she's still—'

Helen pointed a shaking finger at the door they'd just entered through. 'He killed my mum, and now he's trying to kill me!'

Neither Rachel nor Shay turned to check, but at the back, Leona released Belinda long enough to lean back through the door. It took only a second, and her moan of dismay, to add validity to Helen's claim.

Rachel also moaned in distress.

'Help me,' Ben called, 'we have to—'

Rachel rushed him, followed a second later by Shay. The latter used her holdall as a flail, just as she had to smash a way inside. She knocked the hand holding the paring knife, even as Rachel latched onto him, struggling to draw him away from Helen. In his alarm, Ben dropped the knife and metal rack, to try to disengage from Rachel, and was unprepared for the holdall smacking across his face. Something heavy within bashed his cheek, and a fold of the stiff nylon bag scraped his left eye, immediately causing tears to flood his vision.

'You don't understand—' he cried, but the women had witnessed enough to form the wrong opinion. Rachel and Shay grappled him, and even Leona, encumbered as she was carrying the executioner box, jumped to her friend's aid. Ben felt overwhelmed by them. He stumbled with them, dragged away from Helen. Everything was chaotic, everyone shouting, frantic hands yanking him in different directions.

Unbeknown to them, Helen drew her feet under her, and came to her knees. She reached for the paring knife Ben had just dropped, and while he struggled to get free, she took her time relishing the moment.

Ben was encumbered, and the pulling and tugging of the women was enough of a distraction that he didn't at first sense what the cold fire in his abdomen meant. It was another moment before he felt a similar flaring sensation in his gut, and he looked down.

Helen grinned up at him, her face again set in that malicious, self-satisfied grin of before. She held the paring knife. It was bloody all the way to her bandaged hand, and it was as if his blood had oiled the steel, the ease with which she plunged it into him a third time.

THIRTY-SEVEN

Discovering Ben hunched over his wife like something demented, blood splattered, threatening her with a knife in hand, Rachel could be forgiven for misreading the situation. In her struggles to save Helen from him, she took a few bumps and scrapes, accidentally given to her by the thumping elbows and knees of Shay and Leona, as the three tried to drag Ben away from his intended target. Ben also wrenched and yanked his limbs, and he was much stronger than she, so her muscles felt strained and sore within seconds of taking hold of him. Shay struck him several times with the holdall: once it skimmed him and struck Rachel instead, knocking her glasses askew. They were all shouting, none of them making sense, and Rachel's ears rang.

When Helen suddenly rose to her feet, holding out the bloodied paring knife at them, a moment's confusion descended over Rachel, especially when the other two released Ben, stepping away from him with squeals of horror. Rachel pawed her glasses on, and also stepped aside from him; as he'd instantly given up the fight. He took a couple of staggering steps away, and then his back was checked against the kitchen wall. He looked at Helen, and then at Rachel, and his features were stricken. He lowered his gaze and, feeling nausea wash through her, Rachel followed his stare. He cupped his hands over his lower abdomen, but his palms weren't large enough to cover all the wounds in it. Blood spread like the petals of a giant rose in three distinct places, his clothing growing more sodden by the second.

'Oh, nooo . . .' Rachel moaned.

She looked up and caught Ben's eye.

'It's not me,' he croaked for the second time, and this time she believed him.

Helen laughed.

'Which of you whores is next?' she asked, and she stepped forward with the paring knife raised.

'You are!'

Helen barely turned in time to spot the figure lunging around the central island at her.

In the chaos, Belinda had gone unnoticed. The young woman might seem frail, a character whose life had been one of use and abuse, until she'd met Jason, and he'd shown her kindness, support, love and possibly even a future safer from harm. That was until the thing now nestled inside Helen had snatched him away from her. As frail as she looked, it was a lie, because she was also from the streets, and had been forced to fight for the majority of her life. Her existence had been tough, and she'd been in a perpetual tussle to hang on to whatever gains she could make, and this was not the first time she'd been forced to fight tooth and claw to take what was rightfully hers . . . in this case revenge.

'You killed my Jason, you evil bastard!' she screeched, and rammed the chef's knife she'd plucked from under the island into Helen's neck.

Belinda drew it out, and held it, ready to stab again.

Rachel cried out, and behind her Shay and Leona also voiced their consternation. Ben uttered a single cry and sat down heavily, all strength flooding from him at the sight of Helen so viciously wounded.

Instantly, a transformation went over Helen too. The malicious grin fell from her face to be replaced by confusion, and then complete shock, as she dropped the paring knife. Her fingertips went to her neck, and were jetted by a spurt of arterial blood. She searched their faces, even Belinda's, but it was as if she didn't recognise the one responsible for wounding her so badly. Her gaze fell on Ben, and he met it. In that moment of connection, they both knew that the possessing entity had fled them both, that they looked solely on the person they each loved most, but they were about to lose what was most precious to them. Another spray of blood flew from Helen; her knees gave way, and she stumbled forward and fell. Ben opened his arms, catching her, and pulling her into his embrace. Already she was insensible, and he was bare seconds behind.

Rachel yowled and lunged towards them.

Then she turned on Belinda, perhaps expecting the girl to

continue her revenge-driven assault, but Belinda had also noted the change in Helen's demeanour, that she'd struck deep and driven the thing that killed Jason from her, hopefully back to hell where it belonged. Fulfilled, she dropped the chef's knife, like a cabaret artiste performing a mic drop.

The apparent danger at an end, Rachel again rushed to Ben and Helen, and weakly Ben raised his head. Rachel cupped his face as she leaned in, and he tried to register her face close to his, but his pupils juddered around . . . he was on the verge of seeing other vistas beyond the confines of his wrecked kitchen. 'Rache,' he wheezed, his voice so quiet it was barely perceptible. 'You can't help us. You have to finish this . . . and save yourself.'

Rachel wept.

Behind her, Belinda was set aside by Shay with an instruction not to move.

'I'm not going to cause any more trouble,' said Belinda, telling the truth.

Shay next instructed Leona, and then Rachel felt a hand on her shoulder, drawing her from Ben, who had slipped away while she held him. Numb to the proceedings, she allowed herself to be manoeuvred to a safe distance, while Shay began reciting words from an ancient leather-bound book, and making gestures over the doomed couple. She had removed other esoteric items from her holdall, and Leona had lit a tallow candle as she'd been encouraged by Shay.

Rachel had no comprehension of the goings-on, but whatever form the rite took, it was nothing like she had expected from watching too many horror movies over the years. There were no whistling winds, flapping curtains or crashing of flying objects as so often depicted during movie-land exorcisms. There was no sense of a change in the atmosphere, and no lightening of the room when Shay finally sat down on the ground, uttering a final string of archaic words. She drew the executioner box to her, seated it in her lap, and – calling for help from her goddess, Nuit – physically forced a tiny nail through the original nail hole to keep the lid sealed. If she had placed anything inside – personal belongings, sorcerer's tongue, or dead men's string – in the interim, Rachel had missed it.

'It's done,' the occultist announced.

No, Rachel thought, they were far from done, because how were they ever going to explain what had happened there, in a manner that anyone would believe their claims?

She said to her unhearing bosses, 'If we tell the truth, people won't believe us. If we lie, your names will be dragged through the mud. Please forgive me . . .' and again she wept, this time loudly and openly. She wasn't the only one to vent their distress.

THIRTY-EIGHT

'You didn't fetch Belinda with you?' asked Shay, standing in the doorway of her farmhouse five days later.

Rachel shook her head. 'She's off doing her own thing.'

Leona appeared over Shay's shoulder, looking beyond Rachel, whose taxi was just disappearing from sight behind the agricultural sheds. 'You're alone?'

'Yeah, I was just explaining to Shay . . .' Rachel shrugged. 'The truth is, I didn't bother calling for her. Since, well, you know what happened, she's been kind of distant, and I can't say that it doesn't suit me. I know she only intended to destroy the thing inside Helen, but I struggle to see past it. I can't unsee what she did with that knife, or her satisfaction afterwards. The less I have to look at her face, the better.'

Shay peered all around, perhaps expecting to spot an all-seeing eye in the sky spying on them. 'Maybe we should wait until we're indoors before talking about this stuff?'

'I think we are in the clear,' said Rachel.

'It's certainly looking that way,' Shay agreed.

'But let's not take any chances, lassies,' Leona urged, and beckoned Rachel inside.

They convened in the same sitting room as they had when Ben had first accompanied them. Rachel sat in the same spot on the settee, feeling his absence as a tangible weight in her chest. Grief had not struck her yet, but it was only a matter of time. She had not fully released her anguish over losing both her close friends, because the days since the awful events at their home had been filled with questions, and even some accusations, but thankfully none of the latter had stuck.

She would take the time to properly mourn Ben and Helen after they were laid to rest, and she could be certain that the investigation into their deaths was behind them.

She had not been back to their shop after they died. She couldn't face it yet, her memories of what had happened to her in the basement too raw. Perhaps once it came time to put their effects in order, liquidise their estate, and clean out the premises, Rachel would help, but for now it suited her that she didn't need to get close to Belinda's apartment, or the place down below where this entire nightmare began for her. It meant that any opportunity to reconnect with Cezary Nowak was slim, but he'd been conspicuous by his absence lately, and she'd wondered if he had deliberately distanced himself from her. So much so that she'd not seen hide nor hair of him since they'd failed to burn the box in the yard. Not that she cared too much, because initiating any type of romance was something she couldn't countenance just then.

Shay had baked again. This time a gingerbread loaf, and she had served it sliced and spread with butter. Rachel had no appetite.

She eyed the executioner box where Shay had set it under a glass cloche on the fireplace. Mounded around the box and liberally sprinkled on top there were some kind of granules that Rachel assumed was Dead Sea salt, a mineral she'd read was often used in occult purifying rituals. Before they had called the emergency services, Shay had them all recite some words in an archaic language, and declared the binding ritual a success, and smuggled the box away from the scene and into the rear of her van, with the promise she'd take further pains to secure it once she got it home. Rachel had thought she'd have sealed it in a steel drum and sunk it to the bottom of a lake, not depended on a sprinkling of salt to keep them safe. Then again, trying to burn it had proved a waste of time, so maybe it would simply bob back to the lake's surface again and end up in the hands of some innocent and luckless fisherman. Rachel didn't want anyone else to fall victim to the cursed thing.

'Can we trust Belinda not to speak about what happened?' Shay probed after a moment.

'She isn't going to deliberately admit to killing Helen,' Rachel said, not feeling as confident in her assertion as she perhaps sounded. Unfortunately, Belinda was as much a puppet to her vices as Helen had been to the sorcerer's tongue, and who was to say that under an altered state she wouldn't blurt out their secret to somebody? Hopefully, though, if anyone overheard her confession, they'd believe it all a drug-fuelled fantasy, or they would be as stupefied as she was if it happened.

'Hopefully she won't.' Leona sat back, and cradled her broken arm in her lap. 'It's important that we all stick to our stories, and never deviate, or we'll all be in serious trouble.'

It had struck Rachel already that Leona, by proxy of Hettie's use of the executioner box, was responsible for the death of her abusive husband, and if the truth about Helen and Ben was to come out, then so too would the nature of Keiron's killing.

'I'll stick to the story as agreed. But I admit that it hurts that the blame was put on Ben.' Rachel had to catch herself as her eyes welled, and a lump formed in her throat. 'He was a good man, not the monster he's being painted as.'

Ben Taylor was named as the villain of the piece in most versions of the appalling triple killing, and it saddened Rachel that she couldn't defend his name by telling the truth. It was accepted by most that Helen King, her blood infected, and suffering from a fever and lacking control of her actions, had murdered her mother, Gloria, before luring home her husband, with who knew what deviltry in mind. Discovering Gloria's murder, Ben had apparently flown into a panic, and they had argued, then fought, and it had spurred Helen into murderously attacking him too . . . but what kind of a decent man stabs his wife in the throat with a chef's knife, whether she has mortally wounded him or not? He had to have been as crazy as she, most judged him, and that was without being – as she had been – out of his mind with a fever.

The police investigation was more thorough than the conjecture aimed at them via the local community, or even the wider media, but there was nothing in any of the women's stories that proved they'd done anything but try to stop the couple from killing each other. There had been suspicion around how the women had come to arrive at the house together, as they were not previously known to socialise, but they had concocted a story about Ben contacting Leona about returning the valuable amulet he'd found among some of the belongings he'd purchased from her deceased grandmother, and from there had struck up a passing friendship regarding their shared experiences as dealers. Rachel claimed that they had been passing their condolences on to Belinda for the loss of her boyfriend, when Ben had suddenly abandoned her to race home at Helen's summons, and when she'd called her new friends for a ride, Belinda had joined her, knowing how concerned she was by her employers' recent behaviour. Hearing the commotion inside the house, the group had forced entry by a back door, and found the married couple locked in their final moments. That they had wiped it clean of Belinda's fingerprints, and then forced Ben's hand around the chef's knife handle had been important details left out of their testimonies.

Rachel again studied the box under the cloche.

'Are you certain that thing will hold the spirit?' she asked.

'I'm positive.'

'You can't even be certain that it's inside,' Rachel pointed out. 'The tongue, I mean, the chovanó's chipe.'

Shay smiled, nodding in her surety. 'I'm reasonably confident it's in there, but it doesn't really matter now. When I recited the words of binding, and you all repeated them back, it would have broken the connection between the spirit and the tongue and sent the spirit back where it belonged, to purgatory. The mummified flesh itself was only ever a conduit for the spirit to gain entry through to this plane. Whether or not the chipe's in the box, I believe the spirit of the sorcerer is trapped within its own reckoning, and the proof is that none of us has been threatened or molested by its presence since. We stood together, united, all of us who had come in contact with it, and, by the will of Nuit, we pushed it back inside its cell.'

'It just seemed too easy,' Rachel said.

'Spinning heads and pea-green vomit,' Shay laughed, making the signs of the horns with one hand, 'and the power of Christ compels you!'

'I'm sorry, but I don't find it a laughing matter,' said Rachel.

Shay sobered. 'You're right. It isn't. The matter is deadly serious, as we've all found out. That was my first binding rite . . .' She glanced at the box under the glass dome. 'I don't mind admitting, I also hope it's my last.'

'You'll just keep the box there on your mantel like a trophy?' Rachel asked.

'No. I intend to reach out to people more learned in magick than I am, and have one of them take it away and discard it properly.'

'How can you be certain that it's safe to keep here until it's done?'

'You needn't worry. Shay knows her stuff,' Leona put in. 'And like she pointed out already, we were united and severed its link to us. We are finally safe, lassie.'

THIRTY-NINE

Stubbing out his cigarette under his heel, Tymon Nowak exhaled, and then hitched his jeans around his narrow hips. In the week since his cousin's accident he had rarely eaten, and had subsisted mostly on cigarettes, coffee and alcohol. He had lost several kilograms, and it showed in his pale features and how loose his clothing hung on him. Their roommates, Patryk Dybas and Oskar Galewski, weren't as severely affected by Cezary's accident as Tymon was; they were their own men, and weren't dependent on Cezary the way he had become. Tymon knew full well that if Cezary hadn't agreed to accompany him there in the UK, he would never have had the confidence, nor the imperative, to seek employment in a foreign land. It was Cezary who had found them jobs at the fish-packing factory – it was horrible work, but it paid well – and a reasonably affordable apartment where they could live. All Tymon needed to concern himself with was how much of his wages he could save, and how many cigarettes he could bum from his generous cousin before having to buy his own: Ja pierdolę! Cigarettes were so expensive in the UK!

In the little under a week since Cezary's accident, Tymon had seriously considered that his time in England was over. Patryk and Oskar owed him nothing, and it wasn't on them to look after him, and he knew that out of earshot they called him gówniarz, because to them he was just an annoying, immature little shit, and they had only tolerated his presence for Cezary's sake. With Cezary gone, he knew it would only be a matter of time until he was asked, more likely told, to seek lodgings elsewhere. When that time came, he'd be forced to flee home to his mama like a frightened little boy.

He went back inside the hospital and wound his way through echoing corridors that had grown familiar in the past few days and mounted stairs to an upper floor. At a locked entrance door, he waved and was buzzed through, his face now as familiar to the desk staff as theirs to him. He made his way to a private room set apart from the bustling wards across from it. Tymon had been given fluid visiting rights, due to the severity of Cezary's injuries, with free access to come and go in the hospital outside normal visiting hours.

Cezary lay on a bed. He was strapped and bandaged, his neck supported by a plastic collar, and wires adhered to him, feeding vital data to a beeping, flashing computer console. The hose and mask through which he'd been fed oxygen was unstrapped and lay discarded on his left shoulder. Unlike the times before, when Tymon had sat vigil at his bedside, his cousin was conscious, and greeted him with a steady look, and the flicker of a smile.

'Cezary, you are awake?' Tymon rushed to his side, eyes sparkling with delight. 'Thank God you're OK. I thought we had lost you.'

He clutched at Cezary's hand, squeezing it, until his cousin hissed at the pressure and withdrew from his touch.

Tymon blurted his delight in his own language: 'I'm sorry. I didn't mean to hurt you. Oh, Cezary, I am so happy to find you awake. Tell me that you are going to be OK.'

Cezary peered at him steadily.

He frowned.

His lips pursed in silent question.

'Don't you recognise me?' Tymon asked, a feeling of mild dread climbing his chest. 'It's me, Tymon, your little cousin!'

Cezary grunted in acknowledgement. Then he attempted to sit up, squirming as if troubled by discomfort at his lower spine.

'No, you mustn't. You damaged your back in the fall, so you need to stay as flat and still as—'

Cezary snorted, and forcibly shunted his hips and shoulders until he was in a seated position. He studied the wires attached to his chest with tiny sticky patches and his nose wrinkled in distaste. He began brushing at them with the side of his hand, and then when he failed to dislodge them, began plucking at each individually and peeling them off.

'I don't think you should be doing that,' Tymon warned. He reached to gently coax Cezary's hand from the next wire. Cezary grasped his fingers, squeezing, but with a deliberate intention to harm. Tymon squirmed under the pressure, and with a yowl he tore free of Cezary's grasp.

Cezary laughed at Tymon's shocked face and opened his mouth to speak.

Only a dry rasp was emitted, and the foulest of smells.

'Ugh,' said Tymon, grimacing as he studied the dried, withered state of Cezary's tongue. 'Have you been sneaking out and smoking when no one's around? Your tongue is as black as tar.'